AR Quiz#: 147758
BL: 5.7
AR Pts: 12.0

HAYNER F

W9-AFN-708

Also by Matthew Cody

Powerless

THE DEAD GENTLEMAN

MATTHEW CODY

ALFRED A. KNOPF
NEW YORK

THIS IS A BORZOI BOOK PUBLISHED BY ALFRED A. KNOPF

Visit us on the Web! www.randomhouse.com/kids

Educators and librarians, for a variety of teaching tools, visit us at
www.randomhouse.com/teachers

Library of Congress Cataloging-in-Publication Data is available upon request.
ISBN: 978-0-375-85596-2 (trade)
ISBN: 978-0-375-95596-9 (lib. bdg.)
ISBN: 978-0-375-89780-1 (ebook)

The text of this book is set in 11-point Goudy Old Style.

Printed in the United States of America
November 2011
10 9 8 7 6 5 4 3 2 1

First Edition

For Alisha and Willem,
as always

In loving memory of
Lt. Col. James Cody

ACKNOWLEDGMENTS

The process of writing this book was, appropriately, full of twists and turns, and at times we could have used a Cycloidotrope of our own to figure it all out. My deepest thanks go out to my editors, Joan Slattery and Michele Burke, without whom I'd be lost in the ether. Joan helped me begin this book, and Michele helped me finish it—I'm so very grateful to both. And my thanks to Nancy Hinkel and Jeremy Medina for their thoughtful feedback and support and, of course, to my friend and agent, Kate Schafer Testerman, for far too much to list here.

Go to sleep, evening star,
For here comes the bogeyman
And he steals away children who
Don't go to sleep!

—from a traditional Spanish lullaby

PART ONE

We Explorers are, too often, blind to the consequences of our actions; blind to our responsibility for those millions who slumber in ignorance beneath the Veil of Reality. Now is the time for us to open our eyes and recognize that in our journeys we have left too many doors opened.
And dark things have followed us back.

—from the introduction to the
Encyclopedia Imagika,
"On the Profession and Its Associated Perils,"
Sir Bartholomew Wainright, editor

PROLOGUE

TOMMY

NEW YORK, 1901

A mist had settled over the city, the leftovers of the sort of downpour that scrubs manure from cobblestones and soot from buildings. Inside, candles were lit, and outside, gaslights hissed and popped to life. The streetlamps made little difference in the soupy evening fog. But staring up at the Percy Hotel, with its tall windows and new electric bulbs, you'd have thought someone had gone and built a tower of bonfires on the edge of Manhattan.

A new century. It had only just begun and the world had already changed.

Eyeing my chronometer, I triple-checked its charge. I fidget a lot, but it's not that I'm anxious—I just have trouble standing still. Years of living on the streets will teach you that it's dangerous if you stay in one place for too long. You're better off keeping on the move.

I adjusted the paragoggles on my forehead and cinched the leather delver's gloves around my wrists, tight. Any tighter and my fingers would go numb.

"What's the bird say?" asked Bernard, wiping little water droplets from his glasses.

I tried to answer but my words were lost in the hoof steps of a passing horse and rider. The man shouted at us as he trotted by—something about two boys being out after dark and loitering where we had no business, and so on. I answered the man's concerns with a nice, rude gesture.

"Merlin's still on about something," I said again, after the clatter had died down. The clockwork canary on my shoulder gave one of his tin can chirps. "*Something's* funny about that hotel, and I'm betting on the basement." Merlin had been singing up a storm ever since we'd spied the Percy, and the metal bird's squawking usually signaled trouble.

"I don't know," said Bernard. "He's *really* acting up—I've never seen him this twitchy before. Maybe we should go back."

For an Explorer, Bernard was a bit on the cautious side. In his book, there was no situation so urgent that it couldn't benefit from a little extra preparedness. Not a bad way to live if you're looking to make assistant manager by the end of the year at Such-and-Such-Mister-Stuffy-Pants' Bank. And maybe it's fine if you want a really exciting profession, such as . . . an accounts clerk. Or a grocer. But Explorers are adventurers. This may mean that at times we can be a little foolhardy and, yes, even reckless. But if you saw just half the things I've seen, you'd be jumping out of your boots, too.

I promise you, there's just *so* much to see out there—you have no idea.

"Go back?" I asked. "Look, Bernard. Time to get back in the saddle and stop dwelling on the past. Can't worry our way through life, eh?"

"I'm not worried, per se," answered Bernard, his milk-fat cheeks blushing red. "It's just, after the Hidden City, I'd have thought you'd—"

"Let's not talk about that right now, partner," I interrupted. As I said, I'm a fellow of action—I don't care to dwell on the bad stuff of life. And believe me, what happened to the Hidden City was the worst.

"Besides," I said. "We're Explorers, Bernard. Even if we're the last, the title still means something. So let's do some exploring."

Merlin looked at each of us in turn and tweeted.

"See? Merlin's here to protect you if things go south. You keep hold of the bird while I take the lead, and if there's anything in there worth poking into, I'll do the poking. Agreed?"

Bernard nodded, but he was hardly enthusiastic.

I gently scooped Merlin off my shoulder and onto Bernard's. The bird's surprisingly delicate for a creature made all of metal.

Bernard wiped a fresh coat of mist from his spectacles as he frowned at the canary. "Tommy, I've also been doing some reading . . ."

"There's your first mistake."

"The Percy has a history. This very spot was the site of a multiportal event, years before there was even a hotel here."

I squinted at my friend. Now he'd managed to pique my interest. "You mean like a nexus?"

Bernard shrugged. "It's unclear. What is known is that multiple portals opened at once and there were casualties involved. The

Academy declared it off-limits to further exploring. You know, there *are* some doors that are meant to stay shut, Tommy."

"We're just having a quick look-see," I said, clapping him on the shoulder with one of my biggest, most lying-est just-trust-me grins. "We'll be extra careful. I promise."

The basement turned out to be a forest of junk—cluttered trails overgrown with old lobby chairs, cracked clawed tubs and curtain rods. An upright roll of musty carpet marked the entrance, and the exit (if there was one) was lost somewhere in the darkness. As the basement hadn't been wired yet for electric lights, a single gas bulb hung uselessly near the doorway, black with soot. This was a place where things were thrown away, cast off and forgotten about. A graveyard of old lives.

Merlin chirped worriedly as we eyed the room.

Adjusting the chronometer on my wrist, I set it to count backward from ten. The little brass hands whirred and clicked into place before starting the soft ticking of minutes. Then I pulled down my paragoggles and waited a few seconds for my eyes to adjust to the cobalt glow of paralight. Where the room was once hidden in shadow, I now saw distinct blue shapes.

"I've set the clock to ten minutes. That should give us more than enough time to do a little reconnoiter."

"Are you sure?" asked Bernard, squinting beneath his own goggles. He never did have the knack for seeing in paralight. "It looks a bit dodgy, if you ask me. Looks like a perfect place to walk into an attercop web. Or worse."

"If the two of us can't handle a single attercop, then we've got no right to the name Explorers," I said. The awkward way Bernard wore his oversized goggles made him look like some kind of fat, blue-eyed bug. "C'mon, we're wasting paralight."

"Fine," he answered. "But just a quick look. If we're lucky, it's just an ordinary old basement after all."

"An ordinary old basement?" I laughed. "Aren't they always?"

Tiptoeing my way through the maze of junk, I tapped my Tesla Stick on the floor, testing the ground. At the center of the room, I paused in front of an overturned sofa. It lay on its side at a suspiciously awkward angle as if it had been dragged out to the middle of the floor and left there. It was out of place.

"Hey, give me a hand with this," I said, and, with a few grunts, the two of us righted the mildewed sofa back onto its feet, exposing a deep crevasse in the floor underneath. At its narrowest it was maybe a few inches wide, but near the middle it opened into a jagged hole two or three feet across. Where the cobblestone floor was broken away, it had been covered with a thick film of spiderweb. In the blue light I saw, dangling in the sticky strands, bits of animal bone and a few bottle caps. In the middle of everything a single doll's head stared back at me, its eyes chewed out and missing.

"Attercop," Bernard whispered. "Told you."

"Have you ever actually seen an attercop?"

"No," answered Bernard. "And neither have you. But at least I've read about them."

"Well, this web looks old. Maybe he scurried off to a new home. Let's make sure."

Reaching into the shoulder bag at my side, the one marked with the Explorers' symbol—a machine cog with feathered wings—I took out an oddly shaped gun with a net dangling from the tip and tossed it to Bernard.

Bernard looked at the gun and arched one surprised eyebrow at me. "Are you serious?"

I shrugged. "Net for the netter. You can cover me."

As gingerly as I could manage, I stepped within reach of the crevasse. If the attercop was home, he'd be waiting just under the web for his prey.

"Any vibration," Bernard was saying, "even a small one, will bring him to the surface. And he'll come angry. But attercops are built for climbing, not walking, and their short front legs mean that they are ridiculously slow on the ground. Most of the time they're only really dangerous in the web."

Most of the time.

I crouched down low next to the sofa and slowly, very slowly, reached forward with my Tesla Stick, ready to discharge fifty thousand volts of electricity at anything that came crawling out of the web on more than two legs. My heart was beating hard in my chest, but I just couldn't stop smiling. Times like that made me feel alive.

Inching the tip of my pole to the edge—I was a good distance away—I tapped the web. Just a tap. I kept a loose grip on the handle, letting the wrist strap hang. I didn't want the attercop pulling me in along with the pole.

Nothing happened.

I tapped again, harder. The bottle caps jingled against each other as the pole brushed the strands and came away easily. The web had lost most of its stickiness, which was yet another sign that its maker had moved on.

"Looks safe," I said.

It was much tougher than a normal spiderweb, more like spun cotton, and it took a few sharp jabs to break the thing. As I worked, the ghastly doll's head remained suspended by a few stray strands, dangling above the crevasse. Its eyeless gaze settled on me for just a second, before I knocked it into the dark.

Watching the head fall away, I had to shake off the little chill that crept up my neck. With the web cleared, what was left was an open chasm. But if my instincts were right, this was more than that—there was something down there. Even in the para-light, the crevasse looked dark. The walls were uneven and narrowed the farther down they went.

"Hook me up," I said. "I'm going down."

"Do you want the netgun?" asked Bernard as he fastened a thin line to my belt.

"No, that thing's too bulky to climb with, and I've got the Tesla Stick if I have any problems. Besides, if that attercop decides to visit up here, you'll need it more than me."

Reaching back into my pouch, I took out a shining metal ball and handed it, very gently, to Bernard.

He arched his eyebrow again. "A mayfly? What's this for?"

"Last resort. What you said earlier about this place having a *history*? Well, if I don't come back, toss it in and seal up the hole. But make sure I'm truly done for—I wouldn't want to be down there when the mayfly does its thing."

"You're very reassuring," said Bernard, gingerly pocketing the ball and removing his shoulder satchel. "You know I'd never use it."

"Protocol and all. You're the one always quoting me the rules."

Bernard managed a half smile. "You said it yourself: we are the Academy now. We can change the rules as we like. Just be careful, all right?"

Bernard handed me a coil of rope, and, with a satisfied nod,

I slipped over the edge and into the dark. According to the chronometer, I had less than two minutes of paralight left. I'd hoped to at least scout the bottom before having to resort to using a lantern. Even if this turned out to be an ordinary cavern, there could still be something nasty down here, and I didn't want to attract attention with real light until I absolutely had to.

I rappelled my way along the rough dirt wall of the crevasse as Bernard fed me an inch of cord at a time. The seconds took forever to tick by as I was slowly lowered through the basement floor, but to go any faster would risk my losing my balance, or Bernard might lose his footing and I'd fall the rest of the way.

Descending into the unknown, I dreamed about what might be at the bottom. Where did the basement of the Percy Hotel lead? It must be someplace special for Merlin to go on like that. The last really wondrous place I'd explored had led to the Ying Obelisk—an enormous tower hidden among the ice rings of Saturn. The stones drank in the sunlight during the day and shone bright gold at night. The creature who lived there looked like angels with their ice-particle wings, and they sailed along the ether winds of space. It was one of the most glorious places any person could see in all of creation, and I'd discovered it under the bed of an eight-year-old girl.

Though I could still just make out Bernard's silhouette above me, the paralight was fading fast. An unusual panic started to set in the farther I went, as I imagined the walls slowly closing in, tightening like fingers around a bug. I'd have to risk some light after all.

As I fumbled in my breast pocket for a match, I heard Bernard's harsh whisper from above. "Hey, you've stopped! Everything all right?"

Bad enough I was about to light a match, but now we were shouting whispers at each other. "I'm fine!"

With one hand on the rope, I had to pry the match tin open with my teeth, wincing as they scraped the metal. It was a clumsy effort, but after a few tries and some spilled matches I managed to strike one against the rock wall. A quick hiss of sparks and a second later the crevasse was lit by a weak glow.

It took only a few moments for my eyes to adjust, just long enough for me to notice the glint of a solid floor not ten feet below. Its surface was smooth, almost polished. As I put the match to the wick of the small hand lantern clipped to my belt, there was a confused moment as the lantern light was suddenly reflected back at me by four multifaceted eyes not three feet away.

The attercop. It was here after all, and more, it was waiting for me. I spied it just as it was readying itself to pounce, its fangs clicking now in anticipation of this unexpected meal. And here I was, a worm dangling on a hook.

There was no time to think. I pulled the safety hook on my harness and as the creature lunged, I dropped.

The attercop's fangs just missed me as I fell and landed on the hard floor. Something gave way in my ankle, and worse, I heard the crunch of the Tesla Stick snapping beneath me. But I had escaped the attercop's grasp—for a moment anyway. As I rolled across the floor, the lantern sputtered and blinked—but it stayed lit.

The attercop was descending, faster than I would have thought possible with its stubby front legs. I had only a few seconds to act. Bernard was shouting something from above, but the blood pounding in my head drowned out my partner's words.

As the attercop reached the floor, it twisted its grotesque

body around to face me. Next it would rear back on its powerful hind legs and move in for the kill, striking with a bite that would paralyze in seconds.

I managed to sit up—my back to the wall—and raise my lamp at the attercop. Most Explorers use hydro-gas lamps as a backup to paralight goggles. Hydro-gas is safer than lamp oil, less flammable and more reliable. But I keep my lantern filled with old-fashioned lamp oil for a different reason—I've made a few modifications to the device. As the spider beast lurched forward, I flipped a switch on the lamp's handle and a small cylinder of pressurized air began to hiss. The lantern oil was forced out of a tiny spigot on the lantern's front, passing through the open flame as it arched into a stream of liquid fire. I'd turned my lamp into a fiery squirt can. The burning oil landed directly on the attercop's round back, running in flaming rivulets into its face, its eyes.

The crevasse brightened with the flash of fire, and shadows flickered around me as the beast writhed in pain. It squealed in rage as it tried to brush out the flames, but the clinging oil just burned hotter as it caught the fine hairs that covered the attercop's body. My lamp extinguished, I curled up in a tight ball and hugged the wall, avoiding the blind thrashing of the dying creature.

After a few long minutes, the monster stopped its twitching. Though the lamp was spent, the crevasse was still lit by the burning, crackling body of the dead attercop. I almost threw up at the smell of cooking spider meat. My hands were shaky with adrenaline and pain from my injured foot, and my head was spinning with questions.

What was the thing doing down here—waiting for me? Attercops were supposed to be easy opponents because they were *predictable*. Hit the web and the attercop comes running—always. They don't wait in the shadows to get the jump on their victims because they aren't that smart.

Yet this one was. It had waited until I got close enough, dangling from my climbing rope and nearly defenseless. Even then it paused to strike at the last possible moment, as if it was afraid to act too hastily, as if it wanted to stay down in the dark, as if it was guarding something. . . .

For the first time I took a moment to really observe my surroundings here at the bottom of the crevasse. The light cast by the burning attercop was already beginning to fade, but I could see, all around me, flickering reflections. Dirt and rock walls, no tunnels or visible exits except for the way I came down, and the floor beneath—smooth as a mirror. The floor was rock along the sides, but gradually the rough stone gave way to volcanic glass, deep black and flawless except for a single line cut into a six-foot circle in the middle of the floor. And in the middle of the circle was a handle.

It was a door—a door that had been cut into the floor. A door that led straight down.

I felt a shiver that had nothing to do with the attercop. Here was a real mystery.

"Hey, Bernard! Get down here. There's something you've got to see!"

Peering up at the opening, I could see Bernard's silhouette clearly enough—he was still peering over the ledge—but I got no answer. Merlin was uncharacteristically quiet, too.

"Bernard?"

This time he moved. I could see him shuffling around at the top of the hole, though why he was still silent was anyone's guess.

Perhaps he was so thrown by my fight with the attercop that he was too shaken to speak.

"C'mon, Bernard. There was only one of these beasties and I've taken care of him. If you bring down the treats, we can make a roast of it!"

Still, Bernard said nothing. Instead, my calls were answered by a new sound—the crack and rumble of rock sliding.

I had a sudden, terrible image of the mayfly. Once activated, the little bomb would tear through the dirt, rock, whatever it found. In his panic, had Bernard let the mayfly loose, only to leave me here to die? Or was he really betraying me? The tunnel mouth above my head was collapsing, unearthing tons of rock that would close this portal forever—and bury me in the process. My mind wasn't working right. I couldn't accept that my friend and partner would abandon me now. I called, I begged and I cursed. I tried climbing, but more and more earth was falling down, blinding me, choking me.

All that was left for me was the strange door.

Some doors are meant to stay shut. Even then, Bernard's warning hung in my mind. But I'd opened many doors before, followed paths no one had followed. That is what Explorers do—that is our calling, our purpose.

And if I didn't open this one, I'd die.

And so, my mind made up, as the roar of the mayfly above me built to its explosive peak, I grabbed the handle of the black door with both hands and pulled.

But it occurs to me now that I've started a bit late in my story. So many things that come to pass depend on what came before, but I guess that's the way with stories. Still, I should think you would be confused, being dropped into the action like this without so much as an introduction. So before we go any further, I should take a breath, collect my thoughts and put the important stuff in order in my head. Next time, perhaps, I'll back up and start at the beginning.

Here's hoping I have time to finish the tale.

CHAPTER ONE

JEZEBEL
NEW YORK CITY, TODAY

At first glance, the Percy Luxury was a sleek apartment building full of marble floors and shining brass handles. A neatly dressed doorman always waited outside to wave down taxis and tip his hat at passersby, and the smiling elevator man with too-white teeth never had to be reminded which floor was yours. But the marble and the brass were not the originals, and neither were the doorman and the elevator man for that matter—they were all part of a new renovation aimed at transforming the place into a stylish home for the very rich and the very snotty. "New" Percy had been "gentrified"—a word that, in Jezebel's vernacular, meant it was now a good place to own a poodle or some other small, yappy dog that you could stuff into your purse.

Jezebel's Percy was full of peepholes and cracked-open doors. No one said much of anything, she noticed, and each neighbor made a point of seeming totally uninterested as they passed her in the halls—head down, busy examining the mail, no time for a "hello" or "good morning" or even "hiya" when you're staring at your watch. But as soon as they made it inside their apartments, you could hear the click-clack of peephole shutters sliding and the creak of doors inching open. Walking down the hallway meant you were being watched, and if you were being watched, then it only made sense that you were being talked about.

Snobs.

According to Jez's dad it had been a hotel long ago. Its status as an Upper West Side landmark was the only thing that saved it from being torn down when the coffee shops and pay-by-the-hour playrooms started moving into the neighborhood. But the renovations had also exposed part of the real Percy—sections of the old building that remained untouched by double-glazed windows and new crown molding. Underneath the new clothing was a set of very old bones.

On this particular Saturday it was not yet noon, though you wouldn't have known it to look at the sky outside. A thick pallet of black clouds lay over the city like a winter blanket. Sidewalk trees—skinny little saplings planted as part of the gentrification—swayed then snapped in the gusting winds. Jezebel watched out her bedroom window as the storm pummeled the city and churned the waters of the Hudson River beyond. She imagined the tall trees in Riverside Park whipping their branches against the blowing rain, cutting through the sheets of water. The park trees were old and strong, and they would do better in this gale than those poor saplings below.

Jezebel's bedroom window rattled as a thunderclap chased a lightning flash through the sky. That one had seemed too close. She backed away from the window and plopped down heavily onto her bed. Even an epic thunderstorm like this could hold her attention for only so long. She rolled around, sat up and grabbed one of her dad's books that she had started at least ten times. She read for a few minutes before giving up at the same spot she always gave up at, and then laid back down and stared at the unfinished mural her father had started on her bedroom wall. It was a scene from an enchanted forest full of lush green trees, toadstools and fairies. She stared at the open white space he'd taped off that was just begging for a unicorn.

Her dad had to be stopped.

Of course, he meant well—parents usually do. These little gestures reassured him that he was an involved and present father. Jezebel's mom liked to say that fatherhood had hit him like a knockout punch and he'd been reeling ever since. But he'd done what was expected of him, and then some. He'd made sacrifices—trading a painter's career for a job in advertising, for one thing, which was why Jezebel let him have his way with the enchanted-forest mural.

Parents. Her mother feared for her—she worried about the "emotional fallout" left from the divorce. Her father overcompensated by filling their weekends with quality time, but she had survived so far without any deep mental scars, so he must've done something right. She thought that he should accept some culpability for the twelve-year-old baby fat that was turning out *not* to be baby fat at all, and for her nearsightedness and tendency to freckle. In fact, she had a whole list of genetic complaints, but the actual child-rearing part he'd pulled off quite well. She'd told him that once, in those very words, and he'd kind of looked grim and defeated about it. Maybe he just didn't know how to take a compliment.

Jezebel tried once more to go online, but the storm had been messing with the Internet all morning and she waited five minutes just for her profile page to load. Cell phone reception was spotty as well. It was like living in the Stone Age. After the connection timed out twice, she gave up and grabbed her shoes instead.

Time to check out the basement.

The basement had been recently uncovered as part of the renovations. A small door in the corner of the lobby, long ago plastered over and forgotten, led to a basement that no one had seen for maybe eighty years or more. It must have been covered up when the old hotel was converted into apartments, although why anyone would go out of their way to wall off an entire basement was beyond Jez. But then again, that's what made it interesting. It was mysterious. She thought it especially odd that the elevator had no B button, either. Whether it was accidental or deliberate, the basement had been hidden away for a long time. There was no telling what could be down there.

Elevator Man smiled at her as she stepped inside. He was new and Jezebel was terrible with names, but the weather seemed to be his thing, and he was always ready with the forecast—today's, tomorrow's or the ten-day extended. It only made sense that today's unusual storm was a topic of excitement. It was like a little holiday in Elevator Man's world.

"Winds are gusting close to thirty miles per hour," he was saying. "Even though there *was* a zero-point-zero percent chance of any precipitation at all. Can't get 'em all right, I guess. Going to be flash flood warnings all over the place, too. 'Course we don't have to worry about that up here, but down in the subway tunnels? Boy, they better have those pumps working overtime, because . . ." He kept on about the ins and outs of subway maintenance as he smacked his gum. Jezebel had yet to see him when he wasn't chewing on a wad of gum, and if he leaned too close you could be bowled over by the overpowering scent of wintergreen.

"Um, excuse me," Jezebel interrupted. She didn't want to be rude, but he had a habit of talking *at* you rather than *with* you, and for exactly as long as it took to get from your floor to the lobby. If you wanted to get a word in at all, you needed to be bold about it. "I was wondering about the basement they just found," Jezebel continued. "Do you know why there isn't any button for it?"

"Huh?" he answered, apparently thrown by the sudden shift from monologue to conversation. "There's a basement?"

"Yes," said Jezebel. "Well, at least there's a door in the lobby that leads down to somewhere."

"Awfully odd to build a brand-new elevator and not have it go all the way down, but that's architects for you. If my elevator doesn't stop there, then it's not worth the trip. My advice is, stick to floors L through thirty."

At that moment the elevator stopped with a ding. "Ah, speaking of—here we are. Lobby," he said as he opened the gated double doors.

She smiled at Elevator Man as he disappeared back up the shaft, leaving her alone. Despite the gaudiness, the lobby was usually Jezebel's favorite thing about her home. It was always such a bright place—sunlight glittered through the prism of a crystal chandelier, coloring the room in soft rainbow hues that reminded her of one of her dad's paintings. Outside the open entrance, the doorman was always whistling.

But today a pitiful few rays of sun managed to make it through the heavy rain clouds. Tarps had been laid over the crushed velvet rugs to catch the drywall dust that came down as the workmen tore away eighty years of paint and wallpaper. Instead of a shower of light, the chandelier cast a long, dull shadow across the floor. And if the doorman was whistling, Jezebel couldn't hear him over the sounds of the wind and the rain. She went to the foyer and looked for him beneath the awning. Dressed as he was in his rain-slicked, lumpy black overcoat and waving his spindly old umbrella against the rain, he looked more like a troll in a storybook than a doorman.

She thought for a moment about going out to say hello—but the wind was blowing so hard now that it actually seemed to be raining *sideways*. She just couldn't work up the nerve to brave that kind of soaking.

So she went for the basement door instead. It was so deeply set into an alcove beneath the main staircase that it was nearly invisible, even with the plaster taken down. There was a sudden flash of lightning outside, and for a brief second the lobby was lit in the color blue. A second was long enough for Jez to see that the door was open just a crack. A rumble of thunder swiftly followed the flash, and Jez jumped as a hand touched her shoulder.

"What do you think you're doing there, little miss?" said a gruff voice in her ear.

Jez turned around, ready with a kick to the shins, but it was only Bernie, the building's ancient superintendent. She'd known Bernie since her dad moved into the Percy two years ago, and yet he remained one of the sourest human beings she'd ever met. She'd heard once that some people aged like fine wine and some aged like vinegar. Old Bernie was vinegar, through and through.

"I'm just . . . nothing," she said, immediately regretting how guilty she sounded. Why should she feel guilty? Were there laws against looking in the basement of your own apartment building?

"Well, actually I wanted to take a peek in the basement," she admitted, straightening her shoulders. "Is that against the rules or something?"

Bernie let go of her shoulder and scratched at his whiskered chin. He had a face like an old saddle, full of cracks and creases. Bernie had to be at least twice her father's age, but though he walked with a limp and a stout cane, his wits were sharp.

It occurred to Jez then that unlike the nice doormen and smiling Elevator Man, Bernie wasn't a part of this new Percy. He looked out of place against the Italian marble. He was worn and crotchety and creaky, like the building underneath.

"There's no rules against going down to the basement, miss," Bernie said. "But I've been down there and I wouldn't advise you going. It's a dark place, dank and full of roaches. And rats, of course. Big ones. Mean-spirited, too. Definitely not a place for playing." As he spoke he sort of arched one eyebrow for effect.

"There's talk of making it a laundry room," Bernie said, suddenly dropping the drama. "But I doubt they'll ever get around to hooking up the hot water pipes. Why don't you forget about the basement and run along and find someone to play with? I don't see you with your friends much these days. I remember when you first moved in you had a whole bunch of snotty-nosed kids hanging around you. What about your friend Sasha? The one who's always scuffing her shoes on my floors—"

"I'm not ten anymore," was all Jezebel said. She had had a lot of friends once. Bernie would think it was ridiculous, but those two years of difference seemed like a lifetime to Jez.

But surprisingly, Bernie's face softened just a touch, as something gave way in the corners of his frown or the crease of his forehead.

"Of course you're not, little miss," he said. "Roaches and rats and all teasing aside, the basement's really no place to be. Trust me."

Bernie was right. Jez knew that he was right. There was no reason on earth why she should be going down there. No reason at all.

Except that she'd just been told not to.

She put her hand on the basement doorknob. He pursed his lips in disapproval but otherwise did nothing.

Watching him out of the corner of her eye, she pulled the door open a few more inches.

"Wait," he said, disappearing into his little studio apartment around the corner. Jez waited for a moment, her hand still on the doorknob, and peeked down the stairwell. Nothing but blackness. The air smelled different—no fresh paint, just earth and wet stone. And something else she couldn't quite place.

When Bernie reappeared with a large flashlight, she let out a sigh of relief. On second thought, it *would* be nicer to have someone down there with her.

"Here you go," he said, handing her the light. "There's a working bulb here over the steps, but you'll need this if you decide to go any further."

"Oh," she said. "You're not coming?"

"Why should I?" Bernie asked, with that same eyebrow arch. "It's just a basement."

Jez took the flashlight and stood at the top of the steps, staring. Just a basement. Only now that she was getting ready to actually go down there, it seemed somehow different. As she peered down the steps, it looked darker. Deeper. Worse.

The storm must be getting to me, thought Jez. All she had wanted to do was have a look around, but now she felt like she was in the middle of a bad horror film. *Don't go into the basement!*

She flipped the light switch, and for a second the stairwell was a flash as the light sputtered on, followed by a pop as it went dark again.

Bernie shrugged his shoulders. "Bad bulb," he said. "You should come back when I've had a chance to replace it. Like I said, it's no place for stumbling around in. Especially for little girls."

Little girls? Jez rolled her eyes and hit the button on the flashlight—at least that worked. The light was steady, strong. "If I don't come back you can have my stuffed animals, Bernie. And all of my pink socks and hair ribbons, too. You'll look good in them."

She pushed past him and placed a single foot on the top step. It creaked worryingly.

"Have it your way, miss," Bernie said. "But do me this favor— if you see any spiderwebs, let them be. Don't go bothering things best left undisturbed."

"Right. Live and let live," she answered, taking another careful step.

The stairs continued to creak more than Jez would've liked, but there was an old wooden railing that gave her a bit of comfort on the walk down. The steps were surprisingly steep and shallow, shallower than modern steps. It made her wonder if people's feet had grown longer over the last hundred years. She took her time.

The bottom was terribly disappointing. It turned out to be just a basement, after all. An old basement, yes, but still a basement.

There were piles of junk strewn about, a few musty old sofas and recliners, thick with dust. She glanced back over her shoulder and saw Bernie's silhouette still standing at the top of the steps. She waved, but he didn't wave back.

What a weird old guy.

Jez began winding her way through the debris, poking here and there with the flashlight, kicking the occasional armchair with her shoe. The only mildly interesting thing down here turned out to be the floor. Most of it was still the original tile—she guessed that it was probably over a hundred years old. Her father would know. He always knew about things like that.

But in the center of the room was a long patch of slate, obvious despite the grime. It looked newer than all the rest. She wondered, what could have happened to damage the floor like that? It was pretty obvious that the luxurious Percy building had once had a big old hole in its basement.

Maybe Bernie knew something about it.

When she turned around to head back up, she saw something under the stairs. A dark shape was standing just behind the stairwell, next to the wall. It was a boy, and he startled Jez at first. She would've heard someone come down those creaky old stairs, so that meant he must've been down here the whole time, watching her. She nearly hollered when she saw him.

Creep.

"Hey, you. What do you think you're doing?" She shined her flashlight at him to get a better look, even as she took a cautious step backward. He was around her age but dressed in some kind of costume. He wore a long coat, one of those dusters that cowboys wear in the movies, and he had a ridiculous pair of goggles pulled down over his eyes. Yet there was something indistinct about him, kind of fuzzy at the edges. There must have been a lot of dust down there playing with her light.

When he didn't answer right away, Jez began to get nervous.

"Hey, Bernie," she shouted, trying to sound a bit rougher than she really was. "Did you know that there is a creepy kid in a Halloween costume down here trying to scare me?"

That's when she heard the door at the top of the stairs slam shut.

Now her nervousness turned to actual fear. The boy stepped forward. Jez took a stumbling step back. "All right, listen. If you come closer I'm going to call the police and smack your teeth out with this flashlight. And not in that order!"

"It's you," the boy said.

"Oookay, it's me. Now who the heck are you?"

"There're things you need to know," the boy said. "The closet in the dark room—there are monsters in there. The reason you're afraid to let your arm dangle when you're sleeping is because things *are* waiting under the bed for you. The space under the stairs is bigger than the space above it and people do disappear there. Attics can be wonderful or deadly, and when you're alone at home and feel eyes watching you—those are real, too. An overgrown garden's never just an overgrown garden and an old basement's never, ever just an old basement."

The boy stopped talking for a moment and checked a bulky brass device strapped to his gloved wrist. It looked like a cross between a wristwatch and a nautical compass.

"I don't have much time. But you've got to be warned. Keep safe and trust your instincts. Be careful. Be smart. Be afraid. The Dead Gentleman's coming."

The device on his wrist made a small dinging sound.

Then he was gone. He didn't move and it wasn't a trick of the light in this dark basement. The boy just disappeared. Vanished.

After that Jezebel did the only logical thing she could think of—she screamed. She screamed as loudly and for as long as she could, and when she was finished, she screamed some more.

CHAPTER TWO

TOMMY
NEW YORK, 1900

Right, then. Back to the beginning. Let's go back a bit, to when I was still just a cutpurse in the Bowery, thieving out an honest living.

Coachmen are never easy pickings, but their riders are. That was one of the first lessons I learned. I never bothered picking the pockets of Bowery folk, since the people who lived in my neighborhood were no better off than I was. At best you'd lift a few coppers and some pocket lint; at worst you'd end up in a life-or-death street brawl. You see, the poor fight for every penny like it's their last, because it is. The well-to-do, on the other hand, those pretty ladies and their fine gentleman escorts with waxed mustaches and soft hands, they are guaranteed to have a few fat wallets or heavy purses that they can *afford* to lose.

Coachmen, now, they are tricky. The clever ones drop their earnings into a sturdy lockbox mounted beneath the driver's seat, and they don't carry the key. The dangerous ones even carry blades of their own, and not for cutting purses. I nearly lost an ear the first time I reached for a coachman's wallet.

All this is by way of explanation, mind you—don't think I'm bragging. Captain Scott was fond of saying that you should never forget where you came from, because that, more than anything else, will steer your choices in the years to come. Considering where I started out—as an orphan street thief stealing pennies and lifting pies out of widows' windows—on this one point, I hope the Captain got it wrong. And for a while, under his instruction, I did dream that I might amount to something more.

I freely admit to an unsavory background, and many of my current habits probably seem *distasteful* to the soft-bellied types. But thanks to the Captain I am not an uneducated lug—I can string a sentence or two together, enough so that I can tell my story in a pleasing way. And that's useful, seeing as how my circumstances have me thinking a lot about my life—its beginnings and, Lord forbid, its end.

Only let's be clear about one thing—this is not a Last Will and Testament. I do not plan on dying. I am not a quitter. I'm an Explorer.

Some might think the early years of my life a sad tale, but it is hardly unique. Ask a hundred street kids their stories and you'll hear a hundred versions of the same. It goes more or less like this: everyone has a father but I never knew mine. I knew my mother and I like to think she loved me, but the older I got the poorer we got, until we ended up living on the street. She might be alive today, or she might be dead, I don't know. All I know is that one night she left me in a church as she went out to forage for food and she never came back. I left the church to look for her and got lost in turn. I've been fending for myself ever since.

Truthfully, I don't much like talking about her, so I'll just jump to the part that gets really interesting—to Merlin and the Gentleman. To the night I decided to rob a black-canopied carriage clattering through the mist along the Bowery.

I was still a young boy at the time, one of many thieves working the Bowery in Lower Manhattan. I've got trouble when it comes to my exact age, seeing as how I can't remember ever celebrating a birthday. I'll say this, though—I'm still shorter than a squat stool and waiting for my voice to drop, so back then I couldn't have been much older than nine or ten. The night I met Merlin, I hadn't eaten in a day and a half, and that generous meal had been a hunk of stale bread and someone's leftover porridge. So as I watched a fancy carriage approaching my corner, I began to dream of filled pockets and a full belly. This wasn't some open-topped penny cab; this was a grand covered carriage, the windows draped in shiny black silk. The coachman was dressed in the finery of a proper servant befitting a private coach, and anyone who could afford a private coach was certainly worth my time and trouble.

As it never pays to be overanxious, I took a few deep breaths to clear my head and quiet my growling stomach. Even at that tender age, I'd already been on the streets for years as a begging urchin brat, but begging was an unpredictable trade and I'd recently moved into the full-time profession of cutpurse and all-around sneak. I'd found it much more to my liking, but that kind of work needs a set routine and a steady hand. I triple-checked my tools— a sharpened purse-cutter (just a plain old shaving razor with the handle removed) and a cop's whistle I'd lifted from an officer who'd tried to pick me up for truancy. Truancy, of all things!

As I watched, the carriage pulled up not ten feet from the entrance to the Crown, a popular music hall and one of my regular hunting grounds. I was well-placed on the opposite side of the street, just another passerby sifting the garbage for scraps. An unusually thick fog had fallen across the city this night, which could only work to my advantage. In seconds the carriage's doors would swing open and its occupants would be swarmed with ragamuffins and neighborhood kids begging for pennies.

But, surprisingly, the carriage continued past the Crown's front and pulled into a side alleyway. Whoever these rich folks were, they had business that required them to use the back door. My pulse quickened. The possibility of a real score had just increased, but so had the risk. People came to the Bowery because they wanted to do things in private that they didn't want their neighbors to know about. People used back doors when they were up to something they *really* didn't want their neighbors knowing about. Such people could be easy marks, or very dangerous.

I carefully picked my way across the street, and instead of avoiding the piles of horse droppings that littered the cobblestones, I grabbed a handful of the stuff and smeared it onto my shirt. Rich folks are awful fickle about stink, and bad smell could buy me a few seconds if I was unlucky enough to get grabbed.

Slipping down the alley, I hugged the walls. Despite the soot of a thousand stovepipes and chimneys clouding up the sky, there was still just enough moon to see by. The carriage had parked next to a rickety-looking loading dock that marked the Crown's rear exit. Two men in dark cloaks waited there, and one of them held what looked to be a small birdcage, the other obviously keeping guard. I gave a signal and waited as a small tangle of beggar children followed the carriage, calling out cries of "alms" and "pennies, please" as they went. Fever had culled the slums something terrible that season, and among the beggar children I spotted at least three new faces, orphaned by disease.

The coachman shouted curses at the filthy urchins as he cleared a path with his riding crop. This fellow was particularly nasty, and there was something about his sickly, pale sheen that gave me a queasy feeling. Already the beggars were scurrying away with angry red welts across their faces as the coachman spit and lashed at their fleeing backsides, his attention no longer on his precious coach. I'd promised to share a few coins with the kids just to keep everyone happy—we all shared the same turf, and by now they'd learned that they'd get more by helping me than from the pity of the well-to-do. As the carriage's side door creaked open I crept up onto its ledge, the one facing away from the dock.

I crouched there a moment, unseen, with my fingers on the door handle. The younger men of the party—the stronger, faster ones—would exit the carriage first to help any lady companions down the steps. The slower, fatter and older ones (the ones I naturally was interested in) would haul themselves out last. I felt the shift in the carriage's weight as the first passenger exited on the opposite side. There seemed to be some kind of exchange going on between him and the men on the loading dock—I heard the clank of coins changing hands. Still crouching low, I opened the door a crack and risked a peek.

Only one person remained inside the cab. A single man sat in the shadows, facing away from me. Despite the dark, I could spy the glint of rich cuff links and the shine of a gold watch chain. Though the man's face was hidden in shadow, his white-gloved hand was reaching out to take the gilded birdcage of brass and wire. I'd obviously stumbled upon some kind of handoff. And inside the cage was a thing I'd never seen before—it looked like a bird fashioned out of metal, like a child's toy. Only this toy shone with silver and gold and its eyes sparkled like jewels. And it was singing. Its little head pivoted back and forth as it let out a soft, sad tune of whistles in a kind of clock-chime birdsong.

Leather creaked as the gentleman shifted toward the far door. From my vantage point I could see through the open cab and onto the dock beyond, where the coachman now waited with another, hulking figure, presumably the other man out of the carriage. It was now or never.

I let the door swing wide as I pulled myself in, behind the well-dressed gentleman. If I had been bigger I might've been able to reach the man's coat pocket from the doorway, but seeing as how I'm a bit of a runt, I had to climb all the way into the cab. In one swift motion, and careful not to alert the men waiting outside, I reached for the man's waistcoat. In cramped quarters like that, your only hope is a quick snatch-and-run. With any luck, I'd have the man's wallet and watch and be out the door before any of them had time to shout "thief."

But whatever luck I had hoped for that night ran out when the little toy bird in the cage swiveled its head toward me and let out a squawk. I might as well have knocked over a stack of empty tins for all the noise the little contraption made. I tried pulling my hand away, but the gentleman's other glove, the one not holding the bird, was too fast. He wrapped his fingers around my wrist in an iron grip. Reflexively, I pulled out my straight razor and slashed at the man's hand. I'm not one for violence, and I'm certainly no mugger or garrote killer, but the streets are unforgiving and when things go bad there's no choice but to draw a little blood—just enough to give a scare. So I sliced the razor across the back of the gentleman's knuckles. The white silk of the glove slit open, but there was no stain of red underneath, and worse, he didn't even flinch.

Instead the man bent down, his face finally coming out from the shadows, and smiled. A lipless, grinning skull looked at me from beneath the brim of that rich gentleman's cap. Dried flesh was drawn tight over a face like parchment. Patches were missing here and there, and he glared at me with empty, eyeless sockets circled with ragged skin. I was staring right into the face of a corpse in its funeral best, but this corpse still moved. I could feel his hot breath on my cheek as he leaned in close. It smelled like rot. It smelled like the grave.

I don't think my mind was working right, just then—I was looking at something too unbelievable, too horrible to be real. But luckily my body was working just fine and instinct took over. I dropped the useless razor and swung my legs around, kicking with all my might. This corpse-man looked brittle, but his grip was strong and I couldn't shake him loose. Outside, the coachman and his big companion had noticed the struggle. The cab door swung wide open and a bald-headed giant reached inside. His hands were easily the size of my whole head, and he was trying to wrap them around my scrawny neck. But this man, at least, was flesh and bone. I knew how to deal with flesh and bone, even when outsized.

The big man grabbed my other hand, and though I'd dropped my razor in the struggle, I still had teeth. I hissed like an alley cat as I bit down on the man's little finger. The man shouted in pain and anger, bringing his other hand around in a heavy, backhanded slap. I curled my shoulder around to take most of the blow, but the edges of my vision went black with spots. Blood dribbled down my chin, and only some of it belonged to the giant. But suddenly I was free—the force of the man's wild slap had broken the corpse-man's grip as well.

The corpse-man was trying to push past the giant's bulk to make another grab at me, but the two men got twisted up in each other's arms. As I scurried across the seats to the far door, I put a foot on the step, preparing to launch myself out onto the street. But something caught my eye—there on the floor of the carriage was the delicate birdcage. Inside, the little metal bird was looking at me with its head cocked in a curious expression.

Wasting a precious few seconds to grab the birdcage would be the dangerous and reckless thing to do, and maybe that's why I did it. I left the carriage door hanging open as I lunged, wrapping both hands around the cage's wire handle. By the time I made it back to the door, the giant had untangled himself and the corpse-man was reaching for me again. Things had suddenly gotten worse.

I just managed to dodge the man's grab and jump out the door—and into the waiting coachman. He'd come around to cut off my escape while I'd tussled with the giant. If the coachman had tried a grab then I would have been done for, but he tried using his whip on me instead. The whip crack missed my face by mere inches as I rolled under the cab's wheel well. I'd escaped the lash, but now I was trapped beneath the carriage. The coachman was shouting at me from one side; on the other, the giant's tree-trunk legs stomped back and forth. And above, in the carriage, was a grinning dead man.

The clockwork bird gave out a worried chirp.

The copper's whistle was still in my pocket. I stuck it in my mouth and wrapped my legs around the undercarriage, lifting myself up with my free hand, the other gripping the birdcage close. Hugging the underside of the carriage, I cleared six inches between the ground and myself. Then I blew. The whistle cut through the night. It was intended to summon other police officers in the event of a ghastly crime, though here in the Bowery no such help would ever come. But the high-pitched, shrieking whistle did have another, more useful effect—it spooked the carriage horses.

Rearing on their hind legs, the horses shook the carriage loose from its steps and began a panicked gallop down the cobblestone alleyway, taking me with them. They made it as far as Bleecker Street before I dropped to the hard stones, praying that my arms and legs would escape the crushing back wheels. The hard landing knocked the wind out of me, and it was all I could do to lie there and watch the out-of-control carriage disappear into the heavy fog. Before I lost sight of it, the back window shutter slid open, revealing a leering skull behind it.

After a moment, I gathered my wits about me, listening for the sound of approaching footsteps. The coachman and the giant would be in hot pursuit, but this was my neighborhood and I could disappear in its knot of shacks and alleys and never be seen again. I was bruised and sick with shock, and I wanted to get far away from the unholy things I'd seen that night and the memory of a dead man that walked among the living.

But first I held up my prize and risked another few seconds studying it. The cage was bent from the fall, but the bird seemed undamaged.

"I don't suppose you have a name, then?" I asked.

The bird's little glass eyes blinked at me, but it made no sound.

"Well, you certainly are a remarkable little toy. Magical, really."

The bird cocked its head at me.

"Merlin," I said, remembering a story my mother used to tell about a wizard and his boy king. "Yeah, Merlin it is."

Then, as I dusted myself off, I added, "Hope you're worth the trouble."

CHAPTER THREE

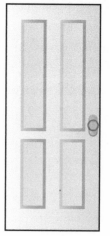

JEZEBEL
NEW YORK CITY, TODAY

Well, it stunk to be insane but it was nice to be loved. And her father, Bernie, and the half of Manhattan who'd heard her screaming now thought Jez was certifiable. In the hours since, she'd begun to wonder if they might be right.

As she lay on her bed staring at the unfinished fairy-garden mural, Jezebel's gaze kept drifting back to her closed closet door. And she remembered the ghost boy's warning.

The closet in a dark room—there are monsters in there.

It wasn't even a particularly menacing closet. Just a plain door. Coat of fresh white paint, cheap aluminum doorknob. It wasn't even a walk-in. The last time Jez checked, it had been full of hanging clothes, a shoe cubby and a few hatboxes of dolls that she was too self-conscious to play with anymore but too sentimental to throw away.

What I should do is go over there right now and open the darn thing up and prove that it is still just a closet. Then I can go to sleep and forget that this whole embarrassment of a day ever happened.

But she didn't. Jez did not get up and swing open the closet door. Instead, she pulled off her shoes and socks and curled up under the covers, not bothering to take off her jeans and hooded sweatshirt. She kept the light on and sat there with a book in her lap, unread. She listened to the sounds of the city outside her window, but she kept her eyes on that door. The storm had weakened to a pitter-patter of infrequent raindrops, and a fog had just begun to roll in. The normal sound track of car horns and traffic had resumed, and every now and then she heard the trot of horses' hooves echoing along the pavement. That was her favorite city sound. Even though she knew that it was just one of the park's mounted police officers or tourists braving a carriage ride, the clip-clop still made the city feel exotic, like a place out of time.

At around ten o'clock her father peeked in to check on her. He had a smear of bright blue just below his lip and a few flakes of red in his hair, which showed he'd been working on one of his paintings. Though working was probably too strong a word for what he had time for—these days he mostly dabbled in the same two or three paintings over and over again. Constantly tweaking, never finishing. Like her bedroom mural.

"Hey, kiddo."

For a moment she actually considered asking him to check her closet. It was something she hadn't done in years—ask her father to give her bedroom the "all clear" before lights-out. It was the kind of thing that little girls asked their fathers to do, little girls who hadn't yet packed away their dolls.

"Hey, Dad."

"Whatcha reading?"

Jez glanced down at the book in her lap. She'd pulled it randomly off the bookshelf in the hall. She hadn't even bothered looking at the title.

"Uh, *Journey to the Center of the Earth*," she said, looking at the gold-embossed binding.

"Oh, yeah? Jules Verne. What do you think of it so far?"

"Well, I . . . I just started it. The jury's still out."

"It's a good one. Ancient secrets, adventure and . . . dinosaurs!"

Jez caught him looking interestedly at the unfinished mural. "No! Do not get any ideas, Dad. I probably won't even like it."

"Hmm, you're right. A T-rex *and* a unicorn would probably be too much."

"Dad! Killing me!"

He laughed. "Joking, Jez."

He sat down on the edge of the bed and set a throw pillow in his lap. It was a frilly, girly thing—out of place in this new room. As he spoke he ran the lace border through his fingers, and Jez wondered if he realized that it had been sewn by her mother. She doubted he remembered it. Jezebel had thought about calling her mother to tell her what happened, but she decided against it. When things went wrong, Jez's first instinct was always to go to her mother. She knew it hurt her dad's feelings, but while she loved them both, Mom was *home*. After he'd moved out, her dad's world had just seemed so alien. Her weekends with him were like visits to another world where she could never quite relax. He tried to make her feel at home but it hadn't worked so far, and it was tiring pretending that it had. But Jez's mother would've handled today's crisis differently than her father had handled it— was handling it. And if given the chance, her mother would've let everyone know it. The two of them, Jez's mother and father, had handled so many things so very differently over the years that they'd ruined their marriage in the end.

To their credit, they were trying desperately not to ruin Jez.

"So, I didn't have a chance to ask you how your session with Dr. Anders went last week," said her father. "You guys getting along?"

Here it was.

"Yes, Dad. He's fine."

"I know your mom said that you can't keep firing your doctors, but if you feel like someone else might be better, then we could always . . ."

"He's fine, Dad. It's not the shrinks, anyway. It's me. Now I'm seeing things."

Her father reached down and stroked her hair. His hands were dry and cracked from the constant washing and rewashing of his paintbrushes. A badge of his trade. "Bernard said that there aren't any other exits from the basement, and he would've heard somebody running up the steps past his door. The draft that slammed the basement door shut came from the lobby. But he'll ask the other tenants to be on the lookout for any strangers hanging around."

"So, I'm crazy."

"Sure, you're crazy. You're crazy-smart, crazy-beautiful and crazy-talented. But you're not crazy-crazy. I know you saw something down there. And you know your mom and I love you no matter what, right?"

She nodded. Of course they loved her. Parents always thought the obvious answers were the profound ones. But they weren't; they were just obvious.

He smiled, though, satisfied. "Now get some sleep." He took the book out of her hands and tucked the blanket up to her chin. "We'll talk more about all this stuff tomorrow. I'm sure it'll make sense in the daylight."

Then he kissed her forehead and switched off the light. He mouthed "I love you" as he pulled shut the door with a soft click, leaving her in a dark room, the light of the city shining through her window like a dim spotlight.

As Jez rubbed at the spot on her cheek where her father's stubbly chin had scratched her skin, a horrible thought occurred to her. It struck her with such force that she nearly bolted upright in bed.

She'd just been *tucked in*.

"No way!" she said as she threw back the covers and marched over to the closet door. She was so mortified by this last, worst indignation after a day of humiliation that she didn't even bother to switch on the light.

She was not a little girl who needed tucking in. She was not a girl afraid of dark closets.

The door stuck at first. It had recently had a paint job and it needed breaking in. It opened on the second try, after Jez gave it a great two-handed heave, and it swung wide on its freshly oiled hinges. Her eyes had adjusted to the low light of her bedroom, but inside the closet it was ink-black.

She half expected a gust of wind or strange faerie light to burst forth, but the air didn't move.

"This is so stupid," Jez said, reaching her hand out to prove, once and for all, that a closet is just a closet, even in the dark.

"Yes," came a small whisper from inside. "Five plump child fingers! We can snap them off and save them for later."

"Shh!" said another voice. "You'll scare her and spoil the treat! She doesn't even have it yet. Fool!"

Jez froze, her hand outstretched just inches from the doorframe, barely a pinky stretch away from the solid black wall of the closet shadow. She couldn't pull her hand back, and she couldn't summon the voice to scream. She felt suddenly unsteady on her feet, like she might fall forward into the dark.

"What's she waiting for?" the first voice asked. "Why isn't she bringing her crunchy and juicy bits in here for us to bite?"

"Because she heard you!" the second voice scolded. "Now she waits to see if she is dreaming. She hopes that she'll wake up with the closet closed and safe and snug in her warm bed."

"Then let's get her first! We can have more than just fingers! We'll leave enough so that she can tell us where the master's bird is."

There was a clatter of movement from within the closet—the sound of something being shifted around, of bodies squeezing past shoeboxes and hangers. At the sound of movement, Jez managed to yank her body back into action, though it felt like cracking a layer of frost from her joints, and she grabbed the open closet door and shoved at it, hard. The door stuck again, but this time it was because of something blocking the doorframe—something small and fat had wedged itself in the way.

"Ouch!" the thing shouted in its full voice, which sounded like the squeal of a chair leg being dragged across the kitchen floor. "She's got me! She's going to mash me in the door! Stop her! Save me!"

The first voice answered from somewhere inside the room, from the nooks and crannies of shadow that the window glow wouldn't touch. "I can't get to her! She's still standing in the nasty city light."

Jez kept her weight on the door, but whatever it was that she'd trapped was pushing back, and it was surprisingly strong. Her arms were shaking with the effort and her mouth had gone dry. Her tongue tasted of metal, of adrenaline.

"Eww! I'm crushing, I'm breaking," said the thing in the door. "Get the shade! Pull the shade and we'll have her!"

There was a scurrying then, as something ran on short legs around the outer edge of her room. It was keeping to the shadows, avoiding the light of the window, hopping over her laundry basket and scampering over her desk. A cup of pens went spilling over the edge and onto the floor, rolling across the hardwood floor like the rattling of bones.

The little creature was almost to the open window shade. One tug on the dangling cord would smother the outside light behind thick vinyl, leaving Jez in nearly total darkness.

Jez gave the closet door one last, strong kick—eliciting a satisfying squeal from whatever was trapped inside—and made a lunge for the desk lamp. Her knee banged against something hard as she skidded and slid on the spilled pens littering the ground. On her hands and knees now, she crawled across the floor. The way suddenly went dark as she heard the rip-cord sound of the window shade drawing shut, and then Jez was moving through blackness, feeling her way to where she prayed her desk was.

The little creatures began to giggle as she heard the thump of plump bodies landing on the floor, accompanied by the pounding of little feet and the smacking of lips and chomping of teeth.

Her hand found the desk leg just as something cold found her ankle. She kicked it off and pulled herself up, frantically feeling for the lamp switch.

She heard the snap of tiny jaws as her sock was pulled halfway off her foot. Several clawed fingers pulled her pant leg up, expos-ing her skinny calf.

She found the switch.

There was a click, then a brilliant flash that left spots in her eyes. When they cleared, she was alone in her room. The shade was drawn, the closet door ajar and pens and pencils scattered along the floor. One sock had been stretched and twisted and now hung limply from her toes. Her left pant leg was hiked up to near her knee. But she was alone.

She pulled herself to standing and grabbed the nearest heavy object—a soccer sportsmanship trophy that she didn't deserve—and examined the innocent-seeming closet. She nudged the door aside with her foot while holding at the ready the marble base of her only trophy. She couldn't stop shaking.

Clothes and shoes. Solid walls and shelves. Nothing out of the ordinary, no more whispered voices. It was a closet, the same as it had been this morning and every other time she'd opened it.

Maybe Jez was really losing her mind. Perhaps all this was just a continuation of the same delusion that had begun in the basement. First she was seeing ghost boys, and now she was bat-tling monsters in the dark. But Jez knew herself better than that. She was not flighty, not prone to fantasies or daydreams. *Someone* had been in that basement today. *Something* had come out of that closet just now.

She opened the bedroom door and peeked down the hall. Her father's light was still on; she could see it beneath his bedroom door, but she could hear his snores even from here. He'd probably fallen asleep reading again.

She gently closed her door and took a look around the room, surveying the damage. A few broken pencils, her desk chair was overturned, but not much else. She wouldn't be turning off her light tonight, that was for sure, but nevertheless there was something that needed doing right away. The window shade was hung between two unused curtain rods and was easily removed. As Jez rolled the vinyl shade up she looked approvingly at her newly bare, unobstructed window. The light of a thousand New York street lamps and neon signs shone down upon her bed, and it would never go dark again.

She stowed the rolled-up shade, appropriately, in her closet behind a hanging shoe rack and some poster tubes. As she did so, she tested the walls for hollow sounds that might indicate a hidden door or false floor. But it all felt solid; there were no exits except for the door itself. It occurred to her as she closed it tight that it was a shame closets didn't lock from the outside. She knew she wouldn't be sleeping tonight anyway, so she busied herself with one last sweep of the room. Trophy-mallet in hand, she peered behind every book, under the bed and in every corner, looking for any trace of her attackers, but there was no sign of them. It was just another rainy night and her closet was just a closet.

CHAPTER FOUR

TOMMY

NEW YORK, 1900

I stared at the bird. The bird stared back at me. This had been our routine for the better part of two weeks. The contest would go on for most of the night until I finally mumbled, "What are you looking at, you stupid bird?" and rolled over, hugging the frayed, moth-eaten woman's coat I'd been using for a blanket, and closed my eyes.

Sleep didn't come easily. It hadn't ever since I'd looked into the face of a dead man and seen him smiling back at me. My dreams had rarely been pleasant things, but they'd lately turned downright nightmarish. Grinning skulls and pauper's graves visited me now. When I was very young, I'd been taught to say prayers for the well-being of loved ones before bed. Since taking to the streets, and since I had no more loved ones to speak of, I'd altered the practice more to my liking and offered up a nightly list of curses instead.

"A pox on Nate the Twist for taking more than his fair share of last week's score," I recited. "May boils burst on Eaglesham the Scrivener for running me off his shop's stoop yesterday. May Quick-Bladed Jenny's knives snap for telling me there were meat pies being tossed out near Brown's Bakery when there weren't any. A curse on Copper Bryant, Copper Scott, Copper Black and that big, hairy-knuckled Copper who walks the beat near Church but whose name escapes me now. A curse on . . ." My little list had been getting longer of late, lasting ten minutes or more until I reached the end: "Lastly, may this squawking piece of junk rust its beady little eyes shut, and may my own eyes be cursed for ever looking upon it. Amen and good riddance." And with this, Merlin would cock its head at me quizzically and let out a long, tired whistle.

In the weeks since my daring robbery of the fantastic clockwork bird, I'd made quite the discovery—that it was impossible to make any money from a fantastic clockwork bird when the entire underworld of New York was looking for it. Sure, I'd been on the lam before, but never like this. Within hours of the heist, word had gone out to every ne'er-do-well and vagabond in Manhattan that something very valuable had been stolen by a common street boy matching my description. The missing item was a shiny metal bird statue, a toy for the very rich, and a very rich man was willing to pay a king's fortune to get it back. And beneath those rumors were darker whispers that this very rich man was actually someone very well-connected and spiteful, and he was preparing to make life hell for all the street folk of Lower Manhattan if he didn't get his pet prize back in a hurry. Greed and fear were working together to make a nasty little brew on the streets out there.

And there were *other* things after me as well. They'd been waiting for me when I returned to my hideout—the small attic of an abandoned tannery near the riverfront. I'd heard their chattering as I perched on the fire ladder that I normally used to come and go. Peeking through the loose slats over the boarded-up window, I made out smallish shapes moving around in the darkened room, but I'd never managed to get a good look—they kept to the shadows, the unused nooks and crannies, the very places where I used to feel safe. I'd heard them several times since then, in back alleys or cellars I'd mistakenly thought empty. Always, I'd be warned just in the nick of time by a low whistle from Merlin. I had to admit, without the bird I'd have been snatched up a long time ago. That clockwork canary had a knack for anticipating trouble, especially trouble of an unusual sort.

Not that the bird's gift excused anything. Because of him, I was now reduced to sleeping under an overturned iron bathtub, wrapped in a moldy coat, with the rest of the crazies who squatted beneath the Brooklyn Bridge. The sounds of the East River, the bells of the barges and the swell of lapping waves, mixed with the smells of campfires and the people there. Few voices competed with the river; mostly it was just hushed whispers and sickly coughing, but every now and then someone would break down crying or burst out in hysterical laughter. The bridge folk were nuts, mostly, but at least they didn't have the wherewithal to chase a bribe, and they were already so far down in the pecking order that you couldn't really threaten them with less. It seemed that the bridge folk were the only ones *not* looking for me, and therefore they were my best bet if I wanted to disappear for a while—at least until the saner folks forgot about me and the stupid bird.

"Hey, you put a deposit on this here tub, or what?"

My eyes popped open as my hand reached instinctively for my missing razor, which was on the floor of a dead man's coach somewhere. A shriveled prune of a face was talking to me, flapping lips working on toothless gums. The face belonged to one of the bridge folk, a well-seasoned one judging by the smell.

Prune-face was tugging hard on my makeshift blanket, trying to get me to move. I tugged back, harder. "Clear off, will you? I'm not looking for any trouble, you crazy old . . . person." I honestly couldn't have told you whether I was talking to a man or a woman. Merlin let out a short whistle that was absolutely no help at all.

Prune-face let me have the blanket but didn't quiet down. "Hey, I'm talking at you. You hear? You gotta leave a deposit with the Duke if you want to sleep here in this tub. So's you don't ruin it. Maybe you leave me that shiny parrot there and I won't tell him."

I glanced over at Merlin in his cage, then at the cracked, muddy, weed-encircled tub I'd squeezed myself under for shelter. It didn't seem like much of a trade. "How am I going to ruin rubbish?" I asked. "And who are you talking about? A duke owns this tub? I suppose that makes you some sort of baron? Or maybe you're the pope himself, right?" I slowly inched my fingers toward the one weapon I did have—a stout ax handle I'd nicked off a lumber cart. So far this crazy seemed harmless enough, but you never knew when they might turn. Then it pays to have a nice piece of hickory at your side.

"Do I look like the pope? I'm just trying to give you some good advice, friend. That there tub belongs to the Duke Under the Bridge, and you don't want to be caught sleeping in it without leaving him a little something. Else he'll take a little something off of you." With that, Prune-face held up a hand, wriggling the stumps of three missing fingers in my face. "Get my drift?"

I got it. This "Duke" person must have been one of the bridge folk who thought of himself as a kind of boss. Maybe he was a thug who was slumming it for a while, bullying the crazies for kicks. Whatever the case, the last thing I wanted was a run-in with him.

"Yeah, well, thanks for the tip," I said as I began rolling up my things. "Like I said, I don't want any trouble, so I'll just be moving on."

Prune-face's face scrunched up even more, if that was possible. "No, you don't get it, friend. There's no time for moving on. The Duke's here *now*!"

"What's this squatter doing here?" asked a voice full of stones. "Lazy sack o' bones enjoying the luxuries of my home without so much as an apple core left out for the Duke?"

He was at least as tall as an elephant, nearly as broad and *fat*. A patchwork robe of stitched-together blankets strained to cover his layers of girth. And atop his square, lumpy head, resting crookedly on two pitted black horns—*horns*—was a dull, dented crown of gold. The Duke Under the Bridge.

He upended the cast-iron tub like it was made from so much newsprint. For once, Merlin had the good sense to remain quiet. As my gaze drifted, very much against my will, up to the pointed teeth that grew crookedly in all directions out of his wide mouth, I had the instant, sinking certainty that Prune-face hadn't lost those fingers to anyone's blade.

The Duke grinned, showing even more twisted teeth. "What's the matter, sport? Cat make off with your tongue?"

Somehow, I managed to find my voice. "Uh, no sir. I . . . I didn't realize that this tub was taken."

"This whole patch of turf is taken. This here bridge and its surrounding parts is mine. And nothing happens here without my say-so, so you'd better pony up tribute to the Duke."

I doubted that the traffic of carriages and carts going to and fro up top had ever even heard of this Duke, much less paid him any sort of tribute. My first guess was right, more or less—the Duke was only a thug, playing big man with the crazies. He was just a particularly nasty, and sort of inhuman, thug. But I had been dealing with thugs all my life.

This insight gave me a scrap of confidence despite the Duke's size and considerable appearance—enough so that my knees stopped shaking, at least. "Well, that might've been my oversight, eh . . . Your Highness," I said, searching my pockets. "Let's see, I've a fine hickory ax handle here, barely a spot of blood on it . . . a nice fur-trimmed coat that would make a grand gift for a lady friend. Just needs a little darning for the holes. Here's a few buttons, some string and a fishing lure . . ." As the Duke scooped up the ax handle and the woman's coat, I subtly put my body between the Duke and Merlin. The big oaf was making small growls of pleasure as he fondled the coat, and I dared to hope that I might just make it out of there if I could keep the beast's attention off the bird.

"Ask him about his shiny parrot, Your Majesty!" shouted a voice from nearby. Cursing under my breath, I spotted Prune-face, looking innocently at the sky.

"Eh?" said the Duke, looking down. "What's this? You holding out on me, son?"

"What? No sir. Of course not. You've got all my best loot right there in front of you."

"That so? I *was* thinking that I'd take this here fancy coat and maybe just a pinky finger. But if you're holding out on me . . . ," said the Duke, letting the coat fall to the ground. "Step aside."

I tried to swallow, but my mouth had gone dry as sand. My alternate plan, which was mostly a lot of running, was looking better by the second. "Sir, I know a very nice scrivener's shop that's an easy mark. Maybe I could get you a few—oof!"

The Duke had heard enough. He poked me in the chest with one thick-clawed finger, which knocked me flat on my back. I landed next to the cage wherein sat the shiny "parrot."

Merlin squeaked with panic, but I couldn't tell whether the concern was for me or for the bird's own well-being. The Duke bent over to inspect the cage, one eye squinting to get a better look, but he seemed to be having difficulty making out such a small thing in the dark. Despite his manhandling of my other goods, the Duke was being surprisingly delicate now, almost cautious.

"Oh, that little thing," I said, rubbing at my sore chest. "That's nothing of interest. Just a bit of junk. A child's toy, is all." If the Duke decided to take Merlin now, there was really nothing I could do about it. And it wouldn't solve my other problems, either. I'd still be hunted. No one would believe that the bird had been re-stolen by some monster living among the bridge folk. They'd assume that I'd hidden it in a safe place, and they would hurt me to make me talk. They would hurt me bad.

As the Duke examined the cage, Merlin suddenly burst into song, flying and fluttering around the bars. It was amazing—I'd never seen the bird do that, and I was pretty sure a creature made up of metal and gears shouldn't be able to do that. Merlin's little show had a different effect on the Duke, though, as he got a good look at the bird at last.

"Eh? What's that? Why, it looks like . . ." In a moment, the Duke's pitted and pockmarked face went from drooling greed to confusion to something like fear, then worse, anger. He was working out something in the slow train of his thoughts. When a creature that big has to think about something that hard, the outcome can never be good. I began to back away, doing a slow crab walk on my hands and feet.

You could almost hear the clank as something fell into place inside the Duke's ugly head. "Spy!" he shouted. "You ain't no street trash! You're working for them! They sent you here to put the squeeze on the Duke." He rose up to his full height and took a giant step toward me. "Well, you can give them this message for me, will you?"

The Duke brought his meaty foot down just inches from my head. If I hadn't rolled at the last minute, my brains would have become so much toe jam. This was obviously my cue. Still on four legs, I scurried underneath the Duke's other foot and made for Merlin's cage. It was ridiculous and very unlike me to be risking my own neck for Merlin a second time. But then again, if you look at the bird as my property rather than, say, my only companion, then it made perfect sense. I always say you need to protect the things that you have rightfully stolen in this world.

The Duke roared in outrage over his inability to squash me into paste. By this time I'd gotten to my feet, birdcage in hand. The Duke gave pursuit.

"I'll have you," he shouted. "And I won't stop with your little finger, either!" He practically chewed the slobbery threat, but I knew that in an open footrace, I had the advantage. The Duke was all girth, much of it sagging around his middle, and those tree-trunk legs just weren't made for sprinting. I'd already put distance between him and me. I even felt cocky enough to wave my intact pinky finger back at him.

Then a voice came out of nowhere. "Not with my shiny parrot you don't!" it said.

I never even saw Prune-face coming, but the wrinkled bridge dweller blindsided me. As I was crushed to the ground, something in Merlin's cage broke with a sharp snap, but I didn't have time to check on the bird's condition. Filthy hands grabbed my arms and legs as more bridge folk, seeing which way the tide was turning, rushed to join the winning side. It didn't take long before I was right and truly pinned.

The Duke came jogging up in a puff—the exercise seemed to have made his mood even crueler, if such a thing was possible. He looked to Prune-face and between gasping breaths said, "Nice . . . tackle, Meg."

Meg. I'd been taken down by an old woman.

"Now . . . then," continued the Duke, his ugly mug leering just inches away. A big, dirty drop of sweat trickled down his brow and off the tip of his twisted, corkscrew nose, splashing against my cheek. I tried pulling away, to put even a few inches between me and that gaping mouth, but the bridge folk held me fast. The Duke grinned, showing teeth. "Now, where's that little finger again?"

I kicked and cursed and fought against my captors, but I was stuck. In my years of thieving, I'd imagined a number of grisly ends. I'd played these scenes out in my head time and time again. Worst I figured, I'd be knifed in a back alley, while the best I could hope for was three squares in a cell somewhere until I was old and gray and useless. But I'd never imagined this kind of death—as a monster's breakfast under the Brooklyn Bridge.

In the distance, I heard Merlin singing like mad. The bird sounded agitated, almost hysterical. In some small way, beneath my own panic, this pleased me. It was nice that there would be someone to mourn my passing, even if it was an addle-brained windup toy.

But I didn't see, at first, the shining flash of metal swooping and diving at the Duke's face. I didn't see the tiny creature valiantly pecking away at the great brute's eyes, heedless of its own safety. I didn't see any of this until, his blood rising in a red-hot and overexerted rage, the Duke swatted at the bird with a reckless, overreaching left hook that missed Merlin and connected, instead, with poor Prune-face's jaw. The shriveled old woman went out like a candle in a gale, spitting out her few remaining teeth on the way down.

After seeing Prune-face's sad end, the remaining stragglers holding on to my arms were only too happy to put some distance between themselves and the Duke's anger, so I had little trouble kicking them off. Meanwhile, Merlin kept up his assault, weaving and dodging between blows and landing several good pecks on the Duke's already pockmarked face, buying me time.

Stumbling to my feet, I made a dash for it. Unfortunately, I was still a bit dizzied, and I didn't have the slightest idea where I'd come from or where I should be going—nothing but piles of junk, campfires and bridge folk in every direction. Luckily, Merlin appeared again. The bird left off its attack on the Duke and soared past my head, circling twice and whistling an urgent tune. I followed the bird at a full run, dodging groups of crazies as we went. I could hear the giant footsteps of the Duke not far behind, his voice bellowing further outrage at being forced into even more exercise.

Together Merlin and I fled through the bridge folks' shanty-town, until we reached the wooden pilings that marked the edge of the East River. The water was a quiet, bottomless black slab in the dark. There was nowhere else to go.

CHAPTER FIVE

TOMMY

NEW YORK, 1900

"Now what?" I shouted. "You've led us to a dead end!"

Still, the bird hooted and squawked and flew out in looping circles over the dark water, urging me to follow.

"That's all fine and good for you," I said. "But I can't swim!"

An exhausted, gasping roar signaled that the Duke was getting close.

Teeth chattering with more than just cold, I waded into the oily river. In just a few feet I was in over my head and chilled down to my bones. Merlin flew excitedly overhead as I struggled to keep afloat with a kind of made-up dog paddle.

I was trapped between the Duke on land and the deep river all around. There was no way I'd survive a swim to the distant far shore, I was sure of that. I'd already swallowed a load of water and my nose was barely above the waves. But just when I thought I was done for, something happened. The water started to bubble and froth all around me, and I cried out as I spotted lights drifting toward the surface like the great, glowing eyes of some beast rising from the depths of the East River to swallow me whole.

An enormous hulk of slime and seaweed broke the surface, lifting me high into the air. Clinging to the top, I barely kept a grip on its slippery, cold surface. Two bright lanterns shone from its front, bathing the shore in electric light. A series of hissing jets vented from the sides, righting it on the churning waves. I hung there for a few terrified moments, clinging to this metal giant, unsure what to do. There was a dull clank, followed by the sound of something twisting, unscrewing—metal grinding against metal. Then the top, just inches away from my fingers, popped open, revealing a hatch filled with warm yellow light.

A man poked his head out of the opening—a big, mustached fellow wearing a strange-looking set of goggles over his eyes. His nose was overly large and red and made him look a bit clownish. But he carried a long whaler's harpoon in his hands with the confidence of someone who knew how to use it.

With a series of nearly gleeful whistles, Merlin landed on the man's shoulder. He gave the bird a smile and a playful scratch under its chin.

"Nice to see you, Herodotus," he said. He had the crisp accent of a Londoner, but it sounded posh and well-to-do, not like the cockney seamen and deckhands I'd encountered before.

He turned to me. "So you're the one to thank for getting our little friend back, eh? Quite a feat, stealing him right out from under the nose of the Gentleman himself!"

I managed to pry my frozen fingers from the hull of the ship, for apparently that's what the thing was—a kind of ship that traveled *under* the water—and stood up. The slick footing was uneven at best and I was afraid I'd tumble back into the river, plus it looked a lot more inviting inside that hatchway, certainly more inviting than my alternatives. I decided to be on my best behavior.

"Uh, yes sir. I suppose so, sir," I said, assuming he meant the dead man in the carriage, though *how* he knew about that was a mystery. "Though I wouldn't call that fiend a gentleman."

He gave a sour laugh. "Yes, you're right. It's a name he hardly deserves, but the Dead Gentleman didn't earn the name; he *took* it."

Merlin, or Herodotus, or whatever the bird's name was, sang a little song and the man paused. He seemed to be listening to the bird, though it was all chimes and tin whistles to my ear.

"Herodotus tells me you've got a special gift for getting out of danger. That you're fast on your feet as well as with your wits."

"Oh, well, that's kind of him, sir," I lied. I didn't believe that this man could somehow understand all that ruckus.

"He also tells me that you're an untrustworthy thief and a sewer rat, and you'd partner up with the devil himself if you thought you could make a profit."

Blast! He could understand it!

"Well, we'll have to work on smoothing out those rougher edges, won't we?"

I blinked, not sure what he was getting at.

"My name's Jonathan Scott," he said, extending a hand. "I'm a Captain First Rank in the Explorers' Society. And I'm offering you a job."

I blinked again. My mouth moved but nothing came out. A job? Aboard a ship that sailed under the water? Things were moving far too fast, and I felt like I was behind the conversation.

"B-but, the Duke . . . ," I stammered uselessly, pointing back to the shore. I saw the retreating shapes of the bridge folk as they stomped out their campfires and broke down their lean-tos. In the face of a giant underwater ship they were, wisely, striking camp. The Duke was nowhere to be seen.

"Oh, that. He was just your run-of-the-mill bridge troll. Usually they stick to creek bridges, abandoned roads, that sort of thing. Every now and then, a particularly big specimen gets a mite full of himself and tries to lay claim to something more impressive. Like we have here. I reckon that now that he's seen the *Nautilus* here, he'll move on. In a hurry."

A troll? Trolls were the stuff of children's rhymes. And yet, I'd seen the Duke with my own eyes. And Merlin. And the Dead Gentleman. I'd seen a lot over the last few weeks, enough that I would never be the same.

Again the man, Scott, chuckled warmly. "No time for sorting it out in your head, my boy. Right now, you've got to make a choice. You can go back to the city, but you'll still be hunted by the Gentleman's cronies. I can't help you there. Or you can come with me and learn to be an Explorer. You've got the makings of a darn fine one, unless I miss my mark. But you've got to choose—time's wasting and we are needed elsewhere."

"Where?" I asked. "The bottom of the sea?"

"No, my boy," said Scott with a wink. "Our journey will take us to a more wondrous place. We are headed for the bedroom of one Miles Macintosh, age nine and a half!"

CHAPTER SIX

JEZEBEL
NEW YORK CITY, TODAY

As Jezebel blinked and stretched herself awake, she remembered something her father was fond of saying: *Never underestimate your ability to surprise yourself.* For example, a person would imagine that after a night spent battling closet monsters in the dark, sleep would be an impossibility. Especially in the same room, next to the very same closet door that those monsters had emerged from. Yes, a person might imagine that.

But that person had obviously never met Jezebel Lemon and Her Amazingly Lazy Body. Her father also liked to remark that Jez could comfortably sleep through an earthquake, and while that had yet to be put to the test, Jez suspected he was right. Somehow, incredibly, Jez had fallen asleep, only to awake to another stormy, cloud-covered day. The weak morning sun barely cut through the gloom outside her window, and Jez awoke with a puddle of drool on her pillow.

Her room was the same unchanged battlefield from the night before. As Jezebel passed her father's closed door she thought about knocking, but what would she tell him? On the heels of yesterday's hysteria, what would he think of this story?

Jez walked into the living room and stood for a while, watching the downpour. It had picked up again overnight. The rain just kept coming in steady sheets. The heavy showers had the effect of blurring everything outside the window so the city looked like a painting that had gotten smeared—there were no hard lines anymore; the whole world had gone bleary at the edges.

She needed help. The boy in the basement had been creepy—scary, even. But those things in her closet had been terrifying. Still, a ghost in the basement? Monsters in the closet? Who would believe her?

Sasha's apartment was just down the hall. The two of them had been friends since Jezebel moved in, and for a while they'd even been best friends. But over the last year or so things had changed. Small things at first, like little disagreements over movies they wanted to see or music they liked. Sasha was getting prettier every day while Jezebel was just getting taller, but that wasn't the real reason for the distance. Sasha couldn't wait to grow up, and while Jezebel wasn't opposed to it in theory, she just couldn't get the hang of it. She wasn't sure what was expected of her or how she should behave.

Their last fight hadn't even been a fight, not really. Sasha called Jezebel at her mom's to tell her that she'd had her first kiss with a boy named Max Perkins. Jezebel had been quiet on the phone, and Sasha took that to mean that Jez was jealous, and in anger she'd hung up on Jez. But Jez wasn't jealous—Max had peach fuzz on his upper lip and called everyone "dawg." Jez didn't say anything because she'd heard the story before; she'd heard the rumors at school just like everyone else. Jez didn't say anything because Sasha, her best friend, hadn't told her first. Or even second or third. She wasn't sure where she fit in anymore among the hierarchy of Sasha's friends, but it was far down the list and getting farther every day.

But right now she was the best hope Jez had.

Jez knocked on Sasha's door, and when no one answered that, she rang the bell a few times. After several minutes she heard the peephole flipping open and the door opened to reveal Sasha's mom standing there, sleepy-eyed. She had a bathrobe on that she was holding closed with one hand; she hadn't even bothered to tie it.

"Jezebel?" she asked. "Is there something the matter? Are you all right?"

"Is Sasha home?" Jez asked.

"Sasha . . . I don't . . . Jezebel, it's six in the morning!"

It was? Jez hadn't even thought to check the time. Well, that explained why her dad was still asleep.

"So, she's not home? Because I'd really like to talk to her. It's important."

Sasha's mom scratched her head. She was obviously having trouble processing information this early on a Sunday.

"Hold . . . hold on, Jezebel. Just wait here."

The door shut and Jezebel was left alone in the hall. After a few minutes she heard voices inside Sasha's apartment, then the door clicked open and Sasha stepped out into the hall. She wore the same groggily concerned expression as her mother, but hers was colored by something else like annoyance or embarrassment. More likely a combination of all three.

"Jez, what are you doing? Do you know what time it is?"

"Yeah, it's six. Your mom told me. Sorry about that."

"You know as soon as I go back in she's going to ask me if you're on drugs."

"Listen, I need to talk to you about something," said Jez, taking Sasha by the arm and leading her away from the door. "But I need you to promise me that you'll listen and not freak out. Or tell me I'm crazy."

Sasha pulled her arm away. "You're already acting nuts, but okay. This better be good."

Jezebel told Sasha the whole story, starting with her trip to the basement and ending with last night's closet monsters. Sasha raised an eyebrow at the description of the mysterious ghost boy, but otherwise she didn't show much reaction.

When it was all over Jezebel took a deep breath—she felt like she'd just swum from one end of the pool to the other without breathing. From the shallow to the deep end.

Sasha just stared at her, her brow wrinkled with thinking.

Please believe me, thought Jez. *Please.*

"Jez," Sasha said after a moment. "Are you jealous of me and Max?"

Jezebel started. She felt she'd just been hit with a case of verbal whiplash.

"What? No! Of course I'm not jealous. . . . Did you listen to a word I said?"

Sasha smiled and winked. "Of course I listened, but you don't expect me to believe that you've got monsters in your closet! Or that you've got a ghost boyfriend who only you can see."

"He's not my boyfriend! I'm telling you something serious is going on, something really scary, and all you can think about is Max?"

"Well, it's obvious you are trying to get my attention. And besides, I know you had a thing for him."

"I did not!"

Sasha placed her hands on her hips. "You gave him your picture."

"I what?" asked Jez.

"He has a picture of the two of you, together. In Mrs. Leonard's class."

"Mrs. Leonard's class? We *all* took pictures of each other on the last day. I even got my picture taken with Mrs. Leonard, and she's like a hundred and hunchbacked!"

Jez was confused. She felt suddenly guilty even though she had nothing to feel guilty about, and the guiltier she felt the guiltier she looked. She probably had her picture taken with Max but she couldn't remember.

Jez felt her face turning hot. Her voice began to crack. "Everybody got their picture taken with every—"

"Max didn't have his picture taken with me!" Sasha said. She poked her finger at Jez, and she was no longer smiling. "He still has it. Yours is the only one he kept."

"Huh?" asked Jez.

"He keeps it in his notebook! I saw it there when we were studying together."

Jez felt her cheeks were on fire. She felt like she was under a hot lamp. "I . . . I don't know! He . . . he has a peach fuzz MUSTACHE!"

The apartment door opened and Sasha's mother poked her head out. "Girls!" she whispered. "It's six in the morning!"

Jezebel wasn't aware that she'd been shouting, but she was suddenly certain that she was being watched through peepholes up and down the hallway.

"Sorry, Mom," said Sasha. "We're finished, anyway." And with an angry glare she went back inside the apartment as her mother shut the door behind her.

Max Perkins? Jez had lost her best friend because Max Perkins had hung on to a stupid photo? It was creepy to think that someone she barely knew was carrying around her picture. Max was creepy. Thanks to his overactive hormones, she now had no one to turn to when she was in real trouble. The universe was stacking against her.

She'd find the ghost boy. She would go to the basement, and the ghost boy would explain what was going on. Jezebel crept back into the apartment and grabbed a flashlight, careful not to wake her father. Outside in the hall, as she waited for the elevator, she worked on bolstering her courage. She'd get some answers. She just had to.

The elevator door opened up and Elevator Man was waiting for her.

As she stepped inside she kept her eyes focused on the floor—everything was still swirling around in her head.

They'd traveled down several floors before she realized that something was different. She'd been so lost in her own thoughts that she hadn't noticed Elevator Man wasn't talking. He wasn't even looking at her; he just stared at the slowly changing floor numbers like normal people do. And he was no longer smiling.

For some strange reason this alarmed her nearly as much as anything else she'd experienced in the last twenty-four hours. She felt like she should make some small talk, break the unnerving silence.

"I missed the weather forecast," she said. "You catch it by any chance?"

"They're calling for sun, but they're wrong," he answered, but the smile was gone from his voice. "The sun's not coming back, not ever. And you'd better tread carefully from here on out, Jezebel. The Gentleman is at the door and it's best not to keep him waiting. He will rise up the dead and buried of this world and throw them against you."

At the mention of the Gentleman, Jez's breath caught in her throat and stayed there. She was suddenly keenly aware of how close they were. Gone was the smell of mint; today his breath reeked of rotten things. It was terribly claustrophobic in here, as close as a coffin.

The door chimed again and Elevator Man opened the gate.

"Bottom floor," he said.

Jez dropped all pretense at friendliness. She bolted out of the elevator without looking back, not even daring to breathe until she'd gotten halfway across the lobby.

She was so panicked she didn't even see old Bernie until she'd slammed into him.

"Everything all right, miss?" he asked.

"The Elevator Man! The Gentleman! He said the dead were coming!" Jezebel couldn't help herself. Her heart was throbbing in her ears and panic had thrown all caution to the wind. It was all just coming out in a rush.

Bernie bent down and put a hand on her shoulder. His eyes peered at her from behind thick plastic glasses. When he blinked he looked like an owl. She'd never noticed that before.

"Who said this? The elevator operator?"

Jez nodded.

"He mentioned the Gentleman?"

Jez nodded again. "He said he was at the door."

Bernie looked sharply over her shoulder and Jez followed his gaze. The elevator door was closed—the numbers up top were slowly rising as it traveled back up the floors.

"Come, little miss," said Bernie, leading her to his door. "Come inside."

"No one will believe me, Bernie," said Jez, and she was surprised that her voice was hoarse. Her body was still shaking with fear.

"I believe you, miss," he answered, and his creaky, tobacco-burnt voice turned soft. "I believe you."

Bernie's little apartment was a junk shop of odds and ends, and bits and pieces of machinery. She could see one uncluttered space in the whole room, a well-worn recliner with patched armrests that looked like it belonged in the trash heap. To the left was a small kitchenette, and set into the far wall was a closet door that Jez had no intention of going near. Every other square inch was covered in piles of scattered newspaper, but they obviously weren't meant for reading; they were to catch the grease and oil of a hundred little cogs and contraptions. His apartment looked more like a machinist's repair shop full of tools and spare parts. Spare parts to what, it was impossible to tell—she had never seen anything like it. Jez didn't consider herself any kind of hacker whiz, but she knew the difference between a motherboard and a memory chip. But this stuff just looked like . . . clock guts. There were no wires to be found, or batteries. Only gears and springs.

Bernie cleared off a portion of the couch for her to sit on and walked over to the closet on the far wall. Jezebel stiffened as he grabbed the handles.

"Don't worry," he said, seeing her alarm. "It's not that kind of closet."

He opened the door to reveal a small space not much deeper than her own closet. But there were no hangers or shoe racks. It was filled with shelves of funny-looking equipment. No spare parts here; these were complete gadgets, though what practical use they might have was anybody's guess. Some kind of old-fashioned-looking gun with a net attached to its front, a number of small boxes covered in dials and strange knobs. There was a pair of goggles with blue lenses, like the kind the boy had been wearing, and they were dangling from a peg on the wall. Everything in there looked old, despite the meticulous condition it was obviously in. It reminded Jez of those antique toys you sometimes see behind collector's glass—all the care in the world cannot erase age.

In the center of it was what looked like a robot bird on a perch. When it swiveled its silver-feathered head to blink at Jez, she nearly shouted.

"What . . . what is that?"

"That," said Bernie, gesturing grandly at his little assortment, "is what remains of the Explorers' Society. A few odds and ends, some tired old tricks and our friend Merlin."

The bird chirped proudly as it settled on its pedestal. Its song skipped like an old scratched record.

"Merlin?"

"Well, he's had several names over the years. Wei-fung, Herodotus. Merlin was what Tommy called him. Tommy being the boy you met in the basement yesterday."

"So, he is real!" Jez said, her earlier fear and trepidation washed away with a feeling of sudden, exhilarating *I-told-you-so*.

"He's real, all right," said Bernie. "Tommy Learner was the greatest Explorer, ever. He was also the last Explorer, *ever*. But that's water under the bridge, as they say. All that happened a long, long time ago. I doubt anyone even remembers his name."

"Remembers his name?" said Jez. "But I just saw him yesterday, and he's no older than I am."

"And that, young miss, is what's so troubling. You see, Tommy Learner has been dead for nearly a century."

Jez stood up, opened her mouth and shut it again. For just this once, she could think of absolutely nothing to say.

"Sit down, Jezebel," he said, "and I'll tell you everything. I promise, all will be revealed."

CHAPTER SEVEN

Tommy

Somewhere in the Atlantic Ocean, 1900

"We're Explorers, Tommy," said Captain Scott as he gave the ship's wheel a turn. The man cut an impressive figure, standing tall in his naval cap and long shipman's peacoat. But I have to admit that my attention wasn't on the Captain himself. I couldn't take my eyes off the enormous porthole behind him and the blue expanse of water beyond. We were bouncing along on top of the Atlantic Ocean.

And I was going to be sick.

The Captain continued. "The Explorers' Society is a unique club. We conquered the last frontier of this planet long ago, but now we navigate far more exciting places. Adventure is always out there—you just have to know where to look!"

I tried answering from my place on the floor, but all I managed was a low moan. The cool metal, at least, felt good against my forehead, and if I closed my eyes I didn't have to see the roiling, lapping ocean outside. Unfortunately, I could still feel the motion, all the way from my toes to my stomach, as Captain Scott's strange ship rode the choppy waves like a leaf in a storm. Each lurch threatened to upend what little remained of breakfast down my front—I'd had to change clothes three times so far since daybreak, and I was now draped in one of Scott's oversized shirts. I would've felt ridiculous if I hadn't been so busy praying for a quick death.

"Still feeling seasick?" asked Scott, in what I suspected was the man's one-and-only tone of voice—that of the booming announcement. He shouted commands as if he were piloting a ship of eighty men, but from what I saw, he and Merlin made up the whole crew.

"Don't worry, it'll get easier," he said.

Something that Scott mentioned earlier suddenly struck me. "What do you mean, you conquered the last frontier of *this planet*? What other planet do you mean?"

The Captain smiled. "Countless others, my boy. Countless! Other worlds, hidden under our very noses. Stuffed away in the folds of time and space!"

"Now you're just talking nonsense," I said. "You're having me on." A fancy underwater ship was one thing, traveling to other planets was another.

"Was that bridge troll nonsense? You think that fellow came from your neighborhood? Or Brooklyn, perhaps?"

I didn't answer. He had a point, there.

"BEGINNING PREPARATIONS TO DIVE! You see, Tommy, that troll came through a portal—kind of a doorway to another world. Most people think of reality as being a dependable, solid thing, but it's actually more like a block of Swiss cheese.

Full of little pockets and holes. Full of doors. Can't say we understand the science behind the portals, but they tend to appear in
the most ordinary places. Old gardens, cellars, behind bookcases,
even. Your troll came here from another world where blokes like
him are commonplace. Probably the world of Faerie, judging by
his looks, or maybe New Hamelin. Usually the doors stay closed,
but it happens sometimes that a creature finds his way through.
Most keep a low profile, since it doesn't pay to draw too much attention. This nasty fellow just got too big for his britches, started
making waves."

My stomach gurgled again at the mention of "waves."

"Besides," the Captain continued. "The vast majority of people wouldn't have noticed anything unusual about him if he were
napping in their own bed. They wouldn't see past the Veil."

"The Veil?"

The Captain nodded. "The Veil is a kind of energy field that
hangs over everything. Invisible, imperceptible, but it's a part of
nature, as real as the open sky or this vast ocean. And it's very
good at reckoning what belongs on Earth and what doesn't. It
softens the harsh realities of things that are too *different*—things
most folks aren't ready to face. It blurs the edges, so to speak, and
makes the unbelievable into something . . . acceptable. It hides
the portals to those other worlds and disguises the beings who
come through them. To the common eye, a troll that crosses into
our world becomes a big, ugly lug of a man, though still just a
man. But the Veil is not all-powerful, and there are those who
can see past it, who can lift the Veil and see the truth. Children
often have the gift, which is why you've been having so much
trouble these last few weeks. I'd say your Veil has been lifted—
and then some."

"I'm not a child," I said, maybe a bit too quickly. "I take care of myself."

"Mm-hmm." Scott nodded. "Of course, my mistake." He looked at me for a moment. I felt my cheeks redden beneath their greenish tinge.

"But as I was saying," he went on. "There are precious few adults these days who can see past the Veil. Some artists manage glimpses, but even they usually blame it all on an overactive imagination in the end. Take this ship, for instance. I knew a Frenchman once who looked out the window of a coastal hotel one blustery afternoon and spotted a great metal ship rising up out of the waves! A ship that had emerged intact from beneath the sea! Being a literate fellow, he immediately put pen to paper and wrote about what he'd seen. But within hours the Veil had worked its magic on him, and instead of the truth, he ended up with a novel!

"Perhaps you've read it? *20,000 Leagues Under the Sea?*"

I shook my head. I had no use for novels. Not that I had any problem with other people enjoying them. After all, it was much easier to lift a man's wallet if his nose was buried between the covers of a book.

"Well," said Scott. "The book made him famous but left him none the wiser to the truth of reality. I rechristened the ship after the name of the one in the novel—the *Nautilus*. Seemed the least I could do.

"There are other, sadder cases of those with the gift, but they are often, well, a bit soft in the head. Take those poor bridge folk of yours. The Duke was able to take over their home because they could see him for what he truly was and were rightly terrified."

I remembered the look in Prune-face's eyes when the Duke

came stalking toward them. How many horrible things had that old woman witnessed over the years?

"And what about you?" I asked. "You saw him. You're not a child. You an artist? Or . . ."

The Captain chuckled. "Neither! It's training, my boy! We Explorers join when we are children, well, *young men* like yourself. Then we train for years to see past the Veil. Some make it. Most, unfortunately, do not. It takes a steel mind to discipline oneself to avoid the Veil . . . ALL HANDS PREPARE TO SUBMERGE! TO YOUR STATIONS!"

I glanced around the empty ship as Scott shouted orders to a crew that wasn't there and wondered, for what wouldn't be the last time in our career together—was it discipline that kept the Veil away, or did this Captain have more in common with the bridge folk than he liked to admit?

But even if the Captain was a touch delusional, the *Nautilus* was certainly real. Scott continued to bark orders as he flipped a barrage of switches, and the entire vessel began to rattle. A bell dinged somewhere in the distance as my eardrums began to crackle and pop.

"What's going on?" I shouted, covering my ears with both hands.

"Shift in pressure," the Captain shouted back. "We're diving!"

The noise of waves chopping at the ship's hull gave way to a muffled roar as it was surrounded on all sides by ocean, aft to stern, top to bottom. The nausea lessoned a tad as the ship's motion steadied, but it was replaced with the cold sweat of absolute terror. I knew we were going to die. The *Nautilus* would sink until the pressure crushed it like an empty snuffbox. I'd escaped a dead gentleman and a bridge troll, only to die in the deep ocean.

Or not.

After a time, when the ship's quivering had ceased and the pops in my ears subsided, I opened my eyes just a squint and risked a peek. The porthole was dark, and the interior lights of the *Nautilus*'s bridge lit up the glass like a mirror. But at least the room had stopped spinning. If not for the constant thump of the ship's engines, I wouldn't have been able to sense any movement at all. We might have been standing still in any posh room in New York.

"Are we really . . . underwater?" I asked.

"Not quite twenty thousand leagues under the sea, but we are deep enough." Scott smiled, his teeth shining white beneath his sandy mustache.

"Have a look." With that he turned a crank on the wheel, and the lights in the cabin dimmed as the floodlights on the outside of the craft blinked and sputtered once . . . twice . . . and lit up with a flash. The deep, impenetrable black of the ocean outside came alive all at once as a school of brightly colored fish zigzagged past the porthole, and for a few seconds it looked like we were in some kind of painter's dream. But they soon cleared, and what was revealed was . . . unbelievable. Never had I imagined such a sight. The *Nautilus* was traveling above a giant trench in the ocean floor. Towering shapes loomed in the distance, which I could only guess were the shadows of some kind of mountain range—a mountain range on the bottom of the ocean! The waters between our ship and those peaks were filled with schools of strange fish swimming through a tangled coral forest. And below, the yawning mouth of the chasm a mile wide, the blue-black ocean disappearing over its edge and from view.

"That is Kraken's Gorge. And at the bottom is a very, very big portal."

At that moment there was a dull rumble somewhere along the hull of the ship.

The Captain must've caught my worried expression. "Not to fear, just the *Nautilus* adjusting to the deep water. A kraken hasn't slithered out of there in a hundred years or more." This was answered by another, more distant rumble that seemed to come from somewhere much lower, somewhere in the depths of the gorge. Merlin, who'd been perched contentedly on the railing, let out a low whistle.

"Of course, no need to sail *too* close, at any rate." The Captain coughed into his hand and turned the wheel, steering the *Nautilus* farther from the chasm's edge. "What I wanted to show you is *there* anyway," he said, pointing to the far edge of the coral forest. "The Lemuria Outcropping."

"The what-what?" I asked. I was glad to see the chasm mouth growing smaller in the porthole, but I was getting awfully tired of understanding only every fifth word out of the Captain's mouth. "I thought you said we were going to some kid's bedroom! What are we doing on the bottom of the ocean?"

"Miles Macintosh lives in England, which is where we're headed. I just couldn't resist taking the scenic route. We are about to pass one of the most awesome sights on this planet. Why don't you look it up for yourself? *L* for Lemuria." Scott gestured to a pedestal that stood a few feet from the Captain's wheel, and resting atop it was the biggest book I had ever seen. It looked old, with sturdy brass bindings and a fat padlock on its front. It was the lock that piqued my interest, of course. Books are nothing to get excited about, much less really big books, but people only put locks on things that are valuable, and I definitely have an interest in valuable things.

The cover was faded and cracked. I could barely make out an illustration of the Earth, surrounded by a ring of other, smaller planets. "Silly drawing," I said. "So, what's the lock about? This thing hollowed out or what? You keep your cash in there?"

"The *Encyclopedia Imagika* isn't worth anything in currency. But the lock does guard a treasure."

I tested the cover—it was unlocked. I felt a familiar itch in my fingertips. "So what sort of treasure? Jewels?"

"Words."

That gave me pause. "Words? Words are your big treasure? You're joking, right?" I flipped open the book, which was no easy task, given the size of the thing, and looked. It was no joke. It was filled with words. There were some sketches of strange buildings and such, but mostly just words.

"Turn to page one thousand five. Under the heading *Lemuria, Ancient.*"

I flipped until I found the page marked one thousand five— which was not even close to the halfway point—and looked it over. About halfway down was a drawing of some kind of temple built into the face of a giant hunk of rock. "This it?"

"Yes. Now read the entry. Out loud, if you please."

"It's all faded," I said, quickly letting go of the page. "Besides, I lost my spectacles in the tussle with the Duke."

"Glasses? You?"

"Fine, I've just never had much use for reading, all right?"

"Fair enough," answered the Captain gently. "There'll be time enough to correct that, I suppose. What it says is that the Lemuria Outcropping was part of the ancient Lemurian civilization, which disappeared thousands of years ago beneath the waves."

"Disappeared? How?"

"No one knows for sure. Could've been an earthquake. Some say it was swallowed by a kraken, though I think that's a load of poppycock. Regardless, the Outcropping is what they left behind. A single shelf of rock, and the ruins of a temple. But what's even more astounding, what makes this place so very special, is that Lemuria never existed on Earth!"

"Sorry?"

"The ruins fell through the Kraken's Gorge portal, but they fell through the *other side*. Into our world. What you are looking at is a chunk of another planet, Tommy."

"Can't see much of anything right now," I said. The view outside the portal was just mostly black water and shadows again.

"Well, let's see what we can do about that." The Captain threw some kind of switch and the powerful floodlights on the outside of the hull grew even brighter, illuminating more of the dark ocean around us.

I'll admit now that I hold on to a few happy memories of my mother. Despite what I said before, there are one or two times that I don't mind talking about. One was the night she took me to see a play. I can't remember the name, or much about the story, even—something to do with gods and heroes. But I do remember the scenery. It seemed enormous at the time, a wall of tall stone columns and ornate arches, lit by flickering footlights and multicolored lanterns. The backdrop was a painted landscape of purple clouds drifting over a burning orange sun. Though my mother explained that the whole thing was just a construction of paint and wood, I hadn't believed her. It was too massive, too solid to be anything but real, weather-beaten stone. It was the most awe-inspiring thing I had ever seen.

All that was gift paper compared to the temple of Lemuria. Perched atop a tall outcropping of rock, the underwater temple dwarfed the *Nautilus*. It was so gigantic that the ship's floodlights could light up only a small portion of the whole thing. A twisting archway, broken in places and barnacle-covered, shone green-gray in the lights. Beyond were the ruins of a once-great building, now a graveyard of toppled statues and crumbled chambers.

But what unnerved me, what caught my breath in my throat and kept it there, were the proportions of the place. They were all wrong. The steps were not carved for ordinary feet. The gates were not built to be opened by human hands.

This was not a massive temple built for men . . . this was a small temple built for something much bigger.

"Giants," I whispered.

"Hmm?" asked Scott. "Oh, yes. I suppose so. The Lemurians were on the largish side. Which, again, makes the kraken theory a bit suspect."

The *Nautilus* slowed as we approached the arch. The water here was hazy and thick with silt. The effect was like driving a carriage through the fog—the diffused light played tricks on your eyes.

"I . . . it's just . . . I've never dreamed . . ."

Scott chuckled. "I know, I know. This is all a whirlwind, Tommy, and for that I apologize. But I had to take quite a detour to come get you, and that's put us behind schedule. You're going to have to learn as you go—"

The Captain was interrupted by a bell dinging somewhere, followed by another even shriller than the first. Merlin began to whistle and chirp in a way that I recognized. I'd heard that song plenty of times in the last few weeks—it meant trouble.

"What's wrong?"

Scott pulled a long cylinder down from the ceiling and peered through a kind of window at its base. It looked like one of those moving-picture boxes you'd see at fairs and the like.

"Unbelievable," the Captain said, clucking his tongue. "Of all the things . . ."

"What?"

"Bit embarrassed to say it, but it looks like we're about to be swallowed by a kraken."

CHAPTER EIGHT

JEZEBEL
NEW YORK CITY, TODAY

Bernie removed his glasses and squeezed the bridge of his nose between his thumb and forefinger as he let out a long, worried sigh.
"I know how it sounds. But you must believe me, Tommy Learner
is long dead and buried."

"It sounds like a load of—"

"Language, now, young lady."

"Forget my language, Bernie. I'm telling you he's not dead. He
can't be—I saw him. He spoke to me!"

"A great poet once said that there was more to this Earth
than is imagined in your philosophy."

"Okay, there is something weird going on—but it has got to
be something explainable! Something to do with, like, magnetic
fields or gas leaks that cause hallucinations or . . . *anything* other
than a . . . a ghost story."

"Would you prefer that? Would you really rather learn that

this is all in your head? A silly daydream, maybe?"

Jezebel started to answer in the affirmative, but she hesitated. What did she want the truth to be? As of yesterday, when she first saw Tommy in the basement, her life had become . . . unique. Terrifying, yes, but also unique. In the last day and a half she'd experienced excitement that had nothing to do with ex–best friends or first kisses or growing up. Her life had suddenly turned mysterious; did she want to chalk all that up to an overactive imagination?

"Then what is the truth, Bernie? What's going on?"

The old man shook his head. "I don't know everything, myself. But Tommy Learner was a member of the Explorers' Society, a secret organization that existed over a hundred years ago. The Explorers are all gone now—disappeared. But if you are right, if that really was Tommy, somehow, miraculously, alive and in the flesh, then he's the very last one."

Jezebel looked at Bernie, this little old man surrounded by bits and pieces of junk, and thought of people who sit in their basements wearing tinfoil hats, afraid the Martians are trying to get into their minds. But if Bernie needed a tinfoil hat, then Jez should start making one, too. She was just as crazy as he was.

"How do you know all this stuff?" she asked.

Bernie walked over to the closet and pulled down a giant, leather-bound book. The old man grunted and groaned as he hauled it over to the table. The mechanical bird whistled at him.

"It's all right, Merlin," he said, through gritted teeth. "I'm lifting with my legs."

The book landed on the table with a loud thump, spilling

newspapers everywhere and sending little springs and cogs rolling in all directions.

"This book," he said, breathing heavily, "is called the *Encyclopedia Imagika*. It's part history of the Explorers' Society, part encyclopedia of the bizarre, and part textbook. You can see it's a bit unwieldy."

Jezebel stepped forward and ran her hands along the spine. It felt old and sturdy. On the cover was a kind of padlock that dangled, broken, from its clasp.

"I know it sounds ridiculous, but according to this book, these Explorers traveled between different worlds," Bernie said.

"What, you mean like astronauts?"

"No, more like *inter*-nauts. They didn't travel through outer space. They traveled through inter-space. You've heard of quantum mechanics?"

Jez nodded. "Sure. A butterfly flaps its wings in Tokyo and somebody's cat explodes here in New York."

"Eh, not quite, but close. At its most basic, it means that everything is connected. And beyond your charming butterfly/cat example, that means that many planets in our great universe are connected by more than just distance. The Explorers called them portals. Today we would call them wormholes."

"Uh-huh," Jez said. "Bernie, ghosts are one thing, but now you're getting all science fiction-y on me."

He held up his hand. "Just bear with me. These Explorers used these wormholes, these little doorways in reality, to travel the cosmos. They are rare, but they are definitely real. Hidden from the perceptions of most people."

Bernie looked over his shoulder at the mechanical bird, and though she couldn't be sure, Jez thought the bird nodded at him, ever so slightly. As if it was encouraging him to continue.

"But the book also talks about something else—a great evil that the Explorers discovered. A thing totally malevolent and filled with hatred of all living things."

Jez went cold as she remembered what the ghost boy had said.

"The Dead Gentleman," she said. "Tommy warned me about him."

Bernie nodded as he patted the book. "I couldn't be sure until just now, but hearing that nearly confirms it. The Dead Gentleman is coming. He may already be here."

"Bernie," said Jez. "How do you know about all this? I mean, where did you get that book, and that . . . Merlin thingy? Who are you? Really?"

Bernie took off his glasses and wiped them on his shirt as he squinted at the little mechanical bird.

"I'm someone who's trying to make up for lost time. I'm trying to set things right, in my own small way."

"Well, that's great, but you still haven't answered my question. I need to know what is going on—last night I was attacked in my own room! Monsters came out of my closet, Bernie!"

"Your closet?" Bernie put his glasses back on and peered at her. "I've long worried about the basement of this old building, but this is a troubling development. Your apartment could be a direct portal to the Dead Gentleman's world. You cannot go back there. It isn't safe."

Jezebel suddenly pictured her father sleeping, oblivious. She imagined her closet door slowly creaking open and a dead, rotted hand reaching out of the darkness.

"Dad! He's still up there!"

Jez turned and started for the doorway. How could she have been so selfish? She had been so caught up in whether or not he would believe her that she hadn't even bothered to consider that he might be in danger, too.

She ran to the stairwell.

"No, Jezebel! Wait!" Bernie started after her, but his leg stiffened up on him. He fumbled around, looking for his walking stick. Jezebel didn't wait for him to find it.

Into the lobby and past the elevator she ran. As she bolted by the elevator doors, Jez noticed that the number was lit on twelve—her floor. It didn't move. It stayed there.

She heard Bernie's voice calling after her, but it soon disappeared as she began sprinting, two steps at a time, up the long stairs.

She was halfway there, and totally out of breath, when things began to slither in the shadows. The stairwell was not very well lit, and the weak fluorescents barely kept the darkness at bay. Jez was careful to avoid the small pools of shadow that had settled into corners and around doorways, for whenever she turned her back on one she'd catch a glimpse of *something* moving. It wasn't a shape exactly, it was more like a disturbance in the dark, like the ripples on a pond when something big comes too close to the surface.

Whether the pounding of her heart in her ears was from exhaustion or fear, she wasn't sure, but she tried to calm her panic and keep going. One foot at a time. Around floor seven she began to hear voices. She was taking the stairs slowly now, her calf muscles trembling in protest, and she'd just slipped past a shadowy spot on the floor when the lightbulb overhead began to flicker. Its strobe light effect made her dizzy. She saw then that on the floors above her, it was all darkness. Beneath the buzz of the faltering lightbulb she heard a low, unintelligible murmuring followed by a single whispered answer:

"Jezzzzzebeeeel . . ."

Once again her arms and legs threatened to turn to stone and she could barely move. Just like her experience at the closet, she was being held in place by more than simply her own terror. Shaking off this strange paralysis was like forcing oneself to wake from a bad dream, but since she'd broken free once before, it was easier the second time.

Willing her legs to move, she hurried for the stairwell exit, but the door wouldn't budge. The fire doors in the stairwells had no locks, and yet this one was shut tight. It wouldn't give an inch. She turned and went back down the steps to the sixth floor, but it was the same thing there—a lockless door locked tight against her.

She turned to continue down when a buzzing lightbulb exploded with a pop and the stairway above her went black. Then the light above her head began to sputter and fail. Something was choking the lights out, floor by floor. Something was chasing her, and all the doors were locked.

She had a quick, involuntary memory of the chattering voices in the dark of her closet. Light had been the thing that saved her then, but the light all around her was dying.

The bulb went pop. Tiny pieces of glass rained down upon her as the light died in a puff of burnt electricity. There was a moment of near-darkness, lit only by the blue-green afterimages that floated in her eyes.

Just then Jez heard a sound moving along the steps on the landing above her. It was the thumping of something large—

heavy footsteps followed by the clitter-clack of claws on marble steps.

She ran. She jump-skidded down the steps. Five floors below her she could make out the dim, day-lit glow of her only hope—the lobby. The stairwell ended in an archway that emptied into the lobby, and there was no door down there. No door to lock against her.

Fast as she ran, she could still hear something thump and clack its way along the steps not more than a hair's breadth behind her. It was so close now. . . .

A bright light suddenly exploded in front of her, blinding her and sending her tumbling. Any farther and she would have careened down a flight of steps. As her vision cleared, she saw Tommy Learner, standing over her and looking the same as he had the day before. The light originated from the small lantern that Tommy held in his hand, and its glow barely extended to the spot where she now lay in a crumpled heap.

There was no sign of the thing following her. Everything was quiet.

"Sorry about that," said Tommy, frowning. "But you should really watch where you're going."

"You . . . ," she said. "You!" She was out of breath, frightened and angry. She was proud of herself for saying that much. Despite what Bernie had said, Tommy didn't look at all dead.

"Sorry," he said. "But we don't have much time. Have you found Merlin? Have you seen the bird?"

Jez shook her head. "What bird? I was being chased and you . . . YOU!"

"Chased? By what?"

"I don't know! Something big! It was right behind me." Jez

pointed to the wall of darkness just beyond Tommy's circle of light. As she did so, there was the slightest sound of something shifting, slowly moving around in the dark. She noticed that the floors below her had gone black, too. The lobby archway was now little more than a pinprick of light at the end of a long, dark tunnel. Tommy's lantern was the only thing in the whole stairwell keeping the blackness at bay.

"Where?" Tommy asked, squinting. Jez frantically pointed again behind her as she pulled herself to her feet. The boy flipped those ridiculous goggles of his down over his eyes. At once they started to glow blue.

"Uh-oh," he said. "Croucher. Big one, too. I see it. Just outside the light."

"What's a croucher?" she asked, inching toward the stairs. Using Tommy's lantern, they could still make it to the lobby.

"It's a kind of evil spirit. They usually crouch over dark doorways or jump out of closets, surprising their victims. Hence the name. Nasty."

"What's it look like?" she asked. "I can't see it."

"You're better off that way, trust me. Crouchers are uglier than anything you can imagine."

"So what do we do?"

Tommy stood on his tiptoes to get a look over the stairwell at the landing below. The blue light goggles grew brighter as he fiddled with a switch on his belt. "Yep, I was afraid of that. There's another one waiting for you on the next floor. They always hunt in pairs."

Tommy scratched his cheek. "Do you have a light source?" he asked.

"No, but you've got your lantern! C'mon!"

Tommy shook his head. "I can't. Can't move from this spot. See, I'm not here. Not really." The strange device on his wrist began to chime. He made a face. As Jezebel watched he began to change—just like in the basement, he was becoming indistinct, fuzzy somehow. A ghost of a boy.

"Okay, you need to listen," he said. "I'm going to disappear in a few moments and I'll be taking the light with me."

"YOU WHAT?"

"Don't worry, those are two *really big* crouchers, so that's in your favor."

"What's in my favor?"

"The bigger the croucher, the smaller the brain. It's the little, devious ones that are really vicious."

Tommy suddenly flickered. For a fraction of a second he disappeared, leaving Jez in a terrifying eye-blink of absolute darkness. When he reappeared, he seemed even weaker, less distinct.

"Sorry," he said. "I have so much I need to tell you, but you'll get through this—just be cleverer than they are. And don't forget the bird. You need to find him. . . ."

Then he was gone, and Jez was alone in the dark. With *them*.

For a few never-ending seconds she stood there blinking, trying to discern shapes out of the inky blackness. Jez could hear something shuffling around her, and she imagined two great beasts—all claws and dripping fangs—circling their prey.

A light sputtered and flashed in the air next to her. Tommy was there again, as insubstantial as sun through a stained-glass window. His wristwatch contraption was dinging with alarming urgency.

"I'm out of time, but I've got to tell you the most important thing! Everything depends on . . ."

He flickered again. Instinctively, reflexively, Jez reached out to grab his wrist. She saw, rather than heard, him mouthing "No!"

It felt as if she'd grabbed the end of a live wire. Electricity coursed up her arm, stopping her heart as the world exploded around her in an agonizing flash of light. Then darkness.

PART TWO

The winds of time spiral about us like the spheres themselves. It will take a grounded mind and keen senses to follow the path laid out before you.

—from the introduction to the
Encyclopedia Imagika,
"On the Profession and Its Associated Perils,"
Sir Bartholomew Wainright, editor

CHAPTER NINE

TOMMY

MILES MACINTOSH'S BEDROOM, ENGLAND, 1900

"Now, from here on out, do as I do and only speak when spoken to," the Captain whispered, careless of the seawater dripping from his mustache. "This place isn't going to be a stroll in the park like the Lemuria Outcropping. Just follow my lead and try to stay quiet."

Then he opened Miles Macintosh's bedroom door.

By this point I was having a much harder time ignoring my own soggy state. My soaked underclothes were bunching up in a most uncomfortable way, and we both stunk of dead fish. Merlin seemed waterlogged, too. The poor bird tried to shake himself dry, but I could still hear water inside whenever he moved—like it was sloshing about in a tin can. Still, I did as I was told, tiptoeing along the hardwood floor as Merlin sat quietly on my shoulder. At least it felt good to be on dry land again.

Miles Macintosh's bedroom was mostly dark, and what light

there was came from a dim fireplace in the far wall. It was early morning outside the window, not yet dawn, and the fire had burned low until it was little more than a pile of glowing ashes. But that dull light was enough to see that one entire wall was nothing but shelves of books, ornate model ships and tin soldiers. A nice soft rug padded the floor. Heavy drapes framed the double-paned window, and beneath that was a large four-poster bed.

I'd heard that people lived like this, but I'd never seen it with my own eyes. In a way, it was nearly as unbelievable as the sunken temple. All that luxury for one boy.

Young Miles snored softly away, oblivious to the pair of water-logged scoundrels standing in his doorway.

"So what'd he do?" I whispered.

The Captain gave me an annoyed glance. "He didn't do any-thing," he whispered back. "Now, be quiet."

"Then why are we nabbing him? This is a kidnapping, right?"

"We are not here for him!"

We both froze as Miles snorted loudly and rolled over. For such a little kid, Miles had a snore like a wood saw. Scott put his finger to his lips and took a cautious step into the room. The floorboards creaked under the big man's weight, but thankfully Miles didn't stir.

Scott's instructions had been clear—I was to guard the door and not let anyone in or out. Who I'd be guarding it from was still a mystery. Miles's parents were sleeping soundly in the mas-ter bedroom a floor down, and if Miles himself wasn't our quarry, then I couldn't imagine who was.

The Captain had been in a foul and secretive mood ever since we'd escaped the kraken. For my part, I was quite happy to be alive after being nearly swallowed by a giant sea monster, and I'd actually been impressed with the Captain's fancy piloting that'd gotten us away from the beast just in the nick of time. But I guess all Scott could see were the Kraken-teeth-sized puncture marks along the outer hull of his precious ship and the gallons of sea-water that had drenched the lot of us. We'd spent hours pumping out the bilgewater, and it would take days yet to repair the out-side damage. We'd docked in Southampton just after midnight and sloshed our way through the empty streets to the Macintosh house—mansion was more like it; they were certainly well-to-do. The locked front door had been a cakewalk (thanks to yours truly), but I shuddered to think what Mr. and Mrs. Macintosh would think when they awoke in the morning to find two sets of seawater footprints staining their fine rugs.

With the door shut behind us, the bedroom was even darker. The weak glow of the fireplace coals did little to penetrate the deep shadows. Anything could be hiding in there. The Captain pulled something out of his bag, and after a few seconds of shuffling I heard a slight click followed by a very soft hum. Scott's eyes suddenly glowed blue beneath the lenses of a pair of oversized goggles.

He looked ridiculous and I had to bite my tongue to keep from laughing, but as I watched the Captain scan the room with those stupid-looking eyepieces, it suddenly dawned on me what he was doing. He was seeing in the dark! This was my first glimpse at a pair of paragoggles in action, and my mind raced with the pos-sibilities. A pair of see-in-the-dark specs could open up a whole world of lucrative opportunities.

I'd just begun to work on a plan to get myself a pair, or at the very least lift the Captain's, when Scott made a sudden move toward the bed. Merlin squawked and the big man grabbed at a handful of air as Miles Macintosh, who'd apparently been faking sleep all along, leapt past him and headed for the door. As Miles ran past the fireplace, I caught a good look at the boy—skinny, with the pasty white skin of a rich kid who didn't spend much time out in the sun, and spindly little arms and legs poking out of an overly large nightshirt. A stupid tasseled nightcap dangled down in front of his eyes.

I cracked my knuckles and grinned. The boy was headed straight for me.

"Make it easy on yourself, Miles," I said. "You've got nowhere to— Uff!"

Scrawny Miles Macintosh hoisted me by the collar and was lifting me up over his head. One-handed.

The boy growled at me as I dangled helplessly. Then he said something in a throaty foreign language as he tossed me the way you might toss an apple core over your shoulder.

Merlin took to flight and I, thankfully, landed on the bed's soft feather mattress, bouncing once before rolling off and onto my butt.

Scott appeared at the edge of the bed, wielding some kind of bizarre-looking gun. There was a pop, and then Miles went down, entangled in a large net.

"Quickly," said the Captain. "That won't hold him."

"What do you expect me to do?" I shouted, my head still spinning and my butt bruised.

"Here," said Scott. A sturdy pole suddenly appeared in his hand. He tossed it to me. Attached to the handle, near the center of the pole, was some kind of hand crank. "Tesla Stick. Give it a crank, and when he makes a break for it, smack him. But don't touch the end yourself."

Cautiously, I took the rod with one hand and turned the little handle with the other. There was a mechanical whir and the pole started to vibrate beneath my fingers. The little hairs on the back of my arm stood up as the tip of the pole began to spit out little blue sparks. It felt better to have a weapon, but I still wasn't terribly confident—not after having been tossed about like that.

Miles was tearing at the netting, biting and clawing at the cords like a trapped animal.

"What's the matter with that kid?" I asked. "He rabid?"

"That's not a kid. I fear we're too late," answered the Captain without looking up. He was busy fidgeting with something else in his shoulder bag.

Merlin gave a warning whistle and I heard the snapping of ropes. Miles had broken free, and as he stood up he raised his arms in the air and growled again. At any other time I might have laughed at the image of a little kid in a nightshirt and drooping nightcap beating his chest like some zoo gorilla. But I'd felt just how strong the little munchkin was, and there was no time for laughter—Miles was making a run for it.

Jumping forward, I swung the staff at Miles's behind. As soon as the pole connected, I felt an electrical jolt of feedback run up my arm as Miles reeled back, his body stiff. The boy staggered and blinked, dazed, but he didn't fall. And my shiny new staff had stopped sparking.

"Stand back," said Scott, appearing at my side. He was holding a pair of glass flasks that were joined at the nozzles so that they looked like a miniature barbell. He gave the nozzle a snap, and as the seal broke, the two clear liquids began to mix and take on a bright yellow glow.

He shook the strange contraption to speed up the process and, with an underhanded windup, threw the entire thing at Miles. As it shattered, the glowing yellow stuff splashed all over the boy. Miles began to shake and shimmer in the yellow light, dissolving like a rock thrown at a reflection in a pool.

Miles was gone and in his place was a large, bucktoothed and hairy man with pointy ears. The overly large nightshirt now fit him like the tiniest of undershirts and his heavy belly spilled out beneath it.

"Hello, Lob," said Scott.

The hairy man squinted at the Captain and gave a forced, awkward grin. "Why, Cap'n Scott!" he exclaimed. "And yer wee bird! Didn't recognize you! So blasted dim in here and all. Me fire's burned down something awful and me peepers ain't what they should be in the dark."

The Captain looked unconvinced. "Tommy, crank up your Tesla Stick, will you?"

I looked at the Captain. "The Tesla—what . . . oh, the pole!"

I hurriedly turned the crank.

"Now, now, let's not us be hasty!" said Lob. "One tickle with that there stick is quite enough, thank you. Me butt cheek's numb as 'tis."

"Where's Miles Macintosh, Lob?" asked Scott.

"I ain't hurt him, Cap'n! I swear."

"Tommy? Tesla Stick, if you'd be so kind."

"Wait! Wait!" shouted Lob as I took what I hoped was a menacing step forward. The Tesla Stick actually felt pretty useless in my hand; its charge obviously gone, the pole barely buzzed, and I doubted that a tap from it would tickle, much less shock. But Lob apparently didn't know that. "He's there, in the cupboard," said the big oaf.

The Captain walked over to a large chest of drawers and, after testing a few, very gently opened the bottom one. Curled up inside was the real Miles Macintosh, snoozing away.

"How long were you planning on leaving him in there?" asked the Captain.

"Look," said Lob. "We were going to come to an agreement, him and me, just as soon as I got a chance. I just didn't want to wake the little angel."

"You know what I think?" asked the Captain. "I think you snuck in here and ensorcelled the boy—that's no ordinary sleep he's in. Then you glamoured yourself to look like him. You were getting ready to throw him into the fire when you heard us coming down the hall."

"Throw him in the fire?" I said. "Why, you murdering thug!" I waved the Tesla Stick at Lob's face, wishing I had enough charge to fry the monster. I think you'll understand when I say that I've got a thing against folks who hurt kids.

Lob whined. Surprisingly, Scott put his hand on the staff and made me lower the weapon.

"Tommy, Lob's a sneak but he's no murderer. Look closer at the fire. Concentrate, and see past the Veil."

Reluctantly, I did as I was told and stared at the fire. I wasn't sure what I was looking for and, at first, all I saw was a pile of hot coals and glowing charcoal. But after a minute the image shimmered like a mirage, and, an instant later, the fire became a round wooden door. The wood glowed red like the coals but it gave off no heat.

"Well, I'll be," I said.

"Lob is a Lubber Fiend. A wanderer," said Scott. "They use fireplaces as portals. If you look them up in the *Encyclopedia*

Imagika, you'll find that they have a fondness for cow's milk and are notorious for thieving saucers from kittens."

At the mention of milk Lob's eyes lit up and he smacked his lips. "You don't have a nice, cold pitcher on you, perhaps? Me throat's awfully parched."

Scott turned back to Lob, ignoring his question. "Normally that's the extent of their mischief, which is why I must beg the question—why were you swapping yourself for Miles Macintosh? Perhaps you were planning on leaving him in Faerie? To become a changeling child or . . ."

Lob let out a terrible cry, like a babe being punished by a parent. "I wasn't wanting to hurt him! But I need a place to hide. Cap'n, I swear! The dead are up and walking!"

Scott's eyes narrowed and he stood for a moment, tugging at his mustache. He gave Merlin a look and the bird cocked its head back at him. Something passed between the two of them, but I had no earthly idea what anyone was talking about. As usual.

It all sounded like a bunch of stuff to me. But then I remembered the smiling corpse. I remembered the smell of rot on his breath. "What's he mean, the dead are walking?" I asked. "Dead means dead, don't it?"

"It does in our world, Tommy," said the Captain. "But there are things from other places. . . . Tell us what you've seen, Lob."

Lob swallowed and wiped his nose with a big, meaty palm. "It ain't what I seen but what I *heard.* The Lubber Fiends are talking, and there are some that has seen things—things moving in the shadows that by rights should be at peace and asleep beneath the earth. Them that can are packing their bags and heading for safer pastures. Why, I heard whole worlds that Lubbers have stopped visiting, small worlds on the outskirts, you know. Places that even you Explorers ain't yet seen. Those places have gotten dark. Dark as a closet, if you get my meaning."

At the mention of the closet, I realized for the first time that Miles Macintosh's bedroom had no closet. A giant dresser and the chest of drawers, but no closet.

Lob looked around as if someone might overhear what he had to say next. "I ain't the only one. You'll see. More of us are getting spooked, and everyone knows that this here's the safest place to be. They say he's building an army, you see. But everyone knows the Gentleman has no sway here. The dead know their place, here on Earth. Like the boy said, dead stay dead."

Scott mumbled something under his breath and then plopped down on the edge of the bed. He seemed for all the world to have forgotten us, and for a time he just sat there chewing on his mustache. In the short period we'd been together, I'd noticed that there seemed to be two Captain Scotts: one was sharp and decisive, and the other seemed nearly as doddering as one of the bridge folk. One could trade places with the other in an instant.

"You, Lob," Scott said distractedly. "Get a move on. Be on your way."

"What?" I said. "We're not just letting him go, are we? He may not have been ready to kill that kid, but he was still getting ready to swipe him! That's like, child endangerment, or something, at least."

"We're Explorers, not policemen!" snapped the Captain. "Miles is safe now. That's enough."

Lob scraped and bowed his way toward the hearth, all the while blubbering a string of apologies and promises. With a grunt he squeezed his fat body through the odd little door and disappeared. Soon the fire was back to being just a fire. Somehow the room seemed darker than before. Colder, even.

"What was all that?" I asked. "All that stuff about the dead walking sounded pretty bad."

The Captain looked at me with unfocused eyes. It was like he was genuinely surprised to find me there, to find that he wasn't alone. A moment later he smiled a tired, tired smile.

"The dead don't walk here, Tommy. Not yet."

The Captain stood, hoisted up his pants and took a deep breath. Just like that, and the fogginess was gone. The old Captain had returned, his eyes bright and mischievous. He held out his hand and Merlin landed, lightly, on his glove.

"We've work to do, it seems," he said. "But first, I need to check on a few things and you need a pair of proper clothes—ones a little less soaked in seawater, I'd say. Come then, back to the *Nautilus!* We have official business at the Academy of Explorers!"

CHAPTER TEN

TOMMY
LONDON, 1900

"Name, please," said a phlegmy-sounding voice on the other side of the door.

"I've already given you my name. I'm Captain Jonathan Scott!"

"The name of your companion, I meant. Know full well who you are."

Captain Scott sighed as he pulled his cap down farther over his eyes to protect himself from the onslaught of rain. As he did so he sent a shelf of collected rainwater spilling down his front.

Looking at my own soaked trousers—pools had formed in the cuffs—I wondered if I'd ever be dry again. I envied Merlin, safe and snug and dry back at the *Nautilus*. The Captain had insisted that he stay there as we made the trip from Miles's bedroom in Southampton to the Academy of Explorers in London. For this leg of our journey we'd relied on the train (a bit of a letdown after traveling along the ocean floor, I can tell you), and we'd just managed to dry off when we arrived at our destination in the middle of a proper English downpour.

When the Captain announced we'd be visiting this Academy, I hadn't figured that meant waiting outside a no-nothing brownstone flat in the London rain. There wasn't even a sign overhead. I'd begun to wonder if Scott had the wrong address as he shouted my name into the tiny peephole for what seemed like the hundredth time. Whoever manned the door delighted in being uncooperative. Either that or he was entirely deaf.

Finally we heard the sound of a deadbolt being slid back and, with a bit of muffled cursing from the other side, the door opened. As we stepped inside and out of the rain we had to walk around a bent, stoop-shouldered old man carrying a heavy ring of keys. The man's eyes were no better than his hearing, and he continued talking to us long after we'd passed him by.

The inside was as unimpressive as the outside, but at least it was dry. The downstairs was made up of a few dusty old sitting rooms occupied by a few dusty old men. Most stared off into space as they sipped whiskey from glass tumblers. A few looked up suspiciously at us as we passed by, but if they recognized Scott they didn't bother to say hello.

The Captain led us up a tall, narrow staircase and into a larger, book-lined chamber on the second floor. Entering this room was an immediate relief, as there was a nice, comfy fire roaring in the fireplace, a soft bearskin rug and no old men anywhere. I made for the fire at once and started wringing out my wet clothes.

"So who's that bunch of geezers, huh?" I asked. "Don't tell me they're Explorers, too."

"In name only, Tommy," answered Scott. "They spend their time bragging about old glories and soaking their regrets in drink. The Veil weighs down on us all. Some bear the weight better than others."

As he spoke the Captain examined a bookshelf near the window, unaware or unconcerned about the dripping mess he was making on the floor.

"Got to tell you," I said, sticking my butt as close to the fire as I dared. "This here Academy is not quite what I'd expected, to tell you the truth."

"This isn't the Academy," the Captain said with a chuckle. "This is only a chapterhouse. One of many."

"Well then, where is it? If it's not in London, then why are we here?"

"Chapterhouses mark the entrances to the Academy, and it doesn't technically matter which one we use. However, there are a few where I am"—the Captain coughed into his hand—"no longer welcome. Here, at least, I am still tolerated."

The Captain pulled a plain clothbound book off the shelf. "Ah, here we go.

"Now, Tommy," he began. "The Explorers long ago discerned the need for utmost discretion in our endeavors. We want to go about our work without worrying about the petty politics of nations. And therefore we wanted to avoid placing our Academy within the boundaries of any single country. As you have seen, our science is a good deal more advanced—knowledge gleaned from our explorations, of course—and we are in possession of an assortment of technologies that could be destructive if given over to the wrong hands. Take the *Nautilus*, for instance. What would naval warfare look like with that ship on one side or the other? Therefore, these chapterhouses serve as . . . secret embassies, if you will, for an Academy that is entirely independent and *off-world*."

I made a face. My behind was beginning to burn and I was bored.

"I tell you all this," said the Captain, "to impress upon you the significance of my allowing you to see the Academy and the importance of this visit!"

I shifted my position at the fire to get a better angle at my most soaked parts. "Look, no offense, but after what I've already seen these last few weeks, it's going to take an awful lot to impress me."

"Hmm," said the Captain. He held up the book and cleared his throat.

I groaned. "What? You going to read to me now?"

"This is a key-book. Just watch. But don't be frightened by what happens next."

Scott opened the book, and out of the pages sprung a long metal coil, like some kind of jack-in-the-box. At the end was a shiny golden key.

"That it?"

"Quiet, you. Now watch." Scott gave me a warning look and continued. "Captain Jonathan Scott, Explorer First Rank, requesting that the door to the Academy be unlocked and passage be granted to two persons of import."

The key snaked along the floor until it found a small hole hidden in the dark wood. The key slipped inside with a quiet click. For a moment nothing more happened, but then I felt, rather than heard, a vibrating hum beneath my feet.

Then a deep voice boomed out. It was coming from the bearskin rug. "Permission granted," it said.

The bear's head began to shift as its mouth opened wide, like an overextended yawn. It kept growing, larger and larger, until the bear's head was soon the size of a man, its toothy maw reaching, opening for me. Coming for me.

With the fire at my back, I had nowhere to run. I scrambled for the Tesla Stick at my belt.

"Wait, wait!" said Scott. "It's all right. Look."

The bear's mouth had opened to reveal a long brick tunnel. Flickering gaslight torches illuminated the way.

"What is that?"

"That, my boy, is the portal to the Enlightened Hidden City, wherein you will find the Academy of Explorers. Come on, it's entirely safe."

The Captain led the way, carefully picking his way past the bear's teeth. I'd never imagined that I'd be entering this Academy by way of a creature's gullet, but I was learning to be ready for anything. We'd gone perhaps fifteen feet when the mouth began to close behind us. There was a flash of light all around as my stomach turned queasy.

"The flash of light signified that we've stepped through a portal. That ordinary bear rug back there is actually what we call a Stitch-Golem," said Scott. "It's a construct, a kind of machine that we use to guard portals to the Academy. Clever, don't you think?"

I pictured the huge mouth opening before me. "And if permission to enter is denied? What happens then?"

"Best not to think of that," the Captain said, shaking his head. "Come on."

The tunnel seemed to go on forever, and as we walked Scott began to explain the true nature of the Academy of Explorers. The very first Explorer was a young scholar's apprentice named

Theophilus of Crete. Theophilus lived in the tenth century, and the story goes that one morning he was out exploring, instead of paying attention to his studies, when he chanced upon an old well. As he peered into the well he saw not a dank, dark shaft but a glorious, shining city. He'd, in fact, discovered a portal to the Enlightened Hidden City, a city on another world.

"In the Hidden City lived a race of wise monks," the Captain explained. "Physically, not so different from you or I, except for the longish earlobes and cow's tails."

"Cow's tails?" I asked.

"It's a mark of wisdom."

"They chew cud, too? Maybe while they're thinking all these wise thoughts?"

The Captain cleared his throat—a subtle warning. I shrugged and let him continue.

"As I was saying, the leader of these monks, the High Father, was immediately charmed by Theophilus, by the young man's adventurous spirit. You see, the monks of the Hidden City used a mystical tool called the Cycloidotrope to study the past, present and even the future of a thousand different planets, without ever leaving their city. With the High Father's guidance, Theophilus learned about the different worlds, about the portals that connected them and about the Veil that hid it all.

"But unlike the monks, he wasn't content to simply study; he wanted to explore. He began seeking out the portals and using them for travel. He discovered many wonderful things—exotic places, wondrous races. He recorded everything he saw in a book, which would eventually become the *Encyclopedia Imagika*. Out of that book was born the Explorers' Society and, in time, the Academy. The High Father graciously allowed the Society to build our

Academy within the heart of the Hidden City so that we could share our knowledge with the monks there."

After a few minutes' trek underground the Captain came to the end of the tunnel and an archway that marked the entrance to a sunlit, open square. I stopped at the arch, suddenly nervous. What was on the other side? The Captain had said that we were leaving our world behind, that this Academy place was on a different planet somewhere out there. I'd already seen so much that was strange and fantastical that you'd think I'd be better prepared, but up until that point everything had sort of happened to me. I'd been thrust into this bizarre adventure without so much as a minute to breathe, and now that I'd had time for it to settle in, I was feeling . . . unsettled.

Now was the time for me to make up my mind. I could decide to take that step out into the sunlight of an alien world, if I wanted to. But I had to do it. No one would push me this time.

"It's all right," said the Captain. "Whenever you're ready."

Turned out that stepping out of that tunnel onto another world felt little different from stepping out of a dimly lighted shop onto Washington Square Park at noon. People bustled back and forth between a number of large, classical-looking buildings surrounding a public square. Green grass and stone benches lined the pathways that led to tall columns and steep-stepped buildings with high, ornate doorways. And looming over one end of the square was a single grand tower of rose marble. There were people here and there, but not nearly as many as I'd expected to see. And not a one of them under the age of forty, by my reckoning. A whole lot of gray beards and fat paunches.

"It's a school," I said, disappointed.

"It's the Academy. You're on another planet, you know."

"What's that I smell? It's sweet."

Scott smiled. "Ginger. Or at least it's close to ginger. No one knows why, but the air smells of ginger here. Like I said, another planet."

"And if this is a school, then where are all the students? And those monks you were talking about?" I asked, wrinkling my nose. *Ginger-scented air?* "All I see are old guys like you. No offense."

"None taken. But unfortunately, new enrollment is *low*, you could say. The Society works on a strict apprentice system, and most Explorers just can't be bothered. As for the monks, well, they've reached enlightenment."

"They what?"

"Beyond the Academy walls is the Enlightened Hidden City, but it's nearly empty now. You see, the monks were immortal, Tommy. They reincarnated themselves in a cycle of birth, death and rebirth until they felt they'd gained enough wisdom to pass on from this world. Which they did."

"Wait a minute," I said. "They spent all that time . . . reincarnating, or whatever, just so they could die?"

The Captain shrugged. "I don't pretend to understand it myself. There were still a handful of them around when I was a young Explorer, but over the years more and more achieved enlightenment. Today, the Academy stands in the middle of a deserted city. The High Father is all that's left."

"He's not enlightened, then?"

Scott shook his head. "Oh, of course he is. He's the wisest being in the known universe. It's just that he has unfinished business. That's what he claims, anyway."

"Sounds about right to me," I said. "He's smart enough to

know that if you can live forever, you *do*. You don't give up. I think he pulled one over on those other monks."

Scott laughed. "Come on. I'll show you around. This Academy was a place to train and learn, once. Now it's more of a museum, I'm afraid. It's the accumulation of centuries of exploring, just gathering dust. The knowledge of a hundred different civilizations rests within these marble and stone roofs. Cataloged and recataloged. Preserved for posterity."

"Sounds like it could all get a bit dull."

The Captain smiled at that. "You have no idea. Come on, then. Better get this over with."

We headed for the rose tower, and I noticed more queer looks thrown our way as we passed. But again, if the Captain was aware of it, he didn't let on. We crossed a great plaza and entered the tower through a set of metal doors. I was shocked to find that the inside was hollow all the way to the pinnacle. There were no floors, just a curving set of staircases that climbed up the rows and rows of books lining every square inch of wall space—all the way to the very top.

"The *Encyclopedia Imagika* is just the Explorers' field manual, Tommy. It's the abridged version of this," the Captain said. "The Tower Library."

And in the center of it all, suspended in air, was a device unlike anything I had seen, or even imagined, before. The *Nautilus* was a wonder, but one look and a fellow could at least figure the purpose of the thing. The *Nautilus* was a boat—a darn strange boat, though still a boat. But this particular machine was . . . weird. At its middle was a giant, shining metal globe. It rested at the center of a web of spokes and wheels, and each spoke led to another, smaller globe. There were hundreds, thousands of them, all made of differently colored metal. And most amazing of all—they were all moving. Every part, every cog of the great machine was in motion. Some very slowly, circling the center globe in lazy orbits, while others flew haphazard patterns at incredible speeds. Everything was moving in synchronicity with everything else—complex, bizarre and perfect.

"That is the Orrery," said the Captain. "At its center you see the Earth. A bit oversized and not quite to scale, I grant you, but it's our favorite, so there you are. And all around it are the numerous planets connected to us—via the portals. Whole other worlds, like this one. It's surely a poor representation, reflecting only a tiny, half percent or so of all there is *to* know, but it's the best we've come up with."

"Unbelievable," I said, not caring that my mouth was hanging open. "It's what, sort of a model?"

"A bit of a model, a bit of a map. But mostly it's the Orrery. No other word for it, really."

I stepped back, craning my neck to take it all in. "Now I'm impressed," I said. And I meant it.

Captain Scott put his hand on my shoulder and pointed out the nearby statue of a man in a scholar's robe. His middle was almost perfectly round and his jowly, smiling face beamed up at the spiraling spheres overhead. "That is Brother Theophilus. But we affectionately call him Fat Theo around here."

As I got closer to the statue I noticed that Fat Theo had a bird on his shoulder, a small, clockwork canary.

"Is that . . . Merlin?"

Scott nodded. "Fat Theo discovered Merlin near the end of his travels, though he obviously wasn't called Merlin at the time. That bird's as old as the Society itself. Probably older. Theo had two passions in life—eating and exploring. As he got older he told people that he didn't fear death, but he regretted that there were still so many worlds out there to see. He left us Merlin as a reminder to never stop exploring. There is always a new frontier."

"So Merlin's sort of the Explorers' mascot?"

Scott laughed. "I guess he is at that—but don't let him hear you say that! Now, wait here. I need to announce your visit before taking you any farther, so stay put and, whatever you do, don't wander off. It's easy to get lost."

Scott walked out onto the marble rotunda and disappeared under the shadow of the Orrery, tipping his cap to Fat Theo as he passed. I stood there in my still-damp clothes, trying to ignore the various stares and turned-up noses of the passersby. After some minutes I finally spied another boy. He was plump, perhaps a few years younger than I was. I was relieved to see him, but at the same time I was also keenly aware of how large this great hall was and how alien everything seemed. I was a master of the streets, the dark alleyways and rooftops. But here, without Captain Scott by my side, I was out of my element. Feeling the desperate need to be doing something, I focused my attention on the ground—the entire floor of this place was covered in words. Though back then I still couldn't read much more than my own name, I knew well enough to recognize letters. But these symbols looked like chicken scratch.

"Don't kill yourself trying to make that out," the boy said. "The floor of the Great Hall is inscribed with one motto, but it's repeated in hundreds and hundreds of languages. That dialect you're looking at there is Atlantean, I think."

I looked up to see that the boy was smiling at me as he wiped his thick spectacles on the lapel of his coat. He seemed amiable enough, but I wasn't in the habit of making friends easily.

I squinted back at the words on the floor. "Oh yeah, Atlantean. Yeah. Yeah, I thought it looked familiar."

The boy arched one eyebrow as he threaded his glasses around his overly large ears. "You read Atlantean? I didn't think anyone studied it these days, considering that the Atlanteans died out over a thousand years ago."

"Well, I didn't say I *read* it," I said, stretching myself up a bit on my feet. It needled me that this boy was obviously younger, and yet he still had several inches on me. "I said that I thought I recognized it. I've just seen it around, that's all."

"Oh," he answered. "Sorry. My mistake."

"And what about you?" I asked. "I suppose you know what it says?"

"Sure. I don't read Atlantean, either, but I know what it says. It says the same thing that all the other words say."

"Oh? What's it say, then?"

The boy cleared his throat and began, "It's the Explorer's Creed. It says:

> *For we are those who open the door*
> *and those who guard it.*
> *We are those who light the dark*
> *and those who curse it.*
> *In childhood the fire is lit,*
> *may we keep it kindled always.*
> *For danger, for knowledge,*
> *for safety and for strength—*
> *we are Explorers all."*

"Huh," I said. "Doesn't really rhyme, though, does it?"

"It's not supposed to," answered the boy. "It's a creed. Like a motto? It's not a poem."

"Still, seems like it should rhyme."

"Look, I know that you're new around here, but people are already talking about you. So, if I could offer you a bit of advice . . ." The boy left his words unfinished as he spotted someone approaching from afar. Growing suddenly serious, he spoke next in a harsh whisper.

"Blast! Here comes Harper! Careful what you say around him."

"What? Who's Harper? And who are you?" I asked.

"The Captain asked me to look after you. Now look sharp!"

A tall, gaunt man in a stovepipe hat was striding across the floor toward us. He was smiling, but there was nothing reassuring about that grin. He reminded me of the oh-so-pleasant privateers who prowled the dockside bars looking for drunks to kidnap into service. Many a man had passed out in the wrong tavern and woke up scrubbing decks at sea.

"So, you must be the boy everyone's talking about," said the man. "Congratulations! The value of the artifact you have retrieved for us is beyond measure."

"The artifact?" I asked.

"The bird." The man smiled. "A clockwork canary. It was stolen from the Academy some time ago, but we're pleased to hear that it's been returned."

"Really? You mean Merlin, that clunky thing?" I said, thinking of poor, waterlogged Merlin back in the ship. Truth was, we hadn't returned him at all. And Scott seemed keen on keeping the bird as far away from this place as possible. But until I knew a little more about this fellow, I saw no need to correct his facts.

"My name is Harper," the man continued. "I sit on the Council of Officers, so on behalf of the Society let me say thank you."

"Oh," I said. "You're welcome. But it wasn't much, really. Just lifted it from a dead-looking gent in a carriage. He had some muscle there, too, but they weren't any bother."

I felt myself puffing up a bit, but I couldn't help it. The attention felt good.

"Death cultists," Harper said, nodding. "Grave Walkers, no doubt."

"Eh, whatever. They just looked like a couple of thugs to me. They weren't all rotted like their boss."

The spectacled boy spoke up. "The Grave Walkers are at least partly human. Normal people who've given in to the Gentleman's power."

"Well, like I was saying," I went on, annoyed at the kid for interrupting my story. "I ditched them, no problem. But then there were these other things—in the shadows, like. I kept ahead of them for most of two weeks. 'Course, then I ran into that Duke, and the Captain helped out a bit, but I was doing all right on my own, I suppose."

"Remarkable," said Harper, quietly.

"Sounds like you interrupted a handoff," said the boy. "Those cultists were handing the artifact, eh, Merlin, over to the Gentleman. You might have just saved the world, you know that?"

The man Harper waved the suggestion away. "Let's not exaggerate. Tommy's actions were certainly brave, but I don't think the consequences of one stolen mechanical bird were quite so dire."

"Indeed they were," said a familiar booming voice from behind us. "They could not have been *more* dire!"

Scott had returned. He still hadn't had a chance to dry off, however, and he looked a bit sad. Harper was neatly dressed, while the soggy Captain smelled of seaweed. Scott seemed every bit as out of place here as I did.

"Captain Scott," said Harper. The man was no longer even pretending to smile. "Of course we can count on you to ratchet up the histrionics, yet again. The Council is grateful to you and the boy for delivering our stolen property. But you realize you had an appointment with us early this morning. You're late."

At the mention of stolen property I gave Scott a look, but he ignored it. We'd technically delivered Merlin—but we'd delivered him back to the *Nautilus,* not the Academy.

"I ran into a bit of a detour," said Scott. "I rescued young Mister Learner here from a particularly nasty bridge troll and that put us behind schedule. We had a further incident near the Lemuria Outcropping . . ."

"Well, that explains the state of your dress! The Outcropping is dangerous!" said Harper. "Gorge krakens still hunt there."

"You know," Scott said, hiking up his wet britches, "I've never given much credence to that kraken theory. Lemuria's too big to be swallowed by a single beast."

Harper cocked his head, ever slightly to one side. "Really? How's the *Nautilus?*"

"Nearly swallowed," said Scott definitively. "By a kraken."

Harper started to speak, but Scott cut him off. "But it was a *Nautilus*-swallowing-sized kraken. And the beast could barely manage that!"

"The point is that you shouldn't have been there in the first place," said Harper, pointing his finger at the Captain. "You risked your own life, and this boy's life, while doing god knows what damage to your ship and *still* you arrived late! You only narrowly avoided a first-class bungle. Again."

"I was out *there*, Harper! Exploring! That's what we do, or have you all forgotten?"

"You dare . . . ?"

The Captain ignored Harper's outrage. "Listen to me. The Gentleman is trying to make his way into the Earth. I've gotten information that very nearly confirms it. I spoke to a refugee Lubber Fiend—"

"A Lubber Fiend? You're going to bring the testimony of a milk-thieving chimney haunter before the Council? You may cry wolf all you want but I can tell you what they'll say—the Gentleman presents no immediate threat to us. The soulless undead cannot walk our Earth for long, you know that. They cannot abide the light of our sun. Therefore he's merely a nuisance, and the Council will treat him as such."

"Then the Council is made up of a bunch of old fools," said Scott. "You're too in love with your rules and your books to see the danger all around us! I demand to see the High Father. Perhaps he'll listen to reason."

Harper smiled. "Do you honestly expect to be admitted to the High Father's Inner Chamber in the state you're in? Perhaps, if you clean up *and* make an appointment, I might be able to pull some strings and get you in for a few minutes. That is, if you'll kindly hand over the bird. *Now*."

Harper held out his hand expectantly, as if the Captain had Merlin stuffed in his pocket.

"I'm afraid not," said the Captain. There was a set to Scott's chin that I'd seen before. It was an expression that I've worn myself more than a few times—he was gearing for a fight.

"I beg your pardon?" said Harper. "The artifact belongs here, where we can keep it safe! It's been stolen once—"

"Right out from under the noses of you and your precious Council," said Scott. "Something big is brewing. The Gentleman's got plans for that little bird, and if not for our dumb luck and the bravery of one young street thief, we'd be seeing that plan come to fruition."

"Surely, you trust the Council to keep it safe," said Harper.

Now it was the Captain's turn to put a finger in Harper's face.

"I trust exactly *three* of the four of us present, and not a one of your stubborn Council. You have your heads in the sand, all of you! And if you insist on denying me access to the High Father, then I'll be on my way. With the arti—er, *Merlin*!"

For an instant I thought the spindly Harper might actually strike the Captain. Indeed, Scott looked braced and almost eager for just that. But the moment passed, and Harper adjusted his tall hat and looked down the bridge of his nose at me instead.

"Good luck to you then, boy. Traveling with Captain Scott can be a hazardous proposition. Just ask any of his former apprentices—if you can find one alive, that is."

Then Harper turned and stalked away, careless of the many eyes now watching us. We'd created a bit of a scene.

As Scott watched the man leave, his eyes turned distant once again, unfocused. He looked as if the air had been let out of him along with his anger. Whatever he was thinking about now, it was worlds away. "We should go," he said absently. "We're not welcome here anymore."

Then he turned and started out the tower door.

Before I could follow, the spectacled boy stepped up next to me and held out his hand. I had forgotten all about him.

"Bernard Billingsworth, Apprentice Explorer Second Class," he said. "It's a pleasure."

"Er, likewise," I said, trotting off after the Captain.

"Welcome to the crew!" said Bernard, huffing and puffing as he struggled to keep up. I ignored him as best I could. I was too focused on the hard stares and upturned noses of the people around us—the Explorers' Society. As far as I was concerned, Scott was the only one I'd seen worthy of the name. I couldn't wait to get away from the Academy in the Hidden City, and I didn't care if I never saw it again.

I thought I was done with the place for good, but I'd soon learn just how wrong I was. Looking back now, I do feel sorry for that soft bunch of gents. I won't lie and say that I was at all impressed by those stodgy old men—by Harper and his lot. But I won't say another bad word about them, either.

I don't like speaking ill of the dead.

CHAPTER ELEVEN

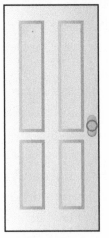

JEZEBEL
THE HOLLOW WORLD, 1902

Jezebel had a migraine once, back when she was little. It was brought on by a bad reaction to a medicine, and it had left her trapped in her room, in the dark, as her father pressed a cool, wet towel down over her eyes. Her head had felt then as if it might split open with the pain, and her body was an exposed nerve causing her to wince at every creaking floorboard, every outside noise. Even the glowing cracks under the door hurt.

She felt like that now. The last thing she remembered before the flash of light was the dark stairwell and reaching out for Tommy. Then she woke up here, wherever this was, with a head full of crawling, stabbing needles.

Again, she was in a mostly dark room. What illumination there was came from a flickering candle nearby, but when she tried to look directly at it, the pain in her head made the light halo and blur, and it was just too hard to focus.

Her father was here with her at least, cooling her forehead with a damp rag, just like before.

"Take it easy," he was saying. "You're sick from the jump, but it'll pass in a few minutes. Just close your eyes and try to think of something pleasant."

Jez did as she was told. She chose one of the pictures he'd given her—the one he'd done on their family trip to Ireland. They'd come across a little fishing village on the western coast where people still spoke Irish. The town was known for the dolphin who lived there in the bay. For a few euros, fishermen would take tourists out to watch the animal dance and play in the boat's wake. On the day that Jezebel looked for him, however, the town's local celebrity apparently had better things to do, and despite three boat rides, he never appeared. That night her father unwrapped a bundle of colored charcoals and drew his own dolphin for Jez, on the back of her mom's map. Jezebel's dolphin was bright green, and he swam with her amid the blue and white waves. The soft colors of the charcoals blurred together like sea spray.

The pain was gone.

She blinked up at her father, but it wasn't her father at all. It was a gap-toothed boy with a dirty face who somehow seemed shorter in person than he had as a ghost. Standing, he might come up to Jezebel's neck, if that.

The famous Tommy Learner was a bit of a twerp.

"I know. Strange, right?" he said, misreading her frown. "Thinking happy thoughts and all that, but it does make the pain go away. Usually that stuff's a lot of nonsense, but when you're talking time travel, it works. The Captain explained why once, but it didn't make much sense. Something to do with good memories being anchors in the time stream and blah, blah, blah. The man did go on."

Jezebel sat up slowly, cautiously, and rubbed her eyes. She was lying on a little cot of pale palm leaves. And the candle wasn't a candle at all—it was a hollowed-out shell, similar to an oblong coconut, and filled with a burning taper of something like black pitch. Whatever the sticky stuff was, the smoke it gave off smelled terrible, like burnt hair and sour milk. A tunnel twisted to the right and disappeared in a faint glow.

"Where are we?" she asked, wrinkling her nose at the nasty smoke.

Tommy stood up straight and gestured around the dank chamber. "I think it was once a trog cave—they're great rock shapers, you know—but it's abandoned now. Well, it looks abandoned, don't you think? Anyway, it isn't cozy but it's home, at least for the moment. But that's not the important part. *Where* is not the most important part."

"You said something about time travel," Jez said softly, but she already feared the worst.

"Yeah. See, I was talking to you from here—which to you is the past, I guess—through a sort of open window in time. And when you grabbed me, you accidentally jumped through. To here. To now."

Jez closed her eyes again and let her head fall back with a small bump. The meager leaf pallet might as well have been solid rock.

"Ouch," she said, rubbing her head. "Okay, putting aside that first part about trogs or whatever . . ."

"Well, I call them trogs. They're a kind of tunnel-dwelling beastie. Big yellow eyes. Sort of like an ape but bad-tempered," Tommy said.

"*Whatever,*" said Jez, ignoring the sudden swell of panic in her chest. "All right, then . . . *when* am I?"

Tommy pointed to a section of wall near the rock where someone had etched a number of hash marks into the stone. Tiny groups of five lines spread out over several feet of earth.

"Well, if my numbers are right, and I'm not sure they are, I've been here for about two months," he said.

He shrugged, and as he did so a clump of tangled hair fell over one eye, giving him a slightly crazed look. "So that means it's on or around January 1, 1902," he said with an uncomfortable laugh. "Happy New Year," he said.

Tommy was still talking, but Jezebel was no longer listening. *1902.* He had to be lying, or delusional, or have a really, really terrible sense of humor.

"Two months ago I walked through a door in the basement of the Percy Hotel," he was saying. "A black door that went straight down, and I ended up here. Well, stranded here is more like. When you saw me just now, I was using a special device called a Cycloidotrope to talk with you in your time, in the future. But when you grabbed ahold of me, something happened—there was some kind of feedback—and you were pulled backward through time and space. Sorry, I guess it's a shock."

Jezebel said nothing. *1902.* She stood up, turned around and walked down the tunnel searching for a way out. Tommy came after her, telling her to stop, to wait and listen to what he had to say, but she didn't need to hear any more. She needed to see for herself.

She found the cave narrowed to a crawl space, which someone had disguised with a wall of those large palm leaves and tufts of some kind of long-bladed grass. The pieces had been tied together into a makeshift camouflage door, but it was easy enough to pull it aside and crawl through.

Outside, the first strange thing was the light. Instead of the clear light of day, this place glowed a dull burnt orange—like a smoky sunset. The source of the illumination was an enormous orb of gas and molten lava that hung like a miniature sun overhead. The air was hot and so thick with humidity that it was a labor just to breathe. Below her, and oddly lit by the lava sun, was a lush valley, full of strange fungus plants and toadstools the size of trees. No breeze blew, and a smell of sweet decay hung in the air like a pantry of food gone bad. It was nearly overpowering.

But it wasn't the alien landscape or the cloying smell that stopped Jezebel in her tracks. Rather, it was the fact that as she looked into the distance, she could find no horizon. Above every tree line, atop every range of hills, it was the same sight—but it wasn't the blue firmament she was used to; it was nothing but grayish-brown rock. She followed it with her eyes, past the burning orb above, and saw that it continued in every direction.

There was no sky.

"We're . . . we're underground," said Jezebel.

Tommy nodded. "Yeah, I guess the *where* is actually kind of important, after all. This is 1902, but it's not 1902 on the planet Earth. This is someplace else. And that sun isn't a sun at all; it's the planet's core. That's where the black door led me, through a portal to this place, and that's where you've jumped back in time to. We're inside a hollow planet."

"That's impossible," said Jezebel. "The inside of a . . . a planet is like a million degrees."

"The inside of our planet might be, sure. But not here. Here, life happened almost exactly like on Earth, only it happened on the inside. I've even seen big lizards here, like dinosaurs! Dinosaurs! Can you believe it? In fact, I've been wondering if maybe *our* dinosaurs didn't die off at all. What if some of them escaped through a massive portal into this place? You know, you can find so many similar species on different worlds. I bet that kind of thing happens all the time!"

Jez gave him a blank look.

"Well, it's a theory I'm working on . . . Anyway, I've been stranded here a long time," he said, looking sheepishly out at the valley. "And now I guess you're stranded with me."

Jezebel turned to Tommy and said, "Listen, I'm going to sit down, and then I think I'm going to faint."

"Good idea."

"When I wake up, you have some explaining to do."

"I know."

"Tell me about that time travel device," Jezebel said, slowly pulling strips off one of the palm leaves. Upon closer examination Jez saw that it was spongy, textured more like a mushroom than like a fibrous leaf.

"Again?" asked Tommy.

"Humor me. I'm slow."

Tommy rubbed his temples and sighed at her. Jez had been grilling him for the better part of an hour, and he was clearly exhausted, but she didn't care. They'd moved back inside the cave and pushed the leaf door open, leaving just enough room that they could spy out over the valley.

"Not a time travel device, exactly," said Tommy. "It's a viewer, like a picture show. The Cycloidotrope. It's like a personal portal, only it can open a hole in space *and time*. But it's meant to be a window, *not* a door. You can use it to see glimpses of the future, or if you concentrate hard enough you can even project an image of yourself into the future—that's how I was talking to you in the Percy. But it *is* just an image, a mirage. A body shouldn't be able to pass through. What happened to you was a fluke. It's a one-in-a-million chance you weren't torn to pieces and scattered along the time stream."

"Yeah, I guess I'm just lucky like that," she answered. "So, you said that you're stuck here, with no way back."

"Well, the door I used was closed behind me, permanently— buried under rock and dirt in the basement of the Percy Hotel. And I've been searching this place for another portal out, but so far I haven't had any luck."

"But that Cycloido-thingy opens windows into other times, right? You used it to see into the future, to see me."

"Sort of. When you get down to it, time is just another dimension, but it's an awfully delicate one. The Cycloidotrope shows certain pictures . . ."

For a second it looked like Tommy was going to say something more, but he let his voice trail off.

"Yes?" asked Jez. "It shows pictures and . . ."

He shook his head, seeming to brush the thought away. "Never mind. It's complicated. It's enough to know that time doesn't take kindly to living things messing about with it, jumping here and there. Like you said, you're very lucky."

"Can I see it? The Cyclo . . ."

"Cycloidotrope," Tommy finished for her as he pulled a small device out of his pouch. It looked kind of like an old-fashioned camera, but smaller. The casing was polished wood and brass, and it held a crystal cube that pulsated gently with a soft glow.

"The ones who made it," Tommy was saying, "the monks of the Enlightened Hidden City—were a peaceful sort, but they were kind of homebodies. They used it for knowledge but never for travel. Too dangerous."

The brass and wood case covered the cube on three sides, and if Jez looked into the open side she could see a tiny, intricate mechanism at the center of the crystal, a turning piece of clockwork. The whole thing fit rather nicely in the palm of Tommy's hand.

"How does it work?" she asked. There did not appear to be an on/off switch as far as she could tell.

"It doesn't," said Tommy. "At least, it doesn't at the moment. It runs on temporal energy—time. It stores up the passing seconds and converts them to energy. Takes a while. It won't be useful for another day or so."

"What's that in the middle? Some kind of miniature nuclear reactor or something?"

Tommy blinked at her. "Nuclear?"

"Sorry," Jez answered. "It's a modern thing. Look, can't we use this to get out of here? I need to get back to my time—my dad could be in trouble."

"I guess I wasn't clear when I said that thing was dangerous. I don't mean dangerous like tossing-dung-patties-at-coppers dangerous. I mean *dangerous*. We can't use it to go anywhere."

"But there's a chance, right? I went through once. There's at least a chance I can go through again!"

"There's a chance you could jump from the Brooklyn Bridge and land on a nice, cushy barge of mattresses that just happens to be floating by. Think of it like that, Jezebel, only with slightly worse odds. I'm telling you, it's a regular miracle that you're alive."

Jez felt her heart sink in her chest. She looked out of their little hidey-hole to the bizarre land beyond, and missed her home terribly. Every now and again she'd hear the roar of some distant animal echo across the valley. Tommy had warned her that this hollow world was full of strange creatures and that very few of them were friendly, although so far she'd spied only a species of large black dragonflies buzzing about the cave entrance. They were harmless, and when smashed they made a pretty effective slow-burning fuel, as Tommy demonstrated by pulping a few and carrying the tarry remains back to refill the makeshift lamp near his cot. When she'd asked what possessed him to try burning the bugs in the first place, he simply shrugged and answered, "I'm a boy."

"So if we can't use the Cycloidotrope to get home, what good is it?" Jezebel asked. "Other than spying on girls, that is."

Tommy threw up his hands, red-faced. But Jez suspected that his embarrassed flush wasn't entirely due to anger. "I wasn't spying on you," he said. "I wasn't even looking for you, not you specifically. I was looking for something someone stole from me and the Cycloidotrope showed me you. I don't know why."

Jezebel thought a moment. "You said this place is another planet, but you came through a door to get here. Are there more doors on Earth?"

"Portals, yeah," said Tommy. "But they always appear in out-of-the-way places. Like the basements of old hotels . . ."

"How about closets?" Jez asked.

Tommy's expression turned grim, but he nodded. "A dark closet only ever leads to one place, and no one goes there. No one living, that is. That's the Dead Gentleman's domain."

The Dead Gentleman. The name made Jezebel remember the

dark and the things that were after her. "He's what you were try-ing to warn me about. Bernie said that the Gentleman is trying to get into our world. He read about him in that book of his."

Tommy looked at her. "Bernie? What did Bernie's book look like?"

"Biggest book I've ever seen. And old, with a broken padlock on the cover. Why? What's it all mean?"

Tommy shook his head. "I knew an Explorer once by the name of Bernard Billingsworth, he was my partner, but it can't be the same person. He'd have to be well over a hundred years old by your time."

"Bernie's an old guy, but he's not that old."

"We'd better hope not. Because if it's him then we're in worse trouble than I thought. Bernard betrayed me to the Dead Gentle-man. He brought that basement portal down around my ears, and I had no choice but to escape through into this place."

"Well, this can't be the same guy. My Bernie is harmless. He's just a crotchety old coot."

"Hmm. I hope you're right," he said. Then he stood up and dusted off his pants. Pulling back the leaf door, he squinted into the red-orange of the outside. "Looks clear. Want to go for a little hike?"

"Out there?" Jez asked. "I thought you said it was super-dangerous with all kinds of girl-eating monsters and stuff."

"It is. But there's more you need to know and, more impor-tantly, see. But the dinosaurs are cold-blooded and they stick to a regular cycle of hunting and sleeping. There's no proper night down here, you see. No proper daytime, either, so right now is naptime. No time's safer."

Ducking to clear the low-hanging entrance, Jezebel followed

him back out into the open. After the hour or so spent in the cave, she felt exposed out here in the open, although it did occur to her that "the open" might be a relative term, since this whole valley was supposedly several miles underground.

"So where are we hiking to?"

"You'll see. It's not very far. Just on the other side of this ridge, in fact."

Without further explanation, Tommy turned and began scrambling up the slope above the cave entrance. It took Jez a while to reach the top, as she wasn't exactly used to this sort of climb. Her parents weren't outdoorsy types, and the few camping trips they'd gone on had inevitably ended in hurricane-force rains and pizza in a hotel room. Still, she managed to make it to the summit without major injury, and Tommy was there to greet her. He had hunkered down behind a line of boulders and was gesturing for her to stay low and quiet.

As she approached on all fours, he pointed over his shoulder to whatever was on the other side of those rocks.

"Take a peek," he whispered. "But keep out of sight."

Jez peered up over the edge of the rock line and saw that it descended to another valley below. Their ridge seemed to cut down the middle of one gigantic canyon, dividing it into two separate vales of roughly equal size. But size was where the similarity ended. Whereas their valley was tangled and overgrown, this one was a dead wasteland. Instead of a lush jungle, Jez was looking down upon a petrified forest. Tall stalks of stone, broken and brittle caps and long stretches of dust filled the valley floor.

And above it all floated a ship unlike anything she'd seen. It was anchored to an enormous petrified mushroom cap, the black chain straining against its mooring. Indeed, the word "ship" was the closest that Jez could come to describing the great hulk, though its shape was twisted and wrong—a mass of rigging, sails and wicked-looking cannons. Atop the center mast, where the mainsail would normally be, was a giant balloon, like the kind used on zeppelins. This seemed to be its main source of propulsion, for it floated in midair above the dead forest. And every detail—every rope, every sail, every plank of wood or length of metal—was solid black. Not polished or shining but matte and dull, like a starless night sky.

"The *Charnel House*, the black ship of the Dead Gentleman." Tommy had crawled up beside her and now whispered out of the corner of his mouth, but his eyes were fixed on that dark vessel. "He uses it to travel between worlds and to carry his army with him."

"His army?" Jezebel whispered back. "What does he need an army for?"

"To kill things. *All* things. *Everything*. That forest down there looked just like the other one before he arrived. He's killed just about everything on this side of the ridge. They say when the Gentleman calls, the dead answer."

At that moment there was a noise like a trumpet, only with a deeper, grating quality. Jezebel covered her ears and fell to her knees behind the rock line. Listening to it felt like chewing on tinfoil.

After it passed, Tommy went on. "It's a hunting horn. Every now and then he lets his followers out to play. The horn means that they've spotted something down there."

"What is he? How could something that terrible exist?"

"Good question, but I don't have much of an answer. The Explorers have known about the Gentleman for centuries, and even we don't know where he comes from. Not really. Some say he came out of the space in between—the blackness between worlds. He showed up when the first Explorer started using the portals, and he's been skulking around ever since.

"Mind you, the first time I met him he was sneaking into a gambling hall through the back door. Not so grand, eh? I lifted Merlin out of his posh carriage on the Bowery—is that still there, by the way? Anyway, he raised holy hell trying to get it back from me, until Captain Scott showed up."

"Captain Scott," Jez said. "He was an Explorer, too?"

Tommy nodded, but he looked away as he did so.

"The thing is, with the Gentleman," he continued, "he shows up on our Earth from time to time but he never stays long. All the old legends are true—the undead can't stand the light of our sun. It's lethal to them. That's because they have no soul—no life, no soul. So when dawn breaks, the Gentleman has to scurry off to the void or be destroyed."

Tommy cocked his head and looked at Jez. "Listen, you said that Bernie had a book, but did you see anything else?"

"Sure, he had lots of weird stuff . . ."

"How about a bird? A little metal bird."

Jez remembered the little mechanical canary perched on Bernie's shelf, squawking and chirping at him like an old friend.

Jez nodded. "Yeah. He called it Merlin."

Tommy was quiet for a minute as he chewed over this information. Jezebel had no idea what any of it meant, but for once she was content to sit and wait.

"It was Merlin I was looking for when the Cycloidotrope showed me you," Tommy said at last.

"Sorry to disappoint," Jez said.

Tommy smiled, but he still looked worried.

"The Gentleman's been after Merlin for years. I don't know why, but it can't be good. He trapped me here because he thought I had the bird with me. But I'd already given it to my partner, Bernard, for safekeeping."

"So if Bernie and Bernard are the same person, then he's had Merlin all these years," said Jez. "Wouldn't the Gentleman have figured that out by now and given up looking for you?"

Tommy shook his head. "Remember, only a couple of months have passed here. If you saw Merlin safe and sound in the future, then that means Bernard's keeping it safe from the Gentleman, and he'll go on doing so. But I think a hundred years from now, the Gentleman finally finds it—in your time. For some reason the future Gentleman thinks that you have it, too. That's why he sent those crouchers after you. It took him over a hundred years, but he's finally close. He knows it's in the Percy; he just has the wrong person. We have to stop him! We have to get to Merlin before he does, but we're stuck here in the past. Over a hundred years too early!"

"But we've got all the time in the world, right? I mean, I hate to say it, but we've got, like, over a century to try and find a way out of here!"

"Time doesn't work like that. It's not linear—it's more egg-shaped."

Jezebel was about to ask him what the heck he meant when a second horn blast rang out through the valley, another cringe-inducing, piercing bleat. As the noise died down Tommy pulled himself back up to the edge of the rock line. "Sounds like they've spotted something. We'd better get back to our side of the valley before the Grave Walkers start scouting up here."

"What are Grave Walkers?" Jez asked. The name alone conjured up a nasty image in her mind.

"The Gentleman uses many different servants—crouchers like the ones who came after you. Worse things, even. But as much as I hate to say it, the bulk of his army is made up of people. Most are a bad sort to start with—murderers, thugs. They are drawn to his crazy death-worshiping cult and become . . . less than human. Not quite alive, not quite dead. The near-dead. The Gentleman keeps them at the edge of death so that he can control them, but they haven't given up their souls yet so they can move around freely in the daylight. They go by different names in different times, but their methods are always the same. They're killers, through and through."

Jezebel hugged herself. She was suddenly cold. "You're right, let's go. I don't want to stay up here."

As the pair made their way down the ridge, Jezebel was careful not to stumble over the nettle vines that snaked across their path or slip on the loose, gravelly dirt. This time Tommy stayed close to her side, never quite offering a helping hand, but close enough to steady her if need be.

"You said the Gentleman trapped you here?" Jez asked as she navigated a particularly crumbly bit of rock.

"The Gentleman set a trap for me and Merlin in the basement of the Percy Hotel. With the help of my old partner, he left me underground with only one way out—the portal to this place. When I got here, he was waiting for me. I think he was hoping that if he couldn't catch me, then one of the native inhabitants would. Careful, watch your step there—that's a tricky drop. The Hollow World is a very dangerous place, and I think he figured that a boy wouldn't last long."

"Well, looks like he figured wrong."

"Yeah, I guess he did." Tommy grinned wide at the compliment. "I've managed to keep a step ahead of him and his goons this long, but it can't last forever. We have to find a way out of here. For some reason the Gentleman seems to think that bird is the key to conquering our world, and you saw what he's done here in just a couple of months! If he's right about Merlin, then our whole world is at risk."

They went the rest of the way down on their butts, in a kind of controlled slide. When they reached the tunnel entrance, Tommy started pacing outside the door. He was animated, excited. He began making plans immediately, filled with new energy and optimism.

"Every world has portals. We just have to find one! Even if we can't get back to your time right away, we can at least get back to Earth. Then we can work on your time problem. Like you said, there's gotta be a way."

Tommy stopped pacing. "If it is Bernard, if he did betray me, then we have a score to settle."

Tommy's gaze drifted down to the valley below. "The Captain said Bernard was weak. But I never thought in a million years that he'd betray us to the Gentleman. It's his fault I've been stuck here these last few months. Worse, he's put the whole world in danger."

"Bernie went out of his way to show me Merlin," Jez said. "He wanted me to know all about you. He's had Merlin in that closet of his for who knows how long and he hasn't told anyone but me. If he's working for the Gentleman, then he's a sucky employee."

Tommy chewed his lip. "That's true."

"I don't know what his game is, but we'll figure it out."

Tommy nodded at her and brushed past. "Just let me get my stuff. There are some hills on the western ridge that I haven't explored yet. Maybe there's a portal there, just waiting for us!"

Then he pulled his goggles down over his eyes and flipped a switch on the side. At once his eyes lit up with a blue glow.

"Don't want to waste bug fuel!" he said, crawling on hands and knees back into the cave tunnel.

Jez was tired of dark holes. She called after him, "Hey, I'll just wait here, since I don't really have any stuff to get. Okay?"

There was no answer.

"Tommy?" Jez called again, but still nothing. Perhaps he'd crawled out of earshot. She bent down and stuck her face in the hole and nearly screamed when she saw several pairs of luminous yellow eyes staring back at her. It was impossible to make out details in the dark except for those round eyes, as big as grapefruits, and a general sense that she was looking at something very hairy.

A grinding noise startled her out of her momentary shock, and she blinked as a sudden avalanche of dust spilled down upon her head. The entrance was closing in on itself, the very rock growing around the hole, shrinking it, until it was little more than a crack. Jez managed to get her leg out of the way just in the nick of time, or else she might have become a part of the hill, her foot planted in the rock like the roots of some Jezebel-sized plant.

As the moving rock settled, she peered into the entrance, now little more than a peephole as wide as her index finger. The tunnel was still open beyond, and she watched as the yellow eyes slowly backed away from the hole and disappeared into the dark.

"Hey," she shouted. "Hey!"

Suddenly, Tommy's earlier words rang, unbidden, in her ears: *I think it was once a trog cave—they're great rock shapers, you know—but it's abandoned now. Well, it looks abandoned, don't you think?*

She kicked the cave, her anger overriding the pain of her suddenly stubbed toe.

"Tommy Learner, you stupid, stupid . . . BOY!"

She pounded on the rock until her fists hurt and her eyes stung with tears. The rock scraped her knuckles raw, but the tears had nothing to do with the pain.

Jezebel was alone. Tommy was gone, taken by those things, and she was on her own.

Something tickled the back of her neck just before it thumped into her head—once, twice. She turned to see a black dragonfly buzzing around her ear.

Thump.

Jez swatted at the pest and sank down to the ground, her back against the rock.

"Stupid," she whispered, and pulled her knees up close, hugging them to her as she stared at the dense, alien jungle looming before her.

CHAPTER TWELVE

TOMMY

THE ENLIGHTENED HIDDEN CITY, 1900

In time, Bernard and I would become friends, but it took some doing. Our first real bit of trouble had to do with our positions aboard the *Nautilus*. As the more experienced apprentice, young Bernard still technically outranked me, and he wasn't above taking advantage of it. After the first week of shining his shoes and making his bunk, I complained to the Captain, and when this didn't help I resorted to a good old-fashioned street thumping (this being sort of a headlock wherein you bump the locked head into the dirtiest manure-laden patch of street you can find). As it turned out, one street thumping was all it took to even the scales, and Bernard never again ordered me to so much as pass the salt at dinner.

That over with, we settled into a routine of . . . wonder. Alongside the Captain and Bernard, I saw twin suns rise over the Sea of Glass while scaling the shoulder of a thousand-year-old petrified giant. I rescued Bernard from the leopard-men of the Obsidian Temple early one morning and nicked their holy Cat's Eye Emerald later that afternoon. Those few months were the happiest of my life, bar none. And I only wish with all my heart that they could've lasted.

All was not perfect, though. The Captain still suffered his gray, faraway moods. He'd sometimes disappear into his cabin by himself for hours, even days at a time. He spent long evenings obsessing over his books or simply staring at Merlin, leaving Bernard and me to our own devices (hence the little detour with the leopard-men). But the Captain really wasn't alone in this. I'd felt the same ominous fear since the moment I'd looked into the Gentleman's black, soulless eyes. Something bad was coming.

So when the distress signal reached the *Nautilus*, I can't say I was all that surprised. The message was garbled and hard to make out, and we didn't even receive it until we'd returned to Earth for a bit of ship's maintenance—twelve hours after its first transmission. The automated beacon was being rebroadcast from the London Chapterhouse on a protected ether-radio frequency in a continual loop. A single, desperate voice calling out:

The Hidden City has been invaded! Academy under attack! All Explorers are ordered to—

That's all there was. Whether it was a call for help or a warning to stay away, we couldn't be sure. It just ended in the middle. Cut off. Slammed shut like a closet door.

We arrived at the London Chapterhouse only to find it already abandoned. Not even the deaf fellow was left to man the door. There was no rain this time, just a cold, clear moon that played its silvery light along the darkened hallways. The lamps were all out and the fireplace, cold. The Captain opened a number of hidden weapons lockers, but they were all empty. The Stitch-Golem still worked, however. The Captain announced the three of us, and the great bear's mouth opened to reveal the passage to the Academy. The Captain stared at it for a long time before he spoke.

"I should have been here," he said, finally. "I should have been here to fight with them."

Bernard started to say something, but I waved him quiet. I could see what the Captain was going through, and nothing we could say would help him. We all suspected the same thing—the Academy was lost. As complicated as his relationship with the other Explorers was, they were still his family, and the Academy was his home. Odds were, that was all gone.

For the first time, I understood the Captain perfectly. He was an orphan now, just like me.

"I'm going in to see what I can find out," he said. "I'll be back in ten minutes. You two keep guard here until then. If there's more trouble than I can handle, I'll send Merlin back through, and then you two are to close this gate, take him and the *Nautilus* and get as far away from here as possible."

He handed me a metal ball the size of my fist. "This is called a mayfly. It's a bomb that is used to collapse portals. If Merlin comes through without me, you twist here." He indicated a very subtle hinge along the circumference of the ball. "Then give it a hard shake. That twist wakes the explosive mechanism inside, and the shake makes it mad for extra effect. Toss it inside the portal and run. You'll have about three minutes of angry buzzing before the thing goes off. It'll seal this portal up tight."

Then I did the darnedest thing. I saluted. Surprised myself

and just about gave the Captain a heart attack, judging by the wide-eyed shock on his face. But then, with a pleased grin, he saluted back.

"Good men," he said. "I'll be right back."

Two hours later and Scott still hadn't returned. I'd scuffed a very clear set of boot marks along the floor with my endless pacing. For some reason I felt compelled to keep checking the window, even though I knew that if any enemies were coming for us, they wouldn't come from the street. It was just a place to look *other* than that hideous bear's mouth—the open portal.

Bernard picked up a book, but I noticed he never turned the pages.

"How long has it been now?" I asked.

"Exactly two minutes later than when you asked last time," answered Bernard, not even bothering to look at his chronometer.

"He's in trouble," I said.

Bernard didn't say anything.

I grabbed my Tesla Stick and planted myself in front of the Stitch-Golem. The dark tunnel was visible just beyond the Golem's teeth. And beyond that, I knew, was the Academy.

"If you are thinking of going in after him, just forget it," Bernard said. "Captain Scott was very clear in his orders."

Bernard was right, of course. The Captain had been clear. Dead serious, in fact.

"We just need to wait," Bernard was saying. "If he was in trouble, he'd have sent Merlin."

No sooner had the words escaped Bernard's mouth than a flickering, fluttering flash of brass came ricocheting through the darkness of the portal mouth. It was Merlin, and he was alone.

The bird flew in a tight circle around my head, squawking

out a tune of short, troubled whistles that I knew too well. After a few frantic minutes, I managed to calm him down enough that he settled on my shoulder. But his head continued to pivot worriedly, back and forth on tiny hinges.

"The Captain?" I asked.

Merlin gave a swift nod.

"He still alive?"

The bird didn't nod, but he didn't shake his head, either. He just blinked at me. Scott was in trouble, but whether he was alive or dead, Merlin didn't know.

I took the mayfly out of my pocket. It was heavy for its small size. Unusually solid.

"Here," I said, tossing it to Bernard. He let out a little yelp as he made an awkward catch with both hands.

"Merlin, can you show me where you saw the Captain last?"

The bird nodded back.

"I'm going," I said. "Same rules apply—if I get in over my head, I'll send Merlin back and then you use the mayfly to seal up the portal."

Bernard looked at me, his eyes wide behind his glasses. "You're going to leave me behind? What if you need help? This is not the Captain's plan!" he said. I could tell that Bernard was torn between his concern for the Captain and his fear of what was on the other side of that portal. I made it easy for him.

"I work better alone," I said. "New plan."

"What new plan?"

I shrugged as I hefted my Tesla Stick and stepped through the Stitch-Golem's mouth. "I'll let you know when I get back. Making this all up as I go!"

When Merlin and I emerged into the Academy, it was night.

But I'm used to sneaking around in the dark, and I hadn't gone two steps before I spotted a patrol of black-robed Grave Walkers armed with some kind of long sickle knives. The Dead Gentleman's foot soldiers. If there had been any doubt as to who had attacked the Hidden City, it was gone now. Luckily, the cultists seemed to dress for effect and not effectiveness, and the large horse-skull masks they wore looked stupidly hot and cumbersome. I could hear their ragged, gasping breathing long before they marched into view. Merlin was normally an excellent scout and could smell danger the way I could smell an overfull coin purse, but something here had overloaded the little bird's senses. Whatever evil those Grave Walkers had brought with them, it now permeated every inch of the Hidden City. Merlin couldn't pinpoint the danger because danger was everywhere.

I didn't see a single Explorer—not alive, anyway. A few had been piled up against buildings to clear the walkways, but most were just left where they'd fallen. Some still held weapons in their dead hands. The grand marble columns of their ancient Academy were mostly toppled and blackened with scorch marks. Only the rose-stone Tower Library appeared intact, but ominous wet stains fouled the steps leading to its doors.

I swallowed the urge to get sick and hunkered down behind an overturned column while we waited for the patrol of Grave Walkers to pass. Once they were out of sight, I whispered to Merlin. "Okay, which way to the Captain?"

The bird surprised me by pointing his beak away from the Library, to the main promenade that led out from the Academy and into the old part of the Hidden City. The deserted city of the monks.

"What?" I began. "Why would Scott head that way . . ."

Then it dawned on me. The High Father. The High Father's Inner Chamber was out there. Upon seeing the masses of Grave Walkers patrolling the Academy grounds, the Captain had decided to check on the High Father, hoping his remote Chamber might have been overlooked.

But he hadn't made it that far.

With Merlin perched on my shoulder, I made my way out of the Academy and into the winding streets beyond. Unlike the straight lines and tall arches of the Explorers' classical Earth architecture, the Hidden City was a twisting maze of enormous, inverted ziggurats. It looked like someone had uprooted all the pyramids of Egypt and balanced them, precariously, upside down on their points. As I snuck my way through the shadows of that alien place, I couldn't help but fear that the whole thing would come toppling down at any second. It just wasn't . . . natural. But then, few things were anymore.

Soon I was thoroughly and completely lost, although Merlin insisted that we were headed in the right direction. We rounded a bend and stopped at a gated trapdoor set into the floor of an open square. Empty crates and barrels were stacked nearby, and I wondered if this might have been some kind of grain silo once used by the monks. The cultists, however, had apparently decided that it'd work better as a place to store the leftover bits. In the dim moonlight I could see that it was full of dead Grave Walkers. They must have been using the place as a sort of mass grave for their fallen comrades. I'd just started to back away when Merlin began digging his claws into my shoulder. Someone was coming. I listened closely and heard footsteps. There were two streets out of this square, and cultists were coming down both of them. I was caught, with nowhere to run. Already I could hear the heavy, tired breathing of their horse-skull masks getting closer. I had only one choice.

I'd barely closed the trapdoor above me when the first Grave Walker appeared. I clung to the underside of the grill, my hands and feet wrapped around the bars like a sloth. Merlin held on next to me, but it was easier for the little bird. Below us was a twenty-foot drop that ended in a pile of bodies. I just prayed that I wouldn't be adding my corpse to it.

Above us, the first of the Grave Walkers stepped onto the trapdoor. His heavy-booted foot missed my fingers by less than an inch. Already my hands were burning from the strain; after a few minutes my biceps started to tremble. Another joined his companion up top.

As the second cultist joined his friend, I had to unwind a foot from the grill or get stepped on. Now I was dangling by my hands and one foot. My fingers felt like they might snap, but still the Grave Walkers wouldn't move. I heard their muffled voices hissing to each other from behind those grotesque masks. In a ridiculous, idle thought I wondered what cultists' small talk consisted of. The cleanest way to cut open a sacrifice? Funereal fashions? At least it was a way to keep my panic at bay.

"Tommmmy . . ."

Something spoke my name in a low moan, barely audible. At first I thought it came from one of the Grave Walkers, but when it spoke a second time, I realized it was coming from below. From the pile of corpses at the bottom of the pit.

"Tommmmmy . . ." Something was crawling around down there as it called out to me. The dead were moving and they knew my name.

"Tommmmy . . ." The voice grew louder, more desperate.

I closed my eyes tight, but I could picture it reaching for me, waiting for me to fall.

A Grave Walker took a single step to the side and onto my left hand. My fingers crunched beneath his heel, but to my credit I managed not to cry out. I did not, however, manage to hang on.

I landed on what felt like a pile of wet leaves. But I knew that there were no leaves down here, just bloated, rotten bodies underneath rotten clothes. Hands grabbed me, pulling at me. I couldn't bear to look, so with my eyes still shut I kicked with all my strength. I wouldn't go without a fight.

"Tommy—oof!"

I stopped kicking. That "oof" sounded familiar. I'd heard it several times before—often in the moments before having to rescue my mentor from yet another tight spot.

When I opened one eye, my fear was quickly replaced with a mix of joy and sinking guilt. There was Captain Scott, purpled and yellowed with bruises and cuts, but alive. He'd obviously been beaten badly, and he was dabbing at a fresh cut on his lower lip where I had just kicked him.

"Ouch," the Captain said.

"Sorry," I whispered. "Thought you were a corpse."

"Perfectly all right. I probably look the part."

The Captain's voice had a wet, wheezing sound to it that I didn't like, like someone on the edge of a cough. That voice worried me more than all the cuts and bruises. I started to look around.

"Don't," Scott cautioned. "Just focus on what's above you. Try not to think about what's beneath."

I nodded, then winced as something gave way under my foot. A pop and a squishing sound.

"How'd you get here?" I asked, trying to keep my mind on other things.

"I should ask the same of you," he said, eyeing Merlin as he fluttered down from his perch and rested on the Captain's shoulder. The bird innocently set about cleaning a bit of grime from its shining feathers.

"I should've left Bernard in charge," he said.

"Wouldn't have stopped me," I answered, and I was glad when he smiled.

"No, I suppose it wouldn't."

He shifted his weight and groaned suddenly in pain. He was hurt worse than he looked.

"I found the High Father, but then the Grave Walkers found us both. I fought them off until he'd had a chance to escape. Then they threw me in here. Probably think it'll soften me up for a bit of interrogation. They're after Merlin, Tommy. They think we delivered him to the Council, but they'll soon realize their mistake."

"So it's begun?" I asked. "The Dead Gentleman is really coming?"

The Captain nodded. "This was just his first move. The opening skirmish in a much larger war."

"Then we have to go," I said. "We have to get out of here, now!"

"Tommy." The Captain put his hand on my shoulder. "Before we were separated, the High Father said something to me. He told me to ask *you* a question."

"Me? I don't even know him!"

"All the same, he mentioned you by name. He said to ask you, *Are you the flea that skitters or the flea that bites?* Do you have any idea what that means?"

"What? No! It's a bunch of gibberish! A flea, for crying out loud."

"Tommy, the High Father is the wisest mind in the universe. He knows the past, the present and the future! His words should never be taken lightly."

Scott looked at me for a long moment, then he took a small folding comb out of his breast pocket and set about smoothing his tangled mustache. He looked absurd sitting there atop a pile of dead bodies, covered in filth, tending to his out-of-place whiskers. But that was the Captain. I figure you don't get to be his age, and see the things he's seen, without earning a few eccentricities along the way.

"Well," he said after a time. "How to get out of here, then? We still need to escape from this hellish place. Any ideas?"

I stood up, careful to keep my balance on the unsteady "ground" beneath my feet. "Do you have any rope?" I asked.

"Always," Scott answered. "Ah, I get your point—Merlin can fly the cord up to the top. But even if we can climb out, there are those guards up there. They wander off every now and then but they're never gone for long. How do you propose we deal with them?"

I pulled the Tesla Stick from my belt and gave it a flick of the wrist, extending it to its full length. Cool, crackling electricity shimmered up and down its length. Despite the mess of corpses under us, and the horror all around us, I found myself grinning.

"Let's answer the High Father's question," I said. "I'm the flea that bites!"

CHAPTER THIRTEEN

THE DEAD GENTLEMAN
THE HOLLOW WORLD, 1902

The Learner boy had help. The Gentleman could feel it—the increase of life, a slight tipping of the scales in the other direction. All he had to do was taste the air to know that the delicate balance between life and death here in this Hollow World, a balance he'd spent a considerable effort to weigh in his favor, had shifted.

He opened his cadaverous mouth and let the subterranean air drift in again, let it flow through his hollow-boned cheeks and across desiccated nasal passages. *A female*. It was a female helping the boy, which was disturbing news. Another Explorer, perhaps? He'd brought their pathetic Academy down on top of their heads. He'd filled its streets with blood while searching for his prize. Had someone escaped? Whoever she was, like Learner, she was not of this world.

The Gentleman reached for the rail of his ship, the *Charnel*

House, and scraped his bony fingertips across the dark, lacquered wood. The five ragged claw marks that he left there, deep-cut grooves in the banister, were the only outward signs of his displeasure. Today's face, a clean skull bleached white by time and the elements, could show no emotion. His latest incarnation was less expressive than some of his others, and not as outwardly grotesque as the Freshly Hung Corpse or Rotted Man shapes that he sometimes wore, but the Skeleton in Black had a certain motivating effect on his minions. And being a creature of tastes, the Gentleman wouldn't be caught dead wearing the same outfit two days in a row.

He tilted back the brim of his top hat and stared up at the molten core with empty eyes. A voice to his left spoke up.

"I wish we could do something about that bloody fireball. Leave it to you to trap Learner in a place where the sun never goes away. Not as bad as real daylight, of course, but I'm still lobster-red, not to mention it's murder on the eyes."

He turned to consider Archibald Macheath, First Mate of the *Charnel House* and the Gentleman's bloody-minded lieutenant. What possessed the Gentleman to make the uncouth, complaining vampire his number one was something of a mystery. Perhaps it was because out of all the Gentleman's groveling followers, Macheath was the single being who didn't care about anything or anyone other than Macheath. That, and Macheath's skill with a knife.

The slowly baking Macheath dabbed at his brow with a dingy white handkerchief. When it came away it was pink with bloody sweat. "You hear the boys brought down that lizard?" said Macheath. "Last one this side of the valley. Won't be long now. Learner's running out of places to hide."

"You think so?" asked the Gentleman in a voice that sounded like wind through a hollow reed. The Skeleton in Black had no vocal cords.

"Sure. The beasties out there are getting desperate, and he'd make a nice bit of snack. If he dies he becomes your property anyway, so it's a win-win. And I've been having the boys spread the word among the natives that if Learner's caught and turned over to us, we'll lift anchor and leave the Hollow World in peace. After all, we can always come back and clean it out later."

The vampire grinned and showed a mouth of missing teeth. Vampires were useful, impervious to pain and nearly unkillable unless confronted with direct sunlight or a stake through the heart. They were tough creatures, but that also made them hard to discipline. Ever the problem solver, the Gentleman had found that pulling one of Macheath's teeth every time he displeased him was an effective way of keeping the vampire in line. But poor Macheath had had a string of bad luck recently and was down to two single fangs.

Nevertheless, Macheath attended his master's side like a beaten dog hoping for a scratch behind its ears, but the Gentleman didn't feel in the mood for compliments. This new female presence was disturbing. Alone, Tommy Learner would surely have perished, but if he now had a companion . . .

"We have a new wrinkle. Someone is with Learner. Someone from the outside."

"Eh? How'd he get here? We've got every known portal covered."

"*She* might have discovered a new one, though it's unlikely. But however she managed to get in, we can't take the chance that Learner will use the same route to get out."

The Gentleman surveyed the deck of the *Charnel House*. Everywhere, black-robed Grave Walkers tended to the masts, the rigging. Guards walked lookout patrols along the rails. All hands made a careful and obvious effort to steer clear of Macheath. He had a reputation for going on binges among the crew—or, more accurately, binging *on* the crew.

But, despite Macheath's overindulgences, the Gentleman still had an army at his disposal. The ship's hands numbered in the hundreds. On the ground, Grave Walkers rode their skeletal mounts in formation drills, eager for the hunt. And since landing here in the Hollow World, the Gentleman had been making special additions to his forces. They all came to serve the Gentleman in the end.

Just beyond one small range of hills was the verdant valley. Somewhere there was Tommy Learner, inching ever closer to escape. Somewhere there was the key to the Gentleman's plan—a delicate bird of clockworks and gears who possessed a secret that, in the Gentleman's hands, would spell the end of everything. He'd opened the throat of every Explorer in the Academy looking for it, only to find that it was *still* in the possession of that thieving boy. He'd been sure the Explorers had reclaimed it. So sure that he'd struck them with all his might, revealing his strength earlier than planned. There was no going back now. The warning would go up across a thousand worlds. The war had begun and he needed the artifact to win!

"There is no more time," said the Gentleman, his voice carrying across the deck like the rattle of leaves in the wind. "We can no longer afford to wait him out. Pull up anchor and set sail for that ridge—tonight we invade the valley. Kill everything in our way!"

Macheath smiled as he called out the order, which was picked up and repeated throughout the troops. The *Charnel House* began to scurry with activity as the ship was made ready to sail. Coal fires were fed and billows of hot air and acrid smoke filled the giant airbag. Such a force took time to mobilize, time the Gentleman feared he would not have. What if this new companion knew the way out? What if she was here to help Tommy Learner escape?

"You said the Walkers made a new kill?" asked the Gentleman, outwardly calm amid the cacophony.

"Yes sir," answered Macheath. "Biggest one yet. It's stowed away, down in the bilge."

"Show me."

Macheath led the way as the pair descended into the bowels of the vessel. The deeper they got, the fewer Grave Walkers they encountered; in the lower decks dwelt the things that would not or could not abide even the weak light of the Hollow World. The dark down here was thick with crouchers and ghouls and things that had yet to be named. They gathered about the Dead Gentleman as he strode along the planks, simpering and groveling for their master's benediction, for his blessing upon their miserable existence.

Macheath struck out at them with his lash. "Get back, you lot! The Gentleman doesn't need your grimy paws spoiling his fine attire."

The throngs parted and the pair continued unmolested to their final destination. There, on the concave floor of the lowermost cargo hold, was a massive shape. The air here was rank with the smell of putrefying flesh. The Gentleman's presence combined with the heat of the lava sun overhead had sped up the decaying process. Macheath covered his nose with his bloody handkerchief. For one of the undead, he was unusually squeamish, or perhaps it was just habit.

"There he is," said Macheath, his voice muffled by the sodden rag. "A real beaut, isn't he?"

The Gentleman stepped forward and gently ran his hand across the shape's hide. He loved the chill of death as a child loves the warm sun on her face. Rigor mortis had already come and gone, and in places the flesh had begun to split and crack as the decomposition caused gases and fluid to burst forth into the open.

"A terrible beauty, yes," said the Gentleman. "But a beauty nonetheless."

The Gentleman followed the curve of the beast's neck all the way to its blocklike head. The lips had receded and the teeth were shut like the bars of a cage. The Gentleman leaned close and, from his own mouth, exhaled. The Skeleton in Black had no lungs to hold air, so what it was that he actually expelled was something else. It was shadow and frost, the quiet of the grave.

A convulsion racked the body of the dead beast. Something stirred deep inside as the parts that had given up were called upon to move again. Its massive heart began thumping once more—a fierce, staccato rhythm—but no blood flowed in those veins. The will of the Gentleman sustained it and that was all.

Macheath had backed up a number of steps, positioning himself securely on the other side of the bilge doorway. The lurking shadows and demons had retreated to their holes. The Gentleman's bony face managed an expression almost like a smile—predators always knew when something fiercer had entered their territory, and this was fiercer by far.

"Find the female," the Gentleman said. "Smell her out and kill her. Bring me Learner alive if you can, but I want her dead."

Horrible jaws opened in the mockery of a roar, but no sound came out as the newly risen *thing* slouched its way out of the bilge in search of its prey.

CHAPTER FOURTEEN

TOMMY

ABOARD THE *NAUTILUS*, 1900

"How's the Captain?" asked Bernard, his whisper just barely audible over the hum of the ship's engines.

I was staring at the blue-black waters of our familiar Atlantic Ocean as it passed the porthole outside, but my head was still back in the Hidden City.

"He's sick, but he'll be all right," I lied. The Captain had indeed healed from the worst of the Grave Walkers' beating, but he'd taken ill with something much worse. The time spent in that dank corpse pit had done something to his lungs. Every breath the man took now crackled like paper. In my time as a street scavenger, I'd seen enough sickness to know the difference between the ones who would get better and those who wouldn't. The Captain was dying.

Thinking back, it might've been wrong to lie to Bernard. It was probably a violation of some Explorer's Code of Conduct, withholding information from a fellow Explorer and all. But Bernard was still reeling from the news that the Academy was destroyed and all the people there, dead. The boy had signed up to be an Explorer, not a soldier. He wasn't prepared for a war. So I decided to spare him the truth of Captain Scott's condition. While I could, anyway.

"Want to lend me a hand and put on a pot of tea?" I asked. With the Captain sick in bed, Bernard was a ball of nervous energy, shuffling from foot to foot, absently drumming his fingers on the brass safety rails. Putting his body to a task might do him some good.

"Sure. How do you take it? Lemon and sugar?"

"It's not for me," I said. "It's for the Captain. And he likes it with a pour of milk."

Bernard nodded. "Of course. Right. I'll be just a minute."

"Take your time. He's dozing."

I watched as Bernard hurried off to the canteen—the small kitchen/dining hall where we took our meals. I waited until Bernard was well out of earshot before opening the giant oval door to the Captain's quarters.

Scott's room reflected the best and the worst about the man. On the one hand, it was as neat and tidy a space as I've seen, especially considering the amount of stuff he had crammed in there. It served not just as the Captain's sleeping quarters but also as a kind of museum of his various adventures. A generous library full of books from dozens of worlds sat on a glass-enclosed bookshelf. Bizarre relics rested on bolted-down pedestals (we were on a ship, after all). Carved idols, ancient weapons and odd devices were displayed everywhere. In one corner rested an original folio of Shakespeare's plays, right next to a dusky glass globe that held a miniature city, peopled with colored pinpoints of light that actu-ally cooed at you when you approached. It was quite a thing.

On the other hand, it was impossible to look around that room and not recognize the Captain's considerable ego—to not get the impression that you'd wandered into a museum dedicated to the life and times of Captain Jonathan Scott, designed and built by Captain Jonathan Scott, and starring Captain Jonathan Scott.

A life that was ending. Surrounded by his trophies and keep-sakes lay the Captain in his canopied bed, covered in sheets of rich silks. His mustache was, as always, perfectly groomed, and he was wearing a ridiculously ornate nightcap patterned with the winged-cog symbol of the Explorers' Society. But the man's cheeks were sunken, and his once-ruddy nose had turned as pale as his linens—its fire all gone out.

Merlin perched on the bed's headboard, his little face tilt-ing this way and that. Scott was awake and watching me through drooping half slits.

"You send Bernard away?" he asked.

"Yes, like you told me. He's off looking for milk for your tea—I've hidden it and it'll take him ten minutes to realize there isn't any."

Scott smiled. "Sometimes I suspect the boy's spectacles only work one way and he's got them on backward."

"Too bad for an Explorer."

"Poor Bernard is not an Explorer and he never will be," said the Captain, wheezing slightly at the ends of his words. "He doesn't have the stuff. Not like me. Not like you."

"That's a bit harsh, sir. He's a wonkish bookworm, but he tries."

"What I'm saying is no slight on the boy's character; he's a fine lad. But facts are facts. Now come closer. I can't keep up all this shouting."

The two of us hadn't been shouting at all, far from it. In fact I'd had to strain to make out everything the Captain was saying. Still, I pulled up a richly embroidered stool and sat down next to him.

"I'm dying, Tommy. You know that, don't you?"

I nodded. I suppose some might expect that I'd protest or even cry, but the truth is, I'd seen enough people die in my young life that I'd given up on tears. Before I'd ever heard of the Explorers, I'd seen death take folks in far worse ways. The one truth of street life is, you never die in a comfortable bed.

No, I'd mourn the Captain in my own way, but I'd be lashed before I'd show it.

"I wish I could've lived to see the wonders of this new century," said Scott. "The things you will witness! Still. I am thankful for the life I've led. I lifted the Veil of reality and saw the truth of the cosmos. But a different sort of veil is falling over me now, and I've still much to tell you. Things you mustn't share with the crew."

The rest of the crew was, of course, Bernard alone. The Captain's grasp on real life had been especially slippery these last few days. That faraway look that sometimes came and went had come to stay.

"You saw what happened in the Hidden City. The Academy destroyed. The Explorers all dead. That must not be allowed to pass here on Earth."

I pictured the Academy as it had been just a short time ago—bright and shining. A bit dull, yes, but still beautiful. And then I remembered what we'd just escaped—white buildings dipped in blood.

"Could such a thing happen here?" I asked. "Surely not. The Academy was made up of a few thousand people, if that. He can't conquer an entire planet!"

"There is no limit to the Gentleman's power except one—the soulless undead cannot walk in the light of the sun. Right now, that is the only protection we have against him. He'd be powerless during the day; it might even destroy him. Yet the Gentleman risked a visit to our world before, to get Merlin. But he failed to keep hold of him, thanks to you and your sticky fingers. It was our good luck that you interrupted whatever it is he has planned for our little friend." With that, he glanced up at Merlin and smiled. The bird answered him with a sweet, sad song.

"Tommy, you have to stop him!"

"Me? But I'm one boy . . ."

"You are an Explorer! That means something!" This time the Captain did raise his voice, and the exertion sent him into a coughing spasm that shook the bed. As he hacked, I could hear the fluid bubbling in his lungs, blood perhaps.

When the cough subsided, I handed him a glass of water from his nightstand.

"Even before the Academy fell, we'd lost our spines," he said after taking a sip. "You said it yourself. We'd become a society of old men or, at best, scribes like poor Bernard. Explorers are supposed to risk everything because that is how everything is won!

"After I die, you'll be the last one. The last Explorer. The only one worthy of the name, and it'll be up to you to make sure that the Gentleman doesn't get a hold on our world."

I swallowed. The responsibility of what Scott was saying loomed large in my brain. "How? How do I do that?"

Scott shook his head. "I don't know. If I did, I'd have done it myself. But even the dead can die. Remember that, Tommy. Nothing is indestructible."

Scott glanced up again at Merlin, who swiveled his head in response. "Start with him. Keep him safe above all else."

"Merlin? Look, I know the Gentleman's keen on getting him back, but why?"

"Merlin is the key to it all, Tommy. I'm sure of it. The Gentleman wants him desperately. He must be more important than we know." He craned his head up to look at the bird. "If only I'd had time to discover your secret, my little friend . . ."

The shiny metal canary chirped once and cocked his head—he looked as harmless as a child's windup toy. Scott sank back into his pillow. His eyelids fluttered and for a second I feared that the man was falling asleep, or worse.

"I wish I had answers for you," said the Captain, at last. "I've been trying to find out for years. Maybe you'll prove to be a better detective than I."

I reached out a finger and gently tapped Merlin's head. The bird seemed to like it, the way a flesh-and-blood canary might enjoy a nice scratch of his feathers. Pleased, he hopped down from his place at the headboard and climbed onto my thumb. Without gloves, I always winced at those pinching little brass claws, but I let the bird be. He began to whistle.

"It's good that he likes you," Scott said.

"Yeah, well."

"He trusts you."

The Captain reached up and put his hand on my shoulder—a familiar gesture, but this time the man's grip was weak. I could barely feel the weight of his hand against my coat.

"I'm promoting you to full Explorer. Bernard will be hurt but he'll understand. Everything is going to you—Merlin, the *Nautilus*, everything." He opened his hand and in it was a small compass etched with waves and a picture of a ship's steering wheel. "Here. As you know, the *Nautilus* is one of a kind. You're her captain now, and she'll come when you call. Find what the Gentleman has planned and stop him . . ." The Captain's words disappeared in a wet coughing fit. After a minute he went on, but he seemed to be talking past me this time, to a roomful of men who weren't there.

"Tell the crew, tell the men that I want to be buried at sea, with full naval honors. Ask McGuire to play "Rule Britannia," on his fife . . ."

Then his hand slipped, falling back to the bed with a heavy thump. Eventually he drifted off and his eyes closed. I pocketed the compass and waited until Scott began to snore (proof that the man wasn't going to die just yet), and then returned Merlin to the headboard, where the bird resumed its silent vigil.

"You whistle if anything changes," I whispered, and let myself out, closing the door softly behind me.

Bernard was waiting for me with a tea tray.

"It's gone cold," Bernard said. "I heard you two talking and it sounded serious so I waited out here. Now the tea's gone cold."

"It doesn't matter. I was just checking on him, but he's sleeping again anyway. We'll have the tea warmed up for him when he wakes."

"He's not getting better, is he?" Bernard asked.

"No," I answered, too tired and suddenly too full of worries to keep up the lie. "No, he's not."

Bernard nodded. "I've never actually watched someone die before. . . ."

I put my hand on Bernard's shoulder and gave it a squeeze, just the way I imagined the Captain might've.

"It's all right, Bernard. I'll do it," I said. "I'll watch for the both of us."

Then I took the tea tray out of his hands and headed to the canteen to find where I'd hidden the milk.

CHAPTER FIFTEEN

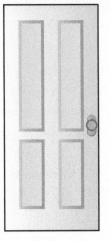

JEZEBEL
THE HOLLOW WORLD, 1902

Something had been following Jezebel for the better part of an hour. She'd first become aware of it as she was picking her way through the high ridge looking for another cave, a back entrance to wherever the trogs had taken Tommy. He'd said that the trogs were cave dwellers, rock shapers. She'd seen the proof of that as they sealed off the entrance while stealing away with Tommy, but perhaps they'd left another one open. It was a long shot, but it was the best plan Jez had been able to come up with so far.

She climbed as high as she dared, choosing to crawl on hands and knees rather than risk walking on the loose gravel. From her vantage point there, she could see the whole valley—the sparse growth of lichens and dwarfish toadstools along the hillside that grew into a thick tangle of fungal forest farther down. Those black dragonflies buzzed around the caps of mushroom trees, and every now and again something would leap up out of the jungle or swoop down from the hazy skies above to catch one in its jaws. Besides serving as Tommy's lighter fuel, the poor bugs appeared to be on the very bottom of the Hollow World's food chain.

Unfortunately, there were no other caves to be found. No cracks or crevices on this side of the valley—none large enough to fit through, anyway. But it was up there on the ridge that she first noticed a strange ripple in the jungle's ceiling of mushroom caps—like the wave caused by something large making its way through the undergrowth. Occasionally she'd catch a glimpse of pale skin as it brushed too close to the canopy, but then it was gone again. This, in itself, wouldn't have been particularly unnerving, not considering the hundred other strange sights and sounds she'd encountered just that morning, except that whatever it was, it seemed to be keeping pace with her. It was sticking to the jungle where the cover was thickest, but it was definitely following her as she zigzagged her way along the uneven ridge. Perhaps it was incapable of climbing the steep slope, or perhaps it was just waiting until it had gained enough ground on her to make its move.

Her worrisome pursuer had just about persuaded her to turn back when she spotted a thin plume of smoke snaking its way out of a ring of giant, fat toadstools.

Someone had built a fire down there. Who knew if they were friendly or even human, but Jezebel thought she stood a heck of a lot better chance with them than she did with the wild animals in this prehistoric jungle. But the smoke was a good several hundred yards into the valley floor, and that meant coming down off this ridge and crossing the path of whatever that thing was down there. Even now it moved monotonously onward, getting ever closer.

She made her decision in an instant and began scurrying down the ridge toward the smoke. She half stumbled, half skidded on her butt, careless of the noise and the dust she was kicking up. Whatever that thing was that stalked her, it obviously knew where she was, so it wasn't like she was giving away her position. She needed to get past the creature chasing her and reach the smoke before it had a chance to catch up. And at first her plan looked like it was going to work. She hit the edge of the forest, and though her pursuer kept on in her direction, it didn't seem to speed up. At this pace she could make a straight line toward the plume of smoke and outdistance the creature easily.

The problem occurred after she'd made it fifty yards or so into the jungle. The giant fungal trees were mostly thicker up top than down below, which meant that there was plenty of room for Jez to travel around their stalks, but the huge mushroom caps all but obscured the sky—and therefore her view of the smoke plume. Without the smoke to navigate by, she quickly became lost among the spongy tree stumps and shaded paths. Every so often she'd find a break in the canopy, but the tiny glimpses of dull red sky did nothing to help her. She had the sinking suspicion that she was running in circles, maybe even winding back into the path of whatever was following her.

She needed to get her bearings, and she wasn't going to do it from on the ground. So she found a tall, sturdy toadstool with a cleft in the cap—a lumpy thing covered in bumpy nodules that made excellent foot- and handholds—and climbed to the top. It was tricky, but after a bit of struggle she was able to lift herself up and above the jungle ceiling, balancing on the toadstool's wide, spongy top. She was covered in powdery mushroom spores and smelled like a day-old sock, but now, at least, she had a view.

Directly in front of her was the ridge she'd just come down from and behind her, as far as the eye could see, was the sprawling mushroom forest. When she peered over her left shoulder, she could see the plume of smoke. It looked smaller now—little more than a dark thread dangling in the haze.

She had been going in the wrong direction. She had indeed circled back on herself and ended up where she'd started earlier that morning—near the trogs' closed cave entrance. All she'd managed to do was to put herself farther away from her destination.

Jezebel cupped her hand over her face to shield her eyes from the molten red glare overhead—the heat really was unbearable down here—and tried to look for signs of movement in the surrounding forest. Nothing stirred. Farther off she could see the dragonflies bouncing about the treetops, but the jungle was strangely quiet. Still. Perhaps it was just reacting to her presence.

Or another presence altogether. Something much larger. And meaner.

Jez felt the tiny hairs on her arm prickle at the thought, and she was suddenly, keenly aware that though she had a good view of the valley, she didn't have so much as a peek at the floor below. The wide mushroom caps obscured everything below her. Something could be standing directly beneath her feet and she wouldn't know it. She might as well have been adrift on a dark, bottomless ocean.

Did her mushroom cap just shake? She thought she felt a slight tremble, but that could have just been the fungus tree settling into her added weight.

But there it was again! The whole thing had definitely shifted, as if something big was brushing up against it. Or climbing it.

Jez had just begun to inch away from the edge when a loud groan, a thick-throated grunt, broke the unnatural silence. It was right beneath her. For a second Jez considered jumping for a neighboring toadstool; perhaps she could leap from mushroom cap to mushroom cap. But even as she began to stand, the toadstool shook again, more violently this time, and it was all she could do to hold on and not tumble off the edge. Her grip was shaky at best, and she found herself sliding inch by inch. She struggled to get her footing, but her feet slipped along the spongy surface until they dangled over the side. As her legs disappeared over the lip, the thing beneath her let out another croaking growl. It had seen her.

She pulled with all her might, but the relentless shaking offered her no purchase. A massive snout appeared at the edge of the mushroom cap. She kicked it with her sneakered foot, but she might as well have kicked a boulder. The snout turned up to reveal a giant mouth, which bit down on Jez's leg just below the knee. It gave a small pull and Jez was yanked off the cap and into the undergrowth below.

She screamed as she was dangled upside down, but after about a minute of panicked thrashing, she realized (to her relief) that her leg had not in fact been bitten off. And, though firm, the creature's grip was surprisingly gentle. The forest floor loomed some ten or twelve feet beneath her, but she was being held, not eaten.

Her captor blinked at her with beady eyes, her leg clamped between its jaws. The creature's head was dwarfed by its enormous body, which was covered in thick green hide. Two rows of red, diamond-shaped scales traversed the length of its back like fins and continued down its tail, where they ended in a cluster of fierce-looking spikes.

Stegosaurus.

She remembered pictures of the small-brained dinosaurs from her biology books, but none of the pictures had prepared her for the creature riding on the reptile's back. Nestled between two fins was a furry, yellow-eyed mammal. It looked a little like an ape, covered as it was in dull brown fur, but the eyes reminded her of some kind of marsupial. They were large and round, and Jez had seen them before. A trog. It held a long spear in one hand and the dinosaur's reins in the other and scratched its head with a third.

A third?

Jez shook her head to clear her eyes. She wanted to make sure she was seeing this correctly as the trog's *third* arm—which was apparently attached to its back squarely between its shoulder blades—gently massaged the top of its head while it studied her.

The dinosaur at least looked familiar, shocking as it was to be chomped on by one in the flesh, but this three-armed trog was absolutely bizarre.

"Well," Jez said. "If you're not going to feed me to your pet, then would you mind putting me down? The blood's all rushing to my head and I'm getting a headache."

Jezebel was not nearly as confident as she hoped she sounded. She was counting on the fact that she remembered stegosauruses to be herbivores, plant eaters. Plus, if the trog had wanted to kill her, he could have done so already with that spear of his. But then again, perhaps these trogs were the sadistic type, and it was going to just dangle her upside down until her brains exploded out her nose.

The trog leaned forward in its saddle and barked something at her in an alien language. It was mostly gibberish and sounded more like the trog was clearing its throat than talking, but amid all the noise she thought she could make out two possible English words, repeated again and again:

Tobby Erber. It sounded a little like a name.

"Tommy Learner?" Jez asked. "Are you trying to say Tommy Learner?"

The trog answered her with another string of unintelligible clicks, excitedly bobbing its head back and forth.

But then all at once it stopped, and the trog's posture turned rigid as it sat up in its saddle and peered into the surrounding jungle. The stegosaurus lifted its head high and sniffed the air, having apparently forgotten about the girl in its mouth.

Jez felt it, too. Something nearby. Something wrong.

It burst out of the trees then, mouth open in a silent roar. Blunt, car-shaped head and long, razor-sharp teeth. Massive clawed feet cut gashes in the ground as it dragged itself toward them. Patches of bone had torn through rotting white skin, and something wet and sticky had started to ooze through the cracks.

Tyrannosaurus rex. Dead. Stinking and decomposing in front of her eyes, but still walking. And it was upon them.

Instinctively, the stegosaurus whipped its body around to put its spiked tail between itself and the predator. It opened its mouth and gave out a low bellow of challenge, dropping Jezebel onto the ground below.

Stunned, Jez barely managed to look up in time to see the trog loose its spear at the T. rex, the blade sinking deep into the creature's left flank. The stegosaurus backed up, swinging its spike in a wild arc to defend against the unnatural beast. But the attack never came. The undead monster, heedless of the spear in its side, lowered its snout to the earth and breathed in deeply. Jez felt her legs go weak as she saw the creature's dead black eyes settle on her. It didn't care about the trog or his mount—Jezebel was its prey.

Its maw opened wide—the stench of death and decay was unbearable—and it lunged for her. It was not fast; it moved in a jerking, halting sort of way, but nevertheless it took only a couple of steps and it was on top of her, bearing down with its teeth.

Had it not been so focused on Jez, it might have seen the blow coming from its side—not that the mindless monster would have cared. The stegosaurus threw its weight into the T. rex, knocking it backward off its feet. In the charge the stegosaurus barely missed trampling Jez underfoot, but she could see the trog deftly manipulating the reins, steering its mount safely away from her.

The stegosaurus and its rider didn't hesitate. As the T. rex struggled to regain its footing, the stegosaurus swung its mighty spiked tail in a great sideways arc, impaling the T. rex through its chest.

But what should have surely been a killing blow did not stop this undead thing, and now that the stegosaurus's spiked tail was stuck in the T. rex's hide, it couldn't retreat. Jez covered her eyes as the T. rex opened its rotted, toothy mouth and reached for the stegosaurus's unarmored neck. She heard a horrible howl and the sound of two great bodies smashing together and tumbling to the ground.

When she opened her eyes the fight was over. The stegosaurus's body lay unmoving and bloody atop the carcass of the T. rex. In its death throes, the poor creature had rolled over the T. rex's legs, crushing the brittle, rotten bones. Everywhere the air was thick with dust and grit kicked up during their battle, and Jez found it hard to breathe without choking on it.

She got to her feet and rubbed her head. Slightly dizzy, she listened. She thought she heard a low moan. Following the sound, she found the trog lying in a heap near the foot of a toadstool. He was alive, but he'd apparently hit his head much harder than Jez had hit hers. His eyes blinked up at her, unfocused and dazed.

A sudden stirring caused Jez to whip around in time to see the T. rex, its legs crushed, its chest impaled on the body of its enemy, twist its head to face her. With its tiny fore claws it scraped at the dirt, trying to pull its ruined body free, trying to finish the hunt. Jez jumped back as it snapped its jaws uselessly at the air.

She thought about Tommy, wherever he was, and desperately wanted to know if he was all right. Then she looked down at the trog who'd just saved her life. The trog who knew Tommy's name.

"C'mon," she said as she pulled the trog to his feet. "We can't stay here."

The trog had short, stubby legs, nearly half as long as his arms. Jez wrapped one of those arms around her shoulder and pulled. The trog used the other two to steady himself and lope along with her as Jez led them back into the forest, away from the monstrous tyrannosaurus and toward the pillar of smoke.

She just hoped that for once she was headed in the right direction.

CHAPTER SIXTEEN

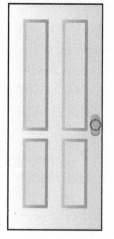

JEZEBEL
THE HOLLOW WORLD, 1902

Jezebel found the smoke, but there was no fire. It drifted out of some kind of giant, oddly symmetrical fungus with a squat chimney of piled rocks on the top. This chimney hole produced the dark tendril of smoke that had drawn Jezebel down out of the hills and into the dangerous jungle. And now that she was here, she didn't have a clue what she should do next.

Her situation wasn't made any easier by the wounded and apparently delirious trog she'd just hauled through half a mile of dense fungoid forest. The strange three-armed creature was still groggy—Jez had made a makeshift bandage out of her sweatshirt and tied that around the red gash in his forehead. Despite the bloody, matted fur, the cut itself didn't appear to be too deep, but he still blinked confusedly at Jez every now and again, all the while muttering in that click language of his. He made no protest; all his earlier bluster and shouting disappeared. Now he leaned on her gratefully while she helped him steer his way through the jungle.

She had half a plan to trade the hurt trog for Tommy. They did that sort of thing all the time in cop movies, swapped one hostage for another. But in order to do that she needed to actually find the trogs first, and this mushroom house did not look much like a trog home. Trogs were rock shapers, Tommy had said, underground dwellers. And while, technically, this whole world was underground, she kind of pictured them living in tunnels like the one Tommy had accidentally trespassed in. A cozy mushroom house just didn't seem very troglike.

"Hey!" she shouted, pounding her fist on the wall. "Hello? Is anybody home? We need help!"

She pressed her ear against the side, but she could hear nothing. She pounded some more and shouted some increasingly less polite pleas for help. But there was no answer from within. Nothing stirred.

"All right, trog, my friend," she said, turning back around. "Where are your buddies . . ."

Jezebel's voice trailed off as she set eyes on the five trogs that hadn't been there before. Each one stood next to a newly appeared hole in the rock floor, and two of them held a net strung between their six arms. Another was tending to her trog, talking to him in their clicking language and examining the melon-sized lump on his head and Jez's bandage.

Apparently trogs did live in mushroom houses. Or, at least, under them.

"Oh, hey," said Jez. "Boy, you guys sure are sneaky when you want to be. You see I brought your friend to you. Fixed him up the best I could. And um . . . I'm here to trade your trog—who I took very good care of, thank you very much—for Tommy Learner. You know, the short kid? Human, like me?"

The two trogs holding the net stepped closer. Jezebel started backing away, keeping distance between them.

"Whoa, now no need for that! Tell you what—keep your buddy *and* Tommy. He's been nothing but a pain since I first . . . hey!"

The trogs tossed the net. It looked almost lazy the way they lobbed it at her, but it somehow managed to twist around her with enough force to pull her off her feet.

The next thing she knew she was being dragged toward a fresh hole in the ground, five trog voices chattering excitedly all the way down.

She was hoisted up between two trogs and bounced along in the net as they scurried through dark tunnels and along teetering rope bridges spanning vast underground caverns. Patches of wet-looking, incandescent cave mold gave barely enough light to see by—the kingdom of the trogs was lit by glow-in-the-dark slime.

But what a kingdom it was. A long network of tunnels served as the superhighways between trog towns, and the trogs managed to traverse these tunnels with surprising speed, using their three arms to pull themselves through—their feet rarely touching the ground. They made their homes in the larger caverns, in huts suspended above underground lakes and heated by burning the cave moss that grew on the surface of the waters. The smoke from these fires was thick and black, and the trogs had apparently developed a complicated venting system that began in the caverns and terminated in giant, hollowed-out mushrooms like the one that Jez had discovered above.

All of which Jezebel saw in snatches and glimpses as she was jostled back and forth between her captors. They traveled a great distance, past the cavern villages and through stranger and darker landscapes where there were no light-giving plants and the blackness was absolute. Even the trogs' eyes, normally a shining yellow, went dark in the total absence of light.

Eventually they emerged again into the open, Jez's eyes hurting in the sudden brightness of the reddish day. The heat of the molten sun felt like a furnace compared with the chill of the trogs' underground world. When her eyes had finally adjusted to the light, Jez looked up to see, looming above her, the underside of a great black ship. All she could do was struggle and plead in vain as the trogs scaled the giant anchored chain and delivered her to the Dead Gentleman's crew.

After being dumped unceremoniously onto the ship's deck, Jez was set upon by a pair of skull-masked Grave Walkers. They grabbed at her with their smelly hands (a rotten odor hung in the air aboard this ship; it clung to everything) and dragged her belowdecks, tossing her into a cell and locking the thick wooden door behind her.

Inside she found Tommy. Far from being happy to see her, he lectured her on her carelessness at allowing herself to be caught. He lectured her, that is, until Jez hauled off and punched him in the arm. She didn't feel the need then to remind him that he'd been captured *first*—the punch had been worth a thousand words.

For the next several hours they waited and debated various plans of escape. None of which seemed very plausible, considering there was only one way out and that was through a heavy, locked door. They were arguing the merits of begging for their lives when they heard the sound of a key turning in the lock.

"Look, don't say anything about Merlin," Tommy was saying. "And don't be scared—the guards here look fierce, but it's just for show. Those crouchers that came out of your closet were a good deal meaner than this lot, and you took care of them."

"And the Gentleman?" she asked, putting her back flat against the wall. "Is he just for show, too?"

Tommy didn't answer her right away; the sound of keys had stopped. "One more thing," he whispered. "Remember, this is the past. Nothing you know has happened yet."

"What is that supposed to mean?" Jez mouthed back, but it was too late—the door was opening.

In walked a pair of scarecrows. At least they looked like scarecrows at first glance, stick-thin with heads as round as pumpkins. But their faces were not the carved grins of jack-o'-lanterns—these frowned and drooped at the edges. And each held a curved black sickle in its hand.

"Harvesters," Tommy said, no longer bothering to whisper. "They used to be crop spirits, a bit dull but all right. Now they work for him."

Behind them walked a man in fancy, if somewhat old-fashioned, clothes. He looked to Jez like a well-off gentleman indeed, complete with top hat and tails. His dress was mostly immaculate, the single exception being a slight spot of something, perhaps leftover breakfast, on the front of his otherwise pristine white shirt. And physically, other than a slight pallor around his cheeks and lips, he was perfectly normal. Handsome, even.

Jez shot Tommy a questioning look.

"He doesn't always look that good, trust me," he said. "He changes."

The man, the Gentleman, smiled at Jezebel as he spoke to Tommy. "The great Tommy Learner escaped my attercop and managed to avoid my Grave Walkers for these many months. Could it be that all along he has had . . . help?"

"I didn't need anyone's help to roast your attercop, and your Grave Walkers are a walking joke," Tommy answered.

Tommy's words sounded solid—there wasn't even a quiver in his voice—but Jez thought she detected something in his eyes that gave him away. Tommy was afraid.

The Gentleman apparently spotted it, too. "I could always put a rope around your throat and swing you from a gibbet, boy. Since I've killed all their crops, I need to give the Harvesters some sport now and again."

One of the scarecrows made a face that might have been something like a smile, but it was hard to tell under all those wrinkles of leathery flesh.

"So, to business," the Gentleman said. "Who are you, girl?"

"My name is Jezebel Lemon," she said, mustering all the steel she had. Name, rank and serial number—that's all they would get out of her.

Jez nearly yelped as she felt Tommy's bony elbow suddenly dig into her ribs.

The meaning of Tommy's warning suddenly dawned on her— *nothing has happened yet*. She'd forgotten that this was the Dead Gentleman of Tommy's time, of the past. The Dead Gentleman who was after her was over a hundred years in the future. To this Gentleman from 1902 she was a stranger, a mystery. He hadn't even known her name until she'd told it to him.

"Jezebel Lemon," he said, trying the words out. He seemed to have a slight problem with speech. Either that or he was choosing his words very carefully. "Pleased to meet you."

The way he looked at her now made Jez acutely uncomfortable. When he'd first entered the room, he seemed to regard her as a nuisance, but suddenly there was genuine interest in his stare. Unable to meet his gaze, she focused instead on his white shirt . . . and the growing crimson stain beneath. What she'd mistaken for a spot of spilt coffee was actually a star-shaped patch of blood, which was spreading along the left of his shirt.

Jezebel gasped and pointed. "You're hurt!"

The Gentleman didn't blink an eye. "No, I am well past that now. I am dead. A knife wound to the back, this time. Punctured lung, nicked pulmonary artery, blade pushed all the way through to the other side. Not a painless way to go." He slowly turned around to reveal a long knife handle protruding from under his left shoulder blade. The back of his coat was slick and soaked with blood. Jezebel put her hand to her mouth.

"You see," said Tommy. "It's different every time."

"I can feel rigor mortis setting in, so we'll need to hurry things along," said the Gentleman, turning back around. Jez was relieved, as that covered most of the gore, but there was still the wet bloodstain in the front. It was hard to take her eyes off it as it crept outward, slowly overtaking the immaculate white linen.

"From your dress I'd say you're not from any place I've ever seen, and I've seen them all," said the Gentleman, examining Jez.

He stepped closer now, his glassy eyes fixed on Jezebel's, as if he was trying to read something there. She kept her best poker face on—she wouldn't give up anything more than she already had. When he reached out a hand to touch her face, Tommy

made a move to intercept. It was a charming, chivalrous and stupid thing to do. He was well within the reach of those Harvester
things, and it seemed they had been waiting for an excuse to hurt
someone. One of them snatched him up by the back of the neck
and lifted him until his tiptoes dangled beneath him. A few tears
squeezed out of his eyes but he didn't cry out.

Ignoring Tommy, the Gentleman took Jezebel's face in his
hand, turning it from side to side, studying it. His fingers were
hard. Cold.

"You are fleshy," he said. "Well-fed and soft. Your clothing
contains synthetic fibers and your hair smells of chemicals. Could
it be you're from . . . the future? Earth's future, perhaps? Now why
would Tommy be peeking around in Earth's future, unless he was
looking for something . . . something that once belonged to me?"

He let his hands drop from Jezebel's face and turned to
Tommy. "You don't have it. Perhaps you never had it? Clever boy.
But where is it, then? You didn't leave it with the Academy. I
spilled every last drop of blood searching that place . . ."

The Gentleman looked at Jezebel. "You know what we are
talking about, don't you? A delicate mechanical bird. You've seen
it, perhaps?"

The Harvester pulled Tommy's head back with a jerk, expos-
ing his throat to its master.

Jezebel started to shout something, but the second Harvester
shot its long, bony hand toward her and grabbed her hair. With
a twist it brought her to her knees. All she could do was watch as
the Gentleman reached around and, with a wet sucking sound,
drew out the knife from his own back. With an awkward stab, he
brought the knife up and sliced open the pouch on Tommy's belt.
The Cycloidotrope tumbled out into the Gentleman's free hand.

"Ah, the Cycloidotrope, of course," he said, holding the device up to his sunken eye. "The High Father's little toy."

With a gesture from the Gentleman, the Harvesters released their grip on the prisoners. Tommy fell to the floor, and when Jezebel took her hand away from her scalp there were fresh flecks of blood on her fingers.

"Let's see where you came from," the Gentleman said. With a pale white hand he rubbed the Cycloidotrope until it started to glow. Images began to flash across its surface, spinning too fast to make sense of.

"Show me the future," the Gentleman said. "Show me Jezebel Lemon."

A beam of light shot out of the cube, and when it cleared they were staring at a three-dimensional image of Jezebel's room. Her bed was unmade and the storm still raged outside. Beyond her window the winds blew ripples across the Hudson River.

"Have you hidden it there, perhaps?" he said. "In your little girl's bedroom?" The Gentleman gave a cock of his head and the Harvester that had held Jezebel stalked toward the picture of her bedroom, hesitating just as it was prepared to step into the frame.

"Go," commanded the Gentleman.

The Harvester turned and took another step forward, but as soon as its spindly leg touched the bedroom floor it shrieked in pain. The image of her room disappeared into a chaotic swirl of color and light. Jezebel covered her ears as the Harvester was pulled into the twisting mass piece by piece. For one second, strips of straw and wood—Harvester parts—hung in the air. Then they were gone, along with Jez's bedroom, the light and everything. The Cycloidotrope sat dark and still in the Gentleman's hand.

"Fascinating," he said, but his face was contorted in a sort of angry frown. Something dark and wet bubbled at the corners of his mouth. His voice sounded like liquid. "But no matter. I'll find the artifact one way or another. And thanks to you, I now know where to look. And *when*. Time is on my side.

"Meanwhile, I'll send my man Macheath down to see what more he can learn from you two. He has a crude touch, but he gets results." He turned and followed the remaining Harvester out of the room. As the door shut behind him he turned to Jez and winked.

"Be seeing you, Jezebel Lemon!"

CHAPTER SEVENTEEN

The Dead Gentleman
Aboard the *Charnel House*, 1902

The Gentleman gazed into the Cycloidotrope's crystal surface and grinned as a six-year-old Jezebel rode her bike, a small pink thing on training wheels, along a tree-lined park street. A woman ran next to her, laughing as she tried to keep up. The woman had dark hair like Jezebel and the same gray eyes. He touched the cube and the image shifted, moving forward in time to an older version of the girl, sitting uncomfortably in a well-furnished office as a man asked her questions. She responded with sullen, mostly one-word answers. The man tapped a pen against his teeth and watched the clock. Again the Gentleman searched ahead, the moments of Jezebel's life clicking past like a slideshow in fast-forward. The images came to another halt on her as she was now, standing in a room full of junk. She was looking into an open closet at a shiny mechanical bird.

"There you are," said the Gentleman. "Hello again."

The artifact. That little bird of metal and clockworks hid a secret so precious, so valuable. To the Gentleman it was the greatest treasure in all of creation, the one thing he'd been lacking in the many millennia of his existence. He bristled at the thought of having to wait a hundred years to get it, but after what had happened to the Harvester, he dared not try stepping through. Time was the domain of forces even greater than he (for now), and he would not risk all on such an impatient act. The girl had managed it, either by accident or by design. If she'd somehow stumbled upon the secret of time travel, then the Gentleman would pry it out of her. If not, what was a century to one such as he? He'd use the years to continue to build his army, to strengthen himself. He'd done enough skulking around in the shadows—when he next returned to Earth it would be at the head of a mighty armada.

Earth. The center of the Orrery itself and the cornerstone of existence. What made that ordinary ball of mud so special was a mystery even to the Gentleman, but to truly kill everything there was, he knew he'd have to start with Earth.

And what a wonderful void of death would be left in its place! He felt himself turn almost giddy at the thought of the quiet, the cold of a universe of dead worlds. All so that he might achieve his fondest, his dead heart's desire . . .

Of course, he may not have to wait a hundred years if the children knew where the artifact was right now, and he had the perfect person to find out exactly what they did know. He wouldn't waste any more time on their lies.

"Macheath," the Gentleman called, and at once the weasely vampire appeared at his side. He was never far.

"Yes, Captain?"

"Spread the word that we are hoisting anchor and setting sail. Fire up the portal engines. We are leaving the Hollow World."

"Leaving?" asked Macheath. "But we've not finished. There's still plenty living out there to kill!"

"What? A planet of mold? This place can wait. Our attack on the Academy has left us exposed, and word will spread quickly between worlds. We need to retreat and prepare for the real prize—Earth. Now that we have Learner and the girl, there is no reason to stay."

At the mention of the girl, Macheath's eyes lit up. The Gentleman had noticed the way the vampire looked at her when she was first hauled aboard. He hadn't had such a fresh young victim in some time.

"I want you to pay a visit to our two prisoners," the Gentleman said. "Find out if they know where the artifact is now. Do whatever it takes, but keep them alive for the time being."

The Gentleman strode past Macheath, palming the Cycloidotrope and climbing down the stairs toward steerage and the engine. Macheath yipped at his heels like a dog.

"What is to become of Learner after that?" he asked.

"I'll keep him around for a time. The High Father is still out there somewhere and the two have obviously been in contact. How else would the boy get his hands on the Cycloidotrope? The High Father escaped my Grave Walkers in the Hidden City, and he could still pose a threat—albeit a small one."

"That little man won't be a problem," said Macheath. "Not without his Explorers around him."

"Never can be too cautious, Macheath. The High Father is old. Nearly as old as me, but he's crafty, that one. A trickster. No, the boy stays alive, for the time being."

"And the girl?"

Ah, here it comes, thought the Gentleman. "What of her?"

"Is she . . . I mean, are you keeping her, too?"

Macheath didn't even try to hide the drool dripping down his chin or the way his lips smacked in anticipation. He was nauseatingly obvious.

The Gentleman stopped walking and Macheath nearly tripped over him. They had come to the real engine of the *Charnel House*. Under a great black curtain it rested, the nerve center of the ship and, next to the artifact, the Gentleman's greatest discovery. He drew back the curtain with his stiff white fingers (he really would have to choose a new shape soon; the rigor mortis was making this one difficult to operate). Underneath was a chunk of stone, a carved doorway cracked with age. Inside the door the air shimmered, a black pool that glowed with a weak, sallow light.

The Gentleman's portal. Built into the heart of the *Charnel House*. Its power fueled the engines of this entire vessel, propelling it not just through the air but between the barriers of reality. With it, he could go anywhere.

For now that meant going home, where no sun had ever shone and there wasn't a breath to draw. There, he would prepare for war. He would wait a hundred years if need be, and then— Earth. At last it would be his. Earth. Then everything.

"My lord?"

"Yes, Macheath, what is it?" The vampire's voice droned in the Gentleman's ear like the buzzing of flies. He wondered if he could endure another century of it.

"The girl, sir. Are you keeping the girl?"

The Gentleman turned and gazed down at the Cycloidotrope

once more. The images of Jezebel's life kept spinning in a perpetual loop. Now she was a baby again, getting a bath from a man with tousled, paint-splattered hair.

"She's yours," said the Gentleman. "After you've interrogated them thoroughly, you may drink your fill. But leave the boy alive."

Macheath practically giggled with gratitude. The obscene vampire bowed and scraped his way out of the Gentleman's presence, hurrying toward the cells, toward Jezebel.

The Gentleman turned back to his miraculous portal and began to ponder what shape he'd take next. Something festive, something celebratory, something especially gruesome. After all, today had been a very, very good day.

CHAPTER EIGHTEEN

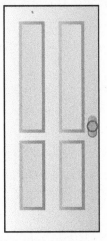

JEZEBEL

ABOARD THE *CHARNEL HOUSE*, 1902

"The way I see it, we've only got one option," Tommy said. "When the guards come to finish us, we've got to take them."

Jezebel gave Tommy a look. His plan, such as it was, sounded like a reliable way to get one or both of them killed. The problem was, however, that she couldn't think of anything better.

"You really think we can overpower those things?" she asked. "Just the two of us?"

Tommy shook his head. "Not really. But it's a chance. The outside walls are reinforced with solid weirdwood, and that stuff's strong as iron. They say it only grows in hangmen's gardens and you need magic to shape it into anything useful. Besides, the Harvesters probably aren't expecting it—two kids charging a pair of eight-foot-tall monsters. . . ."

"I wouldn't," said Jez. "But if we do get free, then I think we should try to find the trogs again. I think they might help us."

"The trogs? Are you kidding me? They captured us in the first place! They're working for the Gentleman!"

"I don't think they all are. In fact, one of them saved my life. And he kept saying your name over and over."

"My name?"

"I think there's more going on here than we realize . . . ," Jez began, but was interrupted by a sound at the door—the jingling of keys in the lock.

"Oh no!" she said, stepping back from the door.

Tommy balled his small hands into fists and stood ready. He looked pretty ineffectual, actually, standing there weaponless. The short kid preparing to face off against the bully—Jez had seen this kind of thing many times before, on playgrounds and in schools. But the sad truth was, no matter how brave the smaller kid was, the bully always won.

She stood next to him and faced the door.

"Don't give them time to do anything," he said. "When they step in, we rush them and then you run."

"You mean *we* run? Together, right?"

Tommy didn't answer. The door handle began to turn.

The door opened and Tommy charged, with Jez right by his side. He swung at the dark shape that had stepped into the room, but his swing went wide. This Harvester was surprisingly nimble and it ducked out of the way, sweeping Tommy's legs out from under him and stepping in front of Jezebel. It sat on Tommy's chest, pinning him, and blinked at Jezebel with bright yellow eyes.

Jezebel stopped—Harvesters didn't have yellow eyes. But this trog did, and it looked up at her from beneath a dirty sweatshirt bandage. Tommy was kicking and scratching at it like a cat, trying to get his teeth around its big, hairy toe.

"Wait!" Jezebel shouted. "I know him! This is the trog that saved me!"

The trog relaxed, and his big mouth opened in a questioning smile.

"Tobby Erber?" he said, looking down at the boy beneath his rear end.

"Excuse me?" said Tommy.

"See," said Jezebel. "You're famous."

"So, he's here to do the Gentleman's dirty work?" Tommy asked.

The trog scrunched his face at Tommy and looked back at Jezebel. His third arm held a ring of keys over her head, and with the other two he gestured to the open door and the hallway beyond.

Jez smiled, understanding. "I think this is a jailbreak," she said. "He wants us to follow."

The trog let Tommy up and stepped several feet out into the hall. He gestured for them, and Jez followed.

"Come on," she said. "I told you, he saved my life. And I kind of returned the favor. I trust him."

"Well, I don't know if I do," said Tommy, dusting himself off. "But I'm sure not hanging around that cell for a minute longer! Lead the way, Mr. Trog."

The hallway outside their cell was more of the same dark wood, lit here and there with what looked like fishbowls of blinking lights. They dangled on chains, these orbs of glass, and inside each one fluttered three or four dots of ghostly light. Their trog rescuer led the way, sneaking down the corridor by pulling his short legs along with two arms, while the third gestured for Jez and Tommy to follow.

They caught up with the trog as he paused to listen at a set of ladder steps. "We need to get off this ship!" said Tommy. "We should make for the hawsehole, where they raise and lower the anchor . . ."

Jez didn't hear the rest of what Tommy was saying—she was focused on the man who'd appeared on the ladder above them. He'd drifted down the rungs, as silent as a ghost. When he spotted Jezebel he showed her his teeth—he was missing all but two. Those that remained were grayish-red, the color her father's turned after he'd had a glass of red wine. They were long and sharp, and Jez felt certain they had been stained by something else altogether.

"Tommy!" Jez shouted, but it was too late. The man dropped down just as Tommy looked up, catching a boot square in the face. The man was fast—in a blur of movement he grabbed the dazed Tommy by the hair and brought a long, curved knife up to the boy's neck. Seeing this, the trog backed away, a low growl issuing from his throat.

"It's good to have friends, ain't it?" the man said, glancing at the trog. "Good for helping you out of tough spots, like cells!"

"What do you want?" asked Jez.

"I want you to come over here, that's all. Come and play with old Archie Macheath," he said. "Or else I open your boyfriend's throat."

Jez couldn't tear her eyes away from his mouth. The man, Macheath, noticed this and pursed his lips in a strange, self-conscious way. "My choppers aren't what they once were, but I can still bite!" He pressed the knife tighter to Tommy's throat. "I just like to use the blade for starters."

Tommy eyes started to focus on Jez. He was coming back to

his senses after the blow, although one eye was already beginning to swell shut.

"D-don't listen to him, Jezebel," Tommy said.

"No one's talking to you!" said Macheath, and he gave Tommy's hair a savage twist to quiet him.

Jez didn't know what to do. She was unarmed, and Tommy was half Macheath's size. Even without the knife he would have been outmatched. She took a hesitating step forward.

"I ain't got all day!" said Macheath, and he dug the knifepoint a little farther into Tommy's neck, just breaking the skin. A small drop of bright-red blood appeared at the blade's edge.

Macheath's face went suddenly slack and his nostrils flared as he sniffed the air near Tommy's head. A low moan escaped his lips as the drop became a trickle. He was sweating now, a disgusting pinkish sheen appearing on his forehead and on his upper lip. He was muttering something over and over again, repeating it like a mantra:

"You can have the girl but leave the boy, you can have the girl but leave the boy, you can . . . BLOOD!"

Macheath became a rabid animal. Dropping the knife, he lunged at Tommy with his jaws opened wide—his eyes rolling back in his head like a shark's just before the kill. Tommy shouted and fought back, punching and kicking, but he might as well have been hitting an unfeeling wall. In his struggle he was managing to make himself a hard target, however, and Macheath was having trouble finding the boy's neck with all that squirming.

Jez ran forward and, not knowing what else to do, scooped up the knife. It was heavy and the handle was greasy and she didn't want to think about what that knife had been used for over the years. She closed one eye, aimed and, using all of her weight, brought it down on Macheath's foot. There was a thump as the blade sank through the man's booted foot and into the wooden planked floor beneath.

Macheath paused for just a moment, looked at his foot now firmly staked to the deck and then with a roar grabbed Jezebel by the collar. One in each hand, he lifted the two kids to his mouth as if he were about to binge from two glasses. His roar changed to a delighted cackle.

The first punch to his face seemed to surprise him but did little more than that. The second, which followed swiftly after the first, knocked him back a step. The third broke his hold on the two kids and sent him to the floor. The trog was on top of him, hammering down with all three fists now into Macheath's face and not letting up for an instant.

Tommy stared, wide-eyed, but Jez kept her head. "C'mon," she said, grabbing Tommy's shoulder. "Let's get out of here!"

They scurried up the ladder, Tommy in the lead. When she got to the top she yelled, "C'mon!" but the trog was already a step ahead of her. Macheath had gotten his arms up in front of his face the way a boxer would, and the trog's beating was having less of an effect. The trog gave him a final smack and then leapt up onto the ladder, his apelike limbs scaling the distance in no time.

There was a sturdy-looking hatchway up top, and as Jez flipped it closed she caught a glimpse of Macheath climbing the ladder after them. Their eyes met, and his fury was palpable as he spit a single, broken tooth out of his bloody mouth.

She shut the hatch and drew the thick bar lock closed. The wooden plank shuddered but it held as Macheath beat on it from below, cursing all the while.

Tommy smiled at the trog. "That's two we owe you!"

"Tobby Erber," he replied.

"Where to now?" Jez asked.

"We need to head for the hawsehole. We'll climb the anchor chain down."

A deep rumble started somewhere in the bowels of the ship. A quiver ran through the walls, the floor. Jez even felt it through her sneakers. Something was happening.

"That sounds like an engine," she said.

"They're setting sail! We've got to go, quick!"

Again the trog led the way, and they ran the length of the lower deck. Once they had to dodge a group of Grave Walkers who were coming down the corridor, but the death worshipers were apparently too busy with their duties to notice the three of them hidden in the shadows.

They reached the hawsehole and found it, thankfully, unattended.

"C'mon," said Tommy. "They'll be here to raise anchor any minute."

Jez went first, wrapping her legs around the thick chain links and not daring to look down. She didn't want to think about the drop or the forest of petrified stone below.

"So, how do you know so much about ships?" she asked, trying to occupy her mind.

"Oh, I've had some experience with boats over the last few years," Tommy said as he climbed down after her. "Remind me to show you mine sometime."

The trog came last, easily navigating the chain.

The three of them were about halfway down when they heard the clink of metal grinding against metal as the chain began to move. Jez risked a look below and saw the giant black anchor being hefted up through the trees. They were still a dizzying height above and a fall from there would surely be the end of them.

"Go faster!" Tommy yelled.

And they did, but they continued to lose ground as the chain was retracted back into the ship's hull. Jez glanced up top and saw that a kind of shimmer had appeared all around them, like she was looking at the ship from the bottom of a swimming pool.

"They've started to sail!" said Tommy, seeing it, too. "The ship's going to jump to a different dimension."

"Which one?" asked Jez, but Tommy didn't answer. He didn't need to; they were both thinking the same thing.

The Gentleman came out of the space in between—the blackness between worlds.

"Go faster!" they both shouted at once. But it was no use; the chain was rising far more quickly than they could descend. They were being hauled back into the Gentleman's ship.

The trog chattered and grunted at them, and Jez waved him away. "I know! But we've only got two hands!"

Then Jez felt something tapping her on the top of her head. She looked up to see Tommy's shoe.

"Hey!" she said.

But he wasn't listening. He was pointing to something in the distance. Two shapes were approaching from over the ridge. They soared high above the hills and swooped as they changed course and headed straight for the climbers.

"No way," said Jez as she got a closer look at the two winged lizards and their trog riders.

Pterodactyls.

Their trog whooped and clicked happily as the two approached, their riders whooping and clicking in return.

The celebrations were quickly drowned out, however, by the ear-piercing roar of grinding machinery. The entire valley echoed with the sound of something building, like an engine being gunned into overdrive. The anchor chain started to vibrate as the last few feet were being hoisted aboard the ship.

The Grave Walkers had wheeled some kind of device to the prow of the ship. It looked like a huge archway surrounding an inky darkness. The valley rang with the Gentleman's voice as he shouted a command, and the arch lit up like a spotlight, shining an ugly greenish light into the underground sky. Where the foul light fell, there appeared an enormous funnel cloud, like some kind of vortex on its side, twisting and swallowing the light of the molten sun overhead. A storm raged at the center of it.

The Gentleman had created a giant portal in the sky—and it led someplace dark.

The trog was shouting something, gesturing wildly at the approaching fliers. Jez held on tight with one hand while trying to cover her ears with the other—the scream of the ship's engines was unbearable as they began sailing toward the dark portal. The Grave Walkers above still hadn't noticed their escape, but it didn't matter—they were about to be pulled back into the ship on its great anchor chain. There was nothing they could do to stop it.

With his two free hands, the trog reached out and grabbed Jez and Tommy by the arms and, with a powerful tug, peeled them off the chain. Jez's stomach jumped into her throat as she fell, only to land with a solid thump on the back of one of the circling pterodactyls.

All at once the sound of the engines stopped, replaced by a

blinding flash of light. Then, just as thunder follows lightning, the whole of the Hollow World was shaken by a tremendous crack.

One Fourth of July weekend Jez's father took her to an air show on the Hudson River. She remembered the sonic booms of the jets as they broke the sound barrier overhead. This was more than that—this was the breaking of the reality barrier as the Dead Gentleman's ship disappeared from the Hollow World altogether.

After a few moments the ringing in Jezebel's ears quieted, and she opened her eyes to see that she was being held tightly by a trog as they soared through the air. A glance over her shoulder told her that Tommy had landed on a similar mount.

The *Charnel House* was gone, but the dead valley below was grim evidence of its passing. The pterodactyls flew in lazy circles now while their trog riders cheered in unison.

"Tobby Erber! Tobby Erber!" they were chanting.

Tommy looked down at Jez from his pterodactyl and shouted. "Hey, Jez! You were right, I'm famous!"

CHAPTER NINETEEN

TOMMY

THE HIDDEN CITY, 1901

The Hidden City was quiet again. The towers had fallen, smashed to ruins and dust. The streets still wound the same paths, but the shining cobblestones were now dusty-brown and filthy—in their slaughter the Grave Walkers had turned them into gutters of blood. Here and there my boot crunched down upon a chunk of solid-gold rubble, the ruins of once-ornate frescoes and rich statuary. But I didn't pocket even the tiniest nugget. I may be a thief, but I'm no grave robber.

The Captain had told me never to return to this forsaken place, but months had passed since the old man's death and I was at a loss as to what to do next. Scott had given me a tall order before he'd died, to find out the Gentleman's plans and stop him. But short of asking the rotted monster himself, I couldn't think of a plan to proceed. I needed a bit of wisdom. Or maybe I just needed something to *do*.

So here I was, returning to the one place in all the universe I never wanted to see again. I was going on a fool's hope that the High Father had managed to avoid capture, but a fool's hope seemed to be the only hope I ever had.

At least the Grave Walkers had all vanished. The walkways that had once swarmed with the cultists were now abandoned. The Explorers were dead, the city was empty, the Academy was in ruins and I had to find one wrinkled old monk in all that mess who, more likely than not, was a corpse now himself.

But sometimes fate smiles on a fool, because I'd not taken two steps when I heard a voice behind me.

"Such a tenacious little flea. It's a wonder you haven't been caught yet in life's scratching."

A short, prunish old man in filthy white robes stood in the middle of the street, looking for all the world as if he'd been expecting company. And perhaps he was—his long white tufts of ear hair were filthy with dirt and dried blood. The little man looked like he'd taken quite a beating. I began to wonder if the Hidden City was truly abandoned, after all.

A long cow's tail flicked back and forth at his feet. The High Father.

"You have no idea how glad I am to see you," I said. "Come on, we're getting out of here."

The High Father smiled at me with an infuriating know-it-all grin, which instantly reminded me of how much adults annoyed me. Captain Scott had been the occasional exception.

"Little flea, little flea," said the High Father. "I'm not going anywhere."

"Look, I'm sorry to tell you this, but in case you haven't noticed, the Academy's a ruin. The fight's over here and I need your help!"

"Yes, yes. The fight is over and we have lost. And the dead that remain now serve the Gentleman. When the sun goes down, they hunt for me, still. It is our nightly ritual of predator and prey. I know this, and yet I will not go."

I took a step forward while trying to keep my voice level. "Look, the Captain's dead! He died trying to rescue you once and I'm not going to let his last act be in vain! You're coming with me!"

"And what are you going to do? Beat me until I agree to go with you?"

The word "yes" was on the tip of my tongue, but I bit it back.

The High Father shook his head sadly. "I regret the harm that has come to your friends, and I honor the spirit of Captain Scott, but look around you. My brothers all passed on to enlightenment long ago. The Explorers are dead. I am all that's left."

"I know. I'm sorry."

"No. You misunderstand me. I am not sad for myself. I can leave this place at any time. I know the portals better than any Explorer. But all things must have their end. If not today at the hands of the Gentleman, then perhaps tomorrow or the next day. Or I might live for a hundred years more. What is certain is that it *will* end. This does not sadden me."

The old man shook his head. "Tommy, I am sad for *you*."

I took a deep breath and started to reach for him. "I don't have time to sit and listen to your little riddles and proverbs; you are coming with me."

"I have seen your future, Tommy, and I know how you are going to die."

I froze.

"You are right, we don't have time for riddles," said the High Father. "Am I being plain enough now?"

For the first time, he wasn't smiling.

"Time is just another dimension, Tommy. Remember that, always."

The High Father reached into his robe and pulled out a strange small box of wood and brass. At its heart glowed a soft light, and fuzzy pictures swirled about its surface—like a shadow puppet show.

"This is the Cycloidotrope," he said. "And it should not fall into the Gentleman's hands, regardless of what happens to me. He has mastered space, but he has no power over time."

He held it out. "You came here for help in your mission to stop the Gentleman. But this is all I can offer you. If you focus on something, moments of its future will appear in the glass, or scenes from its past. If the need is great enough, you may even be able to communicate across the great gulfs of the time stream."

I took the Cycloidotrope in my hands. It was surprisingly warm.

"Know this, though—the future is not set," said the High Father. "Some things you see will be indistinct, changeable. Look for yourself. Focus on your future and see what the Cycloidotrope will tell you."

I didn't believe a word of it, and yet the minute I looked into the cube, the images began to swirl and take shape. I couldn't help but wonder about my future, about what he had said about my death. . . .

First, the image that appeared in the cube was from my recent past. I was standing next to the Captain's empty bed. Bernard was there, too, and he was crying. The picture shifted and changed and now I was seeing a girl. She was my age and she was shouting something but I couldn't make out the words. We were in a bedroom, a girl's bedroom judging by the furnishings, but the style was very strange. Next the girl was tumbling into a dark, yawning portal and I saw myself reaching out to catch her. The image shifted again and I saw a new scene—the same girl on the deck of a black ship with the wind whipping at her hair. Flames glowed and smoke billowed everywhere. She was holding a boy, cradling him in her arms. She was crying, and tears fell on the boy's pale, lifeless face. My face. The scene shifted for a last time, and when it came back into focus all was death. The lands were barren; dead trees and empty cities covered the Earth. The sun in the sky died out, then the stars winked out one by one until all was dark. Just a hollow, empty blackness.

"The less certain the outcome, the more indistinct the picture," said the High Father. "But you have just witnessed the likeliest future. In it, you will save the life of this girl you will meet, you will catch her before she falls into darkness and you will die as a result. First you, then the world."

I looked up; the cube had gone back to its innocent white glow. But the images of the dead Earth had been crystal clear.

"Who is she?"

"You will meet her soon enough," answered the High Father. "She is vital to the future, to your future. Your destinies are intertwined."

"This thing can see into the future. Can I use it to go there? Can I travel in time and stop it from happening?"

"No one has ever tried. The Cycloidotrope was designed to be a window only. You may gaze out through the window. You may even be able to open it and speak to those on the other side. But if you try to jump through you will most likely be splintered into nothingness. The forces of time are unforgiving. The only way to change the future is to live through it."

"So there's no way? Time travel is impossible."

The High Father cocked his head. "I didn't say that. There are no certainties in this universe, Tommy. Merely bad odds. *Very* bad odds."

"Can you do it?" I asked. "Can you travel through time?"

"Yes," the High Father answered, after a moment. "But I won't."

My blood started to rise. "Look, you said you weren't going to play games!"

The High Father held up his hand. "I am not playing a game. Time is not meant to be abused, and just because a person *can* do something does not mean that he *should*."

I cursed as I shoved the Cycloidotrope into my belt pouch. "Live through it, huh? So I'm just supposed to wait until this awful future comes to pass?"

The High Father shrugged. "In the Cycloidotrope you weren't much older than you are now. I doubt you'll have to wait very long."

"What if I change it? When I meet this girl, what if I let her die? Can I save the Earth then?"

The High Father smiled again. "The scene was dim at that precise moment. Foggy. That means that you could, conceivably, act differently. You let the girl die and then—who knows? At that point, as they say, *anything is possible*."

CHAPTER TWENTY

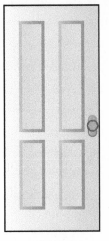

JEZEBEL
THE HOLLOW WORLD, 1902

The trogs flew them to an aboveground camp, a series of small watchtowers on the edge of their subterranean kingdom. Here the trogs corralled mounts like the flying pterodactyls and the poor stegosaurus that had saved Jez's life. As they approached the camp Jez saw her trog gazing at the paddock of dinosaurs. Several trogs were feeding them large mouthfuls of vegetation, while others patted them down and scrubbed their fins clean. The care with which these creatures treated their animals only confirmed what Jez had suspected for some time: the stegosaurus had been more than just a beast of burden—the trog was grieving for a friend.

The reception they received here was certainly nicer than what she'd come to expect. They weren't tied up and jostled around in nets, for one thing. These trogs treated Tommy and Jez more like honored guests. Once on the ground, Jezebel and

Tommy were surrounded by a throng of curious onlookers. Jez even spotted a few infants clinging tightly to their mothers, eyes wide and curious, as they were carried about with that strange arm-walk—two long, powerful arms acting as "feet" while the third held the infant close. It seemed that the trogs' stubby legs weren't good for much more than standing on.

Jez and Tommy were offered food and the opportunity to catch a few much-needed hours of sleep. The meal was a mash of various mushrooms and some kind of grilled meat, which they gratefully accepted. After several days of little to eat, Jezebel didn't care if she was chewing on lizard or bug—nothing had ever tasted so good.

After their rest, the trogs ushered them out of the small camp and up a winding path that twisted its way into the hills. As they climbed, Jez began to feel uneasy. A change had come over the trogs, and their once-excited chatter had reduced to an occasional whisper. Whereas their welcome had felt like a raucous party, this hike was beginning to feel like a solemn funeral march. The last trip she'd taken with the trogs had ended at the Gentleman's ship, and though he and his entire army seemed to have abandoned the Hollow World for who knew where, Jez couldn't help but be afraid. She imagined herself stuffed and tied up like a pig on a roasting stick. Maybe she'd misjudged these trogs and were being led to a giant cooking pot.

Jez breathed a sigh of relief when the trail ended in a shabby little hut. Sitting outside was a harmless-looking old trog tending a small fire. His fur was mangy and long folds of bare skin drooped and dangled from his skinny arms. But he was obviously a creature of importance among the tribe—they all bowed their heads in respect as they approached.

Upon seeing Jez and Tommy, the old trog rose to his feet—

two of his hands leaned heavily on canes while the third waved its curled, arthritic fingers at them to approach. For a moment the picture of the cooking pot loomed large in Jez's mind, but this frail creature looked innocent enough, so she followed Tommy and the trog as they slipped into his little shack.

The hut was bare except for a small pallet where the trog apparently slept and a pile of what looked like rolls of long, dried leaves stacked neatly in the corner. The trog gestured for them to have a seat, offering them the choice of his bed or the hard floor. After eyeing the tiny black bugs hopping about on the trog's filthy straw mattress, they choose the floor. Once they were seated, the trog picked through the rolls of leaves, gingerly choosing one from the bottom. With obvious reverence, the trog unrolled it in front of them and Jez realized that what she had mistaken for just a leaf turned out to be parchment. It was covered in some kind of hieroglyphs, a trog picture language. A book.

The trogs in the pictures were easily recognizable by their three arms. Many of the scenes were of trogs going about their daily activities underground—tunneling, building, fishing the great underground lakes. The old trog pointed at one picture of a lone trog standing on the surface and looking up at the molten sun. Then he pressed one of his hands against his heart and said something in trog-speak.

"Oh!" said Jez, understanding. "That's you. You are the trog in the picture who came up to the surface."

The trog smiled and repeated the gesture—pointing to the picture and then back to himself.

Tommy nodded. "How about that? He's like a little trog explorer! We should give him a pair of silly goggles and make it official."

"Quiet," said Jez. The trog was pointing to a new page.

In it, the trog was standing next to a circle in the ground—a circle of light. A figure was stepping through, a figure with only two arms.

"Is that a . . . ?" asked Jez, leaving the word unspoken.

"Yes," answered Tommy, squinting at the crude drawing. "It looks like it. This old guy found a portal."

The trog continued to flip through the pages, and as he pointed out specific pictures, a story began to unfold. This trog had indeed discovered a portal in his travels, and on the other side of the portal he'd met a man with two arms who'd spoken of the future. The man had told the trog of a black ship that would come and threaten his world. And he'd told the old trog the name of their savior.

The arrival of the Dead Gentleman hadn't been a surprise at all. They'd been expecting it.

"Tobby Erber," he said.

"He's been waiting for you?" asked Jez, smiling uneasily.

"Yep," answered Tommy. "The person on the other side of the portal gave him my name."

"But who would know your name?"

Tommy pointed at the drawing of the two-armed man in the glowing circle. A squiggly line was drawn on his backside, like a tail.

"A cow's tail. Of course," said Tommy. "The High Father."

"The who?" asked Jez.

"It's a long story—it doesn't matter!"

Tommy pointed next to the glowing circle.

"Where?" he asked the trog. "Where is it?"

He was talking very slowly and loudly, the way that people do when they are trying to be understood, as if volume can overcome the barrier of language.

Miraculously, in this case it seemed to work. The old trog peered at the picture and, with a tired heave, pulled himself to his feet. He hobbled over to his little bed and gestured for the two of them to help him. Tommy grabbed one end of the mattress and, reluctantly, Jez grabbed the other. They gave the loosely tied bundle of bug-ridden straw and sticks a shove. Beneath it was a manhole-sized opening, but it was unlike any hole Jez had ever seen. It was filled with a hazy, soft glow, and instead of descending into the earth, it opened out onto a stone courtyard shrouded in clouds. In the distance was a tall tower.

Jezebel's heart jumped when she saw the open portal—this could be a way out! The other portal, the one Tommy had come through, would have just led them to a dead end. Jez remembered the paved-over crevice in the Percy's basement. But this portal might be the first step out of here.

Tommy's face, however, was anything but excited. They might as well have been back in the Gentleman's cell.

"The Academy," said Tommy, slowly shaking his head. "Looks like we're going home."

For Jezebel, the experience of stepping through a portal between worlds turned out to be a lot like throwing up. It was terribly uncomfortable going through—a twisting, churning feeling—but when it was over you felt much, much better.

The most disorienting part of it was stepping down into a hole in the ground and then falling out of the sky someplace else. The sister portal in the Academy was four feet off the ground, so when Jezebel emerged she actually fell and landed on her butt.

Tommy appeared next to her, expertly, on his feet.

"Going through a portal affects different people differently." He shrugged. "Just like some get seasick, but some don't."

"Great," said Jez. "You know, I used to get so sick on long drives that my mother had to crush up these pills in jam so that I didn't taste the bitter . . . What's wrong?"

Tommy was staring.

The Academy was empty. The only sound was the banging of a door somewhere being blown open and closed by the breeze. Whole buildings had been reduced to rubble and shattered glass. Jez didn't spy so much as a cockroach. The Academy was empty, deserted, dead.

"This was once the Academy of Explorers," he said. "But the Gentleman came here with his Grave Walkers and killed them all."

Jez looked over her shoulder at the dark skyline of the empty buildings. "Then where are all the bodies?"

Tommy scratched his chin but he didn't answer. He kept looking, worriedly, at the sky.

"What's wrong?" Jez asked. "Is it those Grave Walker guys?"

Tommy shook his head. "No, they've all gone. This is worse. Look."

Jez followed Tommy's gaze up to the horizon. A pink sun was setting low in the dusk sky. A bank of clouds had gathered just below it, signaling rain. After the hazy molten ceiling of the Hollow World, it was a welcome sight.

"What's wrong? It's a nice sunset."

"That's the problem. We do *not* want to be here at night."

"Why not? What happens at night?"

But Tommy didn't answer her. He was already jogging down

the street, toward the tall rose-colored tower in the distance.

"C'mon!" he shouted over his shoulder. "We have to get to the Tower Library. We need to find a portal. Fast!"

It took them five minutes at a steady jog to reach the tower steps. Tommy paused outside and waited for Jezebel to catch up.

"Before we go in," he said. Reaching up, he removed his goggles and put them over Jez's head.

"Hey—" she started to say. The ridiculous-looking things were heavy, much heavier than they appeared, and they tugged on her hair.

"If it gets too dark to see, just flip this switch, here," Tommy was saying as he adjusted the strap. "They're charged so you'll have about ten minutes of paralight."

"And what about you?"

"Then I'll follow *you*. C'mon, daylight's wasting."

Within, a wreckage of metal globes and wheels lay shattered on the floor. A headless statue of a fat man greeted them as they walked across the rotunda. Piles of books lay scattered about, their pages torn and covers stained with something awful.

"The Orrery," said Tommy, gesturing to the debris. "And the statue of Fat Theo. After the Academy fell, the chapterhouse portals were all closed, except for just a few. There should be one in this tower!"

Even at a whisper their voices carried through the hollow tower like an echo chamber. As if in response, there was a sudden sound from above them—like the dropping of a book on the stairs—followed by the patter of running feet.

"Wait!" said Tommy, and the two of them gave chase up the steps. Whatever it was ahead of them, it was fast and managed to keep the distance between them all the way to the top of the tower. By the time they reached the summit, both Jez and Tommy were winded, heaving and holding on to the wall for support.

At the top of the tower steps, they found a lone wooden door that opened onto the roof. The sun by now was little more than a bright-red sliver against the dark sky. In a matter of minutes it would disappear completely. Black clouds gathered and a light rain had begun to fall, hastening the sunset. With the exception of a short three-foot wall, the tower's crown was open on all four sides, allowing for a 360-degree view of the once-magnificent Academy.

And waiting for them up top was a small boy in a man's over-sized robes. He was breathing lightly, normally, and smiling at the winded pair.

"Hello, Tommy," the boy said.

"Who's . . . that?" asked Jez between gulps of air.

"I don't know," answered Tommy.

"But . . . he knows who you are!"

"Hello, Jezebel," said the boy.

"Huh," said Tommy. "Looks like he knows who you are, too."

"Tommy," said Jez. "He's got a tail."

"Is what you do not see unreal?" said the boy, flicking his bovine tail playfully in the air. "Does the ocean disappear just because the mountain blocks your view?" He had a smug, irritating smile that made Jez instantly dislike him.

Tommy's eyes narrowed. "A tail? Wait a minute . . ."

"Tommy, who is this kid?" asked Jez. The boy couldn't have been older than four or five, but he *felt* . . . older.

"I am the High Father of the monks of the Enlightened Hidden City," the boy answered, pleased with himself.

"The High Father is an old man!" Tommy said to the boy. "Not a . . . toddler!"

"I am what I am at the moment, Tommy Learner," the High Father said. "Having recently died, I was born again into this body. It is the way of the monks of the Hidden City to endure a cycle of reincarnation until our appointed task in this universe is complete. Only then may we become one with the cosmos."

He winked conspiratorially. "It drives the Dead Gentleman to a most furious distraction. He has killed me several times since you and I last spoke, Tommy, but alas, I refuse to stay dead."

"So why are you here?" asked Jez. "Where did you come from?"

The High Father shrugged. "I came here to find you two. I knew you would come, but I had hoped you'd arrive a bit earlier." He gestured to the darkening sky. "I'd hoped we would have a chance to talk before the Gentleman's army awoke."

"What army?" asked Jez, and at that moment the glimmer of western sun vanished in the sky, swallowed by storm clouds. Night had finally settled over the Academy.

At first the noise was just a distant shuffling, like the brush of fabric on stone. It had been disguised by the steady rhythm of the falling raindrops, but within minutes the city was alive with the sounds of doors opening and wooden floors creaking under the weight of shuffling footsteps. Hundreds and hundreds of footsteps. Thousands.

"I'm sorry, my friends," said the High Father. "But *that* army. The Explorers who died defending this place. Their souls are at rest, but what's left serves the Gentleman."

Jezebel and Tommy ran to the wall and peered into the gloom

below. It was too dark to make out many details, but something was moving on the streets down there. Silent and steady, shapes were stirring everywhere, and they were all headed toward the same place—the Tower Library.

"The dead are coming for you. Your warmth, your *life*, burns like a fire in their eyes and they hunger for it," said the High Father. "There is no place safe here for you now."

"What do we do?" asked Jez.

The High Father held out his hand. In it was a small, familiar device.

"A Cycloidotrope!" said Tommy. "I thought there was only one!"

"There are as many as I deem necessary at any given time," said the High Father. "No more, no less. And since the Gentleman took yours from you, I have decided that there should be another."

He continued to hold out his hand and the Cycloidotrope glowed golden in his small child's palm. "You must use it," he said. "You must jump through time."

Neither Tommy nor Jez said anything for a second.

"Jump through a Cycloidotrope?" said Tommy, finally. "Are you out of your little reincarnated skull?"

"I once explained to you, Tommy, that at certain points in time the future is not set. There, different choices can affect the entire timeline, yield different outcomes."

The High Father leaned in, his small eyes bright and shining despite the darkening night. "This moment we are at one of those crossroads," he said. "Tonight, if you activate the Cycloidotrope you will see the place you are trying to go. I believe if you jump through you will arrive there safely."

"You told me that traveling through the Cycloidotrope was almost certain death!" said Tommy. "You said I'd be torn into a million pieces."

"I did not lie," said the High Father. "The odds of survival are grim. And yet, it is what you must risk if you are to survive this night."

"It worked for me," said Jezebel. "Maybe it'll work again."

"A once-in-a-lifetime break," answered Tommy. "You saw what happened to that Harvester. We'd be ripped to bits in the time stream."

"Most likely," the High Father agreed. "But if you don't jump you will *certainly* be ripped to bits here. At least the Cycloidotrope offers you a chance, however slim."

With that the High Father activated the little device, and once again they were gazing at the future, at Jezebel's bedroom.

"Does everyone have a Cycloidotrope that peeks into my bedroom?" Jez snapped.

The High Father didn't answer.

Jez walked over to the bedroom hologram. It looked so real, except for the rain—as the rain fell from the sky it created little shimmers in the image. She had jumped through once, and though it wasn't at all pleasant, she had survived. Could she beat the odds a second time? If she closed her eyes all she saw was the memory of that Harvester being torn apart.

Tommy and the High Father were arguing.

"You expect us to jump through there just because you say so?" he asked.

The High Father's smile faded. "Actually, no. I knew you would not believe me, but I had to try."

Jezebel thought she heard the creaking of steps from somewhere below. Running to the door, she listened. Someone *was* definitely climbing the stairs. More than one, from the sounds of it, and they were getting closer.

When she turned back, Tommy and the High Father's argument had become heated. But the rain was coming down harder now and it was difficult to hear what they were saying. Their voices were drowned out by a thunderclap in the distance, but from the way Tommy was gesturing, it was obvious they were talking about her.

There was no time for this. The crack of thunder was followed by the crack of splintering wood, like a small crash from somewhere not far below. Jez poked her head through the doorway, but in the failing evening light the tower had gone pitch-black—she couldn't see a thing. She remembered Tommy's paralight goggles strapped to her forehead.

Self-consciously, she pulled the goggles down over her eyes. At first there was nothing different about her vision, just a slight bluish tinge. She flipped a switch, and it was like seeing the world through a lightning flash. Everything was illuminated in a washed-out blue, including the tower stairs beneath her.

Standing there on the steps not ten feet away was a human corpse in a tattered Explorer's uniform. Its leering face was mostly bone, with only a few strips of flesh clinging to the skull. It was reaching, awkwardly, for her, but its foot had fallen through a weak spot in the stairs, and the splintered wood was clamped around the rotted meat like a bear trap.

And behind it, more corpses as far as the eye could see. They lined the stairs—a scrambling, squirming mess of putrid arms and legs. The only thing keeping them at bay was the one stuck up front. He was creating a bottleneck, but not for long. As soon as they spied Jezebel they surged forward, trampling the leader underfoot. Jez heard the breaking of bones, like the cracking of dried twigs, as the mindless masses crawled over each other to get to her.

With a scream she slammed the door. She looked around for something to barricade it with, but there was nothing.

"Tommy! They're here!" she shouted, but her words were lost in the roar of the winds and rain. He was so busy arguing with the High Father that he wasn't paying attention to her or to the doorway.

The door creaked as something smacked against it. The handle began to turn.

"TOMMY!" Jez put her weight into the door. Still Tommy didn't hear. The storm raged around them so fiercely that her own words sounded muffled in her ears.

A push and the door opened an inch, despite Jez's efforts. A rotten hand slipped through the gap, wriggling and grasping at nothing. With a shout, Jez gave the door another shove, throwing her shoulder into it. She felt, rather than heard, the crunch as a pair of gray-fleshed fingers snapped off at the knuckle. They landed at her feet but refused to stop moving. They inched toward her like grotesque worms.

A shudder tore into the door as a second body joined the first. Jez nearly lost her balance as the wood begin to splinter and crack. Her shoulder had gone numb from the effort, and she knew she couldn't hold it a second time.

When the next blow came, she was ready for it. Instead of resisting, she jumped out of the way as the door came crashing down and two rotten corpses spilled out onto the ground, their broken bodies in a tangle.

I'm crazy, she thought. *This is it, I'm officially crazy.*

Then she flipped up the goggles—she didn't want to see what she was about to do—and ran. She ran straight at Tommy. He turned and saw her and the throng of dead Explorers spilling through the doorway. He shouted something, but she wasn't listening. She was too busy yelling "I'm crazy!" as she tackled him into the light of the Cycloidotrope.

PART THREE

All paths lead to the same place.
But it seems that Man is destined
always to choose the rockier way.
It is his defining trait.

—*from the* Observations of the High Father
of the Enlightened Hidden City

CHAPTER TWENTY-ONE

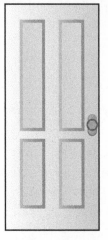

JEZEBEL
NEW YORK, TODAY

Jezebel awoke just as the pain hit her, a spike of agony straight down the center of her skull and a cramping nausea deep in her stomach.

"Happy thoughts, happy thoughts," she repeated over and over.

Pizza for breakfast. Discovering a drive-in movie theater on a family road trip to Florida. Sitting on the car's hood between her parents as they watched *Psycho* on the big screen and burying her head in her father's arm during the scary scenes, but still peeking past his jacket at the reflection in the car window. Somehow it seemed less frightening that way, watching the mirror of the real thing.

The sickness passed.

"I'm home!" said Jez, sitting up. She looked around and saw that the room was just as she'd left it—the unmade bed, the scattered pencils and broken trophy. And there was the forest mural on the wall. Best of all, she was in one piece.

Tommy lay next to her, hugging his knees to his chest, his face contorted in pain.

Jez pulled him to her and whispered in his ear. "Happy thoughts," she said. "You told me yourself, you have to picture happy thoughts to make the pain go away."

Eventually his face unclenched and he began to relax. His eyes fluttered open and he looked up at Jez. "I once discovered a barrel of pickles that had fallen off a delivery cart. I ate as many as I could stand and when I'd gotten sick from the smell, I sold the rest for a penny per. Felt like an honest businessman for a day. Even ran a special on the broken bits and pieces—handful for a half penny."

He sat up and squinted at the room. "Unbelievable," he said. "We're alive."

"We did it." She smiled and hugged him close. He returned the hug with a halfhearted backslap—for a boy thrilled to be in one piece, he seemed awfully subdued. He looked around the room like he'd been tossed back into the Gentleman's dungeon.

"You know this place?" he asked.

"Of course," answered Jez. "This is my room! Why, what's the matter?"

Tommy shook his head and offered her an unconvincing smile. "Nothing's wrong. Just a bit of a surprise is all." Still, he looked troubled. Jez decided to chalk it up to future-shock and got to her feet.

"Dad?" Jez called, ducking out into the hallway. She ran through the apartment, from room to room, but all were empty.

Maybe he was out looking for her, or maybe . . . no, she wouldn't consider the other possibility.

"I'm sure he's all right," said Tommy as she returned to her bedroom. He was staring out her window at the dark city. "Keep a chin up."

"We still have time," Jez said, nodding, wiping at her cheeks. She didn't want him to see the tears. "We can still find Bernie and get Merlin back."

Tommy shook his head and pointed at the window. It was dark outside. "We have other problems."

"What? So, it's nighttime! We might have lost a few hours, but that doesn't mean—"

"No, look." Tommy pointed to the sky over the Hudson River. Just past the river were the bluffs of the New Jersey shoreline, and above that was a twisting, yawning vortex of black clouds and crackling lightning—the Gentleman's portal. The storm raged everywhere, and the winds were blowing into Manhattan like a typhoon through the streets.

"He's here," said Jez. "He's coming for us."

Tommy shook his head. "*We* don't matter anymore," he said. "It's Merlin he wants."

Jezebel ran to her desk and powered up her computer, the little laptop's battery whirring to life.

No signal.

The light of her desk lamp flickered for a moment but then came back on. Outside, windows were going dark everywhere. Whole buildings had blacked out—across the river the lights from New Jersey still burned bright, but the growing storm was quickly eclipsing even those. And here in Manhattan the dark buildings looked like dead fingers pointing at the sky. She grabbed a watch from her desk drawer—the time read 4:36 a.m. There was still at least an hour before dawn, plenty of time for the Gentleman to recover his prize.

"There's no Internet, and whole blocks are losing power," said Jez. "I bet this storm is even messing with the satellite signals. He's completely cutting off Manhattan from the outside world."

Tommy scratched his head. It was obvious he didn't understand half of what Jezebel was talking about, but he got the drift.

"Manhattan is an island," he said.

Jez nodded. "It's the perfect place to start an invasion. Thanks to the weather, there's going to be so much chaos that people won't even realize what's happening until it's too late."

Tommy stared out the window at the widening funnel cloud, laced with streaks of lightning. He seemed, for once, contemplative, even lost in his own thoughts. Jez, on the other hand, couldn't calm the racing of her own heart. They needed to be doing something, to be out there trying to stop the Gentleman, not sitting here in her bedroom as the world ended.

"So?" she asked. "What do we do next?"

Tommy picked up a picture that had fallen over on her desk. It was a shot of her and her dad at Disney World some years ago. In it a giant mouse was tickling her while her dad pretended to cower in fear.

"This your dad?" he asked.

Jez swallowed the lump in her throat and nodded.

"He looks nice. Not sure about the big mouse, though. Think I'd kick him in the shins if he tried that on me."

"Tommy, we're running out of time—"

"My mom used to take me to the theater, when we could afford it," said Tommy, ignoring her. "We'd have to stand, but someone always hoisted me up on their shoulders so I could see."

He looked at her. "At least I think that happened. Sometimes it's hard to tell the difference between the things that happened and the things I wish had happened."

Jez started to answer but was interrupted by the sound of the front door opening and closing. She turned and looked at the dark hallway outside her bedroom. Her own door was slightly ajar, obscuring her view, but she could hear footsteps.

Tommy bent down and picked up the heavy marble trophy and moved in front of her. "Get back," he whispered.

Jezebel reached out and snatched the trophy from his hand. "That's mine," she said, stepping forward.

"Dad?" she called out hopefully. For a minute there was no answer and she held up the trophy with both hands, ready to swing.

Then a familiar voice said, "Weather looks bad today. Showers of blood and zero percent chance of sun."

The bedroom door creaked inward, and standing there was Elevator Man, only changed. His skin had a sickly greenish tinge to it and his normally bright eyes were bloodshot; dark, baggy circles hung beneath them.

"You don't look so good," said Jez.

"Today is the coming of the Master," Elevator Man said, smiling. "I have never felt better."

"He means the Gentleman," said Tommy. "He's one of them."

"Yeah, I figured that much."

"The Master wants you. He said he wanted you alive." Elevator Man stepped into the doorway. "But surely one is enough. One alive for the Master and one . . . for me!"

Jezebel screamed. But this time it wasn't out of fear or even surprise—this time it was out of anger. She was home, but instead of a tearful reunion with her dad, she had stepped into the middle of the apocalypse. That was quite enough crazy for one day, thank you.

Her sudden scream startled Elevator Man, and he hesitated just long enough for her to give the bedroom door a good kick—catching him in the face.

With a snarl Elevator Man shoved the door back open, one hand going to his ruined nose. He didn't seem to be in pain so much as surprised . . . and angry. Jez remembered what Tommy had said about Grave Walkers—not quite alive, not quite dead.

Jezebel swung the trophy. In his rage Elevator Man charged forward like a bull, presenting the top of his head to her all teed up and waiting for a trophy-smack.

She brought down the marble trophy on his skull with a thunk and he collapsed on the floor.

"Nicely done," said Tommy, eyes wide.

"Thanks," answered Jez.

Elevator Man lifted his head up off the ground and snarled.

"Hit him again!" Tommy said.

Jezebel readied another swing, but Elevator Man rolled away and climbed to his feet.

"Here!" Tommy shouted, and Jez turned just in time to see Tommy tossing her bedsheet like a net. Suddenly blinded, Elevator Man staggered forward as Jezebel swung with the trophy again. And again. She never missed, but with each hit Elevator Man only seemed to get angrier and angrier. He was blinded and confused, but he wasn't slowing down.

Finally he lashed out and knocked the trophy out of Jez's hand, shoving her to the ground. With a howl of triumph he grabbed Tommy by the throat and lifted the small boy high in the air. Tommy's face was already turning purple as he struggled to catch a breath. Elevator Man stepped toward the window.

"Can you fly, little Explorer?" he snarled.

Tommy kicked at him, but his blows weren't having any effect.

Jezebel grabbed her desk chair and pushed as hard as she could. The chair connected with the back of Elevator Man's knees and he stumbled, dropping Tommy onto the bed. Elevator Man was off balance, and as he tumbled over, he grabbed Jezebel by the arm.

The two of them fell over backward into the closet door.

The thin door crushed under his weight, and Elevator Man sank into the closet.

Only there wasn't a closet anymore. Behind the door was a gaping black hole that spilled into an empty void. Elevator Man scrambled to keep himself from falling, but it was too late. He was sliding into the void and Jezebel was tumbling after him.

She was halfway through when Tommy caught her feet. He'd stopped her slide, and she could hear him struggling to pull her back into the light. The dark was bitter cold, and she felt something moving there in the blackness, shifting and slithering and touching her hair. . . .

She was vaguely aware of Tommy shouting something as she was pulled out of the closet and back onto the floor of her room.

"What were you thinking?" asked Tommy, panting for breath and red-faced.

Jez was too cold, too frightened to speak. The adrenaline was already giving her the shakes.

At first she thought he was just flushed from the exertion of pulling her back in, but she soon realized he was red-faced with anger. He was furious.

"You could've been killed! Or worse!"

Jezebel sat up. As the warmth returned to her body so did some of her spirit. "Hey, I was saving you! If not for me you'd be out the window—"

"I DON'T NEED SAVING! NOT FROM YOU!"

Jez was stunned. While it was true that they'd known each other for only a short time, she'd still come to think of them as a team. They were partners in this—partners in saving the world.

Tommy took a deep breath and stood up. He walked over to her desk and righted the picture of her family, which had fallen over a second time. Then he pointed to the yawning black portal that used to be her closet.

"All the portals to the Gentleman's world are opening up," he said, not looking at Jez. "Dark closets, old graves, the spaces beneath the stairs—the Dead Gentleman's domains. It'll happen all over the world."

In the distance, they heard the rumble of thunder, followed by a louder crash—like an explosion. Just beneath the wind and the rain Jez thought she could make out the sounds of screams.

"The bogeyman's coming for us all," he said.

Plopping down on the desk chair, Tommy began tugging at his boot. "The trogs took all of my weapons away when they captured me, but they missed this." He picked at the heel of his boot until it slid open, revealing a hidden compartment. A small, dirty compass fell out onto the floor.

"Been meaning to give this thing a polish anyway," he said as he rubbed the case on his shirt. Flipping open the lid, he pressed a button on the side.

For a moment, nothing happened and Tommy's face fell. But then Jez heard a soft ping. Then another, slightly louder. And another and another.

"Atta girl," Tommy said, staring at the compass's face. "Come home, *Nautilus*. Come home."

He yanked on his shoe and popped the compass into his pocket. "She'll be here soon," he said. "Find Merlin, if the Gentleman hasn't gotten to him first. Then hide. You know this building better than I do. Find someplace safe and just hide."

"Hide? That's your great plan? We've been together in this so far and now you want me to run away and hide? You know you'd still be squishing bugs for your fire if not for me!"

"You're not coming with me," he said, walking out of the bedroom. "And that's that."

"Hold on! Stop!" shouted Jez. "You can't do this on your own! And you can't tell me what to do!"

"Good luck, Jez," he called back as he headed for the front door. "And keep the goggles. They suit you."

CHAPTER TWENTY-TWO

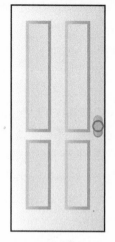

JEZEBEL
NEW YORK, TODAY

The front door slammed shut, and for a moment Jezebel was speechless. Part of her was furious, indignant—who did he think he was? But the other part of her was wounded and hurting. She thought he'd depended on her the way she'd depended on him, despite his crooked, cocky smile and all that swagger. They'd escaped the Gentleman's cell together. They made a good team. Didn't they?

The kid didn't think, he just . . . did things. It was a wonder he was still alive, and he needed her help whether he wanted to admit it or not. She may not be an Explorer, but the two of them were in this together and she was going to tell him so.

But as she started toward the door something caught her eye. It was the mural—it was changing. Even as she watched, the colors began to swirl and darken. The green of the leaves started to bleed at the edges and mix with the browns of the tree bark.

The various flower petals twisted and grew, spiraling round and round. Jezebel stood there, transfixed, watching the morphing oil paints as they started to shimmer and glow.

Shimmer and glow.

"It's a portal," Jez said. Then, louder this time, "It's a portal! Tommy, it's a portal!"

She could barely tear her eyes away from the changing landscape, but she needed to tell Tommy. Running down the hall, she felt her heart pounding with excitement. What were the odds of her bedroom having two portals? It had to mean something.

She threw open the door and instantly froze. A large shape stood in the doorway, blocking her path out to the hall. Thick, bug-eyed glasses stared down at her beneath arched eyebrows.

"Everything all right, little miss?" asked Bernie.

Jezebel took a step back. She wished she'd kept ahold of her trophy-club.

"Everything's fine," she answered. "Why do you ask?"

Bernie was carrying a bulky knapsack slung over one shoulder. She could hear the elevator descending. Tommy must've just gotten in as Bernie was coming out of the stairwell where he'd been hiding, waiting for Jezebel.

Jez shoved the old man as hard as she could. Startled, he let out a cry as he toppled over backward. She leapt past him, careful to avoid his flailing arms, and ran for the elevator. As she bolted away she heard the sound of jingling keys and scuffling boots. Jingling keys, scuffling boots and . . . birdsong.

Jez whipped around to see Bernie, kneeling on the floor and cradling a bent and broken birdcage. A shiny metal canary fluttered around excitedly inside.

"Merlin!" Jez shouted.

"He's okay, he's okay," said Bernie. "It'll take more than my fat behind to hurt this little fellow, thank goodness."

Bernie had apparently been holding the cage behind his back when Jez pushed him—he'd literally sat on it.

"Where's my dad, Bernie?" Jez demanded.

"The Gentleman doesn't have him, if that's what you're worried about, at least not yet. When he woke up and you were gone, he got worried." He gestured to the storm outside. "He's out there somewhere, looking for you."

Jezebel took a breath. If Bernie was telling the truth, then that was something of a relief.

"Hand the bird over, Bernie. I'm warning you." Jez felt ridiculous threatening him like this. After all, she was weaponless and despite his feebleness he was still twice her size. It was only the added advantage of surprise that had allowed her to escape him the first time.

But far from laughing at her, Bernie just sighed. "Whatever you say, little miss. Whatever you say." Then he unlatched the cage, forcing the bent door open, and Merlin hopped out, resting lightly on the man's wrist. "Go on, then," Bernie said to the little bird. "Go to Jezebel."

Merlin cocked his head at Jezebel but didn't budge.

"Sorry, he's a bit shy with strangers."

"Your full name's Bernard Billingsworth, isn't it?" Jez said. "You were Tommy Learner's partner. Tommy told me about you, Bernie. He told me you betrayed him."

Bernie groaned as he struggled to his knees. "Give me a minute, will you? When someone my age takes a fall like that, you're not always sure if you'll be able to get back up."

"Bernie, tell me the truth."

"I am Bernard Billingsworth. *Junior.*"

"You're . . . his son?"

Bernie nodded. "My father was Tommy's partner. An Explorer, like him, though he never made it past apprentice. After Tommy disappeared my father went into hiding. I inherited his equipment, his books and his stories."

Bernie straightened up and adjusted his glasses. "But he was no traitor. Bernard Billingsworth Senior may not have been a brave man, but he was no traitor. It was the Gentleman who trapped Tommy in the basement of this very hotel. To hear my dad tell it, the two of them were exploring an attercop web— Tommy, of course, had gone first. But Tommy was ambushed and, when he fell to the bottom, the tunnel began to close in on itself. It must have been part of the Gentleman's trap, so that if the attercop didn't finish Tommy, the closing tunnel would."

Merlin sang a quiet song while Bernie went on. "My father failed him. We Billingsworths are not natural heroes, I'm afraid. And with the attercop and the tunnel collapsing, well, my father just didn't move fast enough, I guess. He froze. He never forgave himself."

Bernie shrugged. "He tried to put the Explorer's life behind him after that, but he couldn't forget. It haunted him for years and he ended up here, partly, I think, as a kind of penance for a crime he didn't commit. But he never lost the faith— he kept an eye on this place, just in case Tommy ever made it back out. And most importantly, he kept Merlin here, safe. First him, then me. This bird's been in the family for two generations."

Merlin cocked his head and flapped his wings, taking to the

air. He fluttered in circles around their heads and landed with a squawk on Jez's arm.

"Ah," said Bernie. "Now see there? He does like you."

Jez petted Merlin's head with her finger. His feathers were rough and felt like wrinkly tinfoil.

"When my father finally passed away, I took over as the building's super," said Bernie. "I honestly thought of all this Explorer stuff as ancient history. I cared for Merlin, kept him well oiled and such, but I was content just to look after the old Percy and change the occasional blown fuse. Never gave much thought to anything else.

"When they uncovered the basement during the renovations, well, I just didn't have the courage to go down there. Too much history, you know? Then you came along and you saw . . . what you saw."

"Tommy," Jez said.

Bernie nodded. "So is it true? Does Tommy's ghost haunt this place?"

"No, Bernie, he's alive. And he's here to stop the Dead Gentleman. You were right when you said before that the Gentleman was trying to get into this world. We haven't figured out exactly why, but Merlin is the key to his plan."

Bernie glanced at the hallway window and the dark storm blowing outside. "Doesn't look like he's waiting for the bird."

"He knows he's close," said Jez. "I guess he's so sure of himself that he's starting the invasion a little early."

"So what now, little miss?" asked Bernie. "Do we hide away with Merlin and hope for the best?"

His question went unanswered as the windows suddenly shook with an ear-splitting crash. It sounded like an explosion.

"The river!" Jez said.

Several doors down, a frightened face peeked out. Jez's once-friend, Sasha, looked fearfully around and, spying Jezebel, let out a heaving sob.

"Jez! What's happening? Is the world ending?"

Jez bit back the urge to tell her to call Max and ask *him.*

"Everything's going to be all right, Sasha," Jez said. "It's just a storm. Go back inside and stay away from the windows. Get into the bathtub like they tell you to."

"I can hear things . . . moving around in my closet," Sasha said.

"Close your bedroom door and block it with something. Grab flashlights, anything with batteries, go to your parents' room and stay there."

"What are you going to do?"

"I don't know," answered Jez, then turned and went back into her apartment.

Through her window she could see that the sky over the Hudson was now totally obscured by the massive, swirling cyclone. Flashes of lightning were going off, rapid-fire, inside the cloud, and the air seemed to vibrate with the sound of crashing explosions. The prow of a ship was just visible at the edges of the portal— a great black ship was coming through from the storm.

"That doesn't look like any storm I've ever seen," said Bernie, coming into the room.

"It's not," answered Jez, pointing to the mural on her wall.

The mural was gone and in its place was a portal. On the other side was the deck of the *Charnel House,* but it had changed with the times. The great wooden prow was gone, replaced with a sleek metal hull. Heavy gun turrets lined the side where cannons once stood. Though it had been no more than a few hours to Jez, a hundred years had passed since the twisted airship had left the Hollow World. In its place was a modern, armored zeppelin, as black as midnight.

As they watched, the *Charnel House* was rocked by an explosion that had nothing to do with the thundering storm around them—a shining, strangely ornate submarine had broken past the waves of the Hudson and placed itself between the Gentleman's black ship and the city. Grave Walkers scrambled here and there along the zeppelin's hull, some manning the guns and some struggling to put out fires. All around the two vessels was a great wall of dark clouds.

"It's him," Jez said, and she knew in her heart that she was right. "It's Tommy. He's fighting the Gentleman."

"My god," whispered Bernie.

At the mention of Tommy's name, Merlin began to squawk and wind his little head back and forth.

"What's wrong with him?" asked Bernie.

"I don't know," answered Jez. "I think he's worried about . . . NO!"

Jez reached for Merlin, but she was too slow. The little clockwork bird leapt off her shoulder and flew straight for the portal, singing all the way. In an instant he was gone.

"They'll get him," Jez said, her voice cracking. "He thinks he's going to save Tommy, but he's running straight into the Gentleman's hands. . . ."

Jez turned away. Her fists were balled so tight that her fingernails were cutting into her palm, but the pain didn't matter.

"Find Merlin and keep him safe," she said. "That's all he asked me to do, and I couldn't even do that right."

Jez looked at the portal. She watched as the *Charnel House's* one hundred guns wheeled around, slowly taking aim at the ship below, the ship that was standing between it and the city.

Jez took a step toward the portal. The Gentleman wouldn't kill Tommy. Not while she was still able to do something. Not while she could still fight back. They wouldn't lose this easily.

"Wait," said Bernie, grabbing Jez by the shoulder.

"Let go, Bernie," she said. "I'm going. I've got to get Merlin back or we'll all die."

"I know," said Bernie. "I wish I could . . ." He stared at the portal—the swirling clouds, the deathly black ship—and leaned heavily on his cane, shaking his head.

"It's not your fault, Bernie. And for the record, I don't think there's a cowardly bone in your body."

Bernie nodded. "But you shouldn't go unarmed. I can do this much at least," he said as he took the knapsack from his shoulder and opened it on the floor. He pulled out a long leather jacket. A symbol was stitched across the breast—a clockwork gear with wings.

"Slip it on," he said. "It might be a bit big, but it's padded—it should give you some protection."

As Jez put on the jacket—it *was* big; she practically swam in it—Bernie pulled out an odd-looking gun.

"Netgun," he said. "Just point and shoot. It's only got four loads left, so try not to miss."

"*Netgun?*" asked Jez. "Really?"

Bernie just shrugged. "But this is a real weapon. And by that I mean it's dangerous, so be careful."

He handed her a solid, tennis ball–sized orb of metal.

"It's called a mayfly," said Bernie. "Give it a crank like this."

He made a twisting motion. "And throw it. It's a portal closer—very destructive—and only to be used in an emergency."

Jez very carefully stowed the mayfly in her jacket pocket. She adjusted the paragoggles on her forehead and hefted the gun, which was lighter than it looked. She felt ridiculous, but Bernie was right—it was better than nothing.

"I have to have a talk with Tommy about updating the Explorers' equipment. This stuff is nuts." Jezebel looked at the portal again. The ship's cannons were nearly in place.

"No more time to lose," she said. "If you see my dad again, Bernie, tell him . . . oh, I don't know . . ."

"I'll tell him, Jezebel. And good luck."

Jez nodded, then she stepped up to the portal, took a breath and jumped through.

CHAPTER TWENTY-THREE

TOMMY AND JEZEBEL
NEW YORK, TODAY

The *Nautilus* heaved to starboard just as an alarm began to whistle somewhere overhead. I'd asked too much of the old girl with that last maneuver, firing up the engines to full throttle too quickly and banking right despite a twisted propeller blade and a hundred years' worth of silt that had built up on her hull. She was a wonder of engineering, but she was old and uncared for.

What a mess I'd gotten myself into this time. It was a miracle that the *Nautilus* had remained undisturbed for all these years, buried at the bottom of New York Bay. But it was even more miraculous that she was still seaworthy, and that she'd answered the compass's call. I felt more than a little sad for her, knowing as I did that this would be her last mission—that I'd summoned her only to be destroyed.

I could practically hear Scott's voice shouting at me from somewhere far off, scolding me for my foolhardiness. But I could also picture the glint in his eye and the man's barely suppressed smile, and I knew, deep down, he'd be proud of me. The Gentleman wasn't going to take our world without a struggle. Tommy Learner and the *Nautilus* would be the first to fight back. We'd show the rest how it was done.

A warning light blinked at me. I tried to remember—that one had something to do with the steam power intake/outtake flow. Or was it air quality? It didn't matter. I didn't have the time to do anything other than pilot; repairs were useless now.

Light artillery bounced off the armored hull like raindrops on a tin roof. The Grave Walkers were firing down on me with whatever small arms they had handy, but I knew there wasn't anything to fear from them. That ship's heavy guns, on the other hand . . .

Opening up the forward porthole, I got a good look at the *Charnel House*. It was a risk—the porthole window was a full six inches of glass, though it was still just glass—but I needed a view of the battlefield with my own eyes. The *Charnel House*'s underside was already torn in two different areas, both places pockmarked and riddled with holes from my surprise attack. We'd broken surface underneath it, getting off a clear shot with the *Nautilus*'s guns at the ship's exposed belly.

I wouldn't get that advantage again. And though the giant zeppelin was badly damaged and the venting black smoke meant fire on several decks, it was still aloft. A wound like that would have sunk any normal sea vessel. But the *Charnel House*'s heart was its air engine; even this newer, armored version relied on the great gas-filled bag at its top—and the ship wouldn't fall until that was destroyed.

Through the spray of river water and drifting fog I could see that the *Charnel House* was pulling around, bringing its guns to bear.

"Emergency dive!" I shouted. "All hands brace for incoming!"

Wresting the wheel again to starboard, I cranked the dive-shaft. Every single remaining warning light went off, blinking and beeping in rhythm with the screeching sirens. As I shouted orders to the imaginary crew, I heard the Captain's voice in my ears, telling me to give her all I've got.

Just as crazy as the old man.

The *Charnel House's* guns fired overheard.

The first thing Jezebel heard was the din of gunfire, the first thing she saw was a cloud of smoke that made her eyes sting and the first thing she felt was the scrape of metal against her cheek as the portal deposited her face-first onto a catwalk some forty feet above the main gunner's deck. Directly below her, black uniformed Grave Walkers ran back and forth between the many gun turrets, some firing automatic weapons into the waters below, others tending to repairs. Above her roared the ship's engine as it pumped superheated gas into the giant armored airbag. The whole contraption was bound together on a grid of thick, steel-wrought rigging.

Though she couldn't see him past the smoke, Jez knew that Tommy was somewhere below them in the Hudson, piloting that strange submarine. But he didn't know that Jezebel was above him, in the very ship he was trying to shoot down from the sky.

She needed to get Merlin back and then get off this zeppelin, and that meant getting belowdecks and finding where they'd taken the bird. She could shimmy down one of the steel cables, but that would just leave her out in the open, surrounded by

Grave Walkers. Above her was nothing but the airbag. She didn't know what to do next, and she could barely hear herself think above the roar of the propeller, fueled by the churning engine.

The engine . . .

She began to climb. If she could shut down the engine and bring the *Charnel House* out of the sky, then she could use the resulting chaos to find Merlin. Plus she didn't like the look of those guns that were taking aim at Tommy below.

She took hold of the nearest wire and hauled herself up into the rigging, eyes fixed on each span of cable ahead of her, climbing just a few inches at a time. The wind whipped her hair about her face, and the netgun slung on her back got snagged more than a few times, but all in all she made steady progress as she pulled herself along, hand over hand, toward the rear of the ship, where the great engine roared.

She shinnied up and through a doorway into the engine platform, a monstrous compartment near the back, and found herself face to face with a grease-stained, pallid engineer. He looked half dead like the rest of the crew. Seeing Jezebel, he pulled out a long monkey wrench and grinned with rotten yellow teeth as he approached. Jez didn't know which way to go—the engine was there behind him, a massive wall of dials and pressure gauges—but the engineer was nearly upon her. She held her ground and drew her netgun.

I managed to get the aft under the surface just as the first volley of gunfire hit the waves. Cushioned by the churning water, most of the shots rang off the *Nautilus*'s hull with a loud echo. But enough of them had found their mark that the ship was taking on water as the engines screamed at me in protest. A three-foot tear in the

Captain's quarters had swamped the bridge with a foot of river water before I'd managed to get the flood hatch closed. I imagined the Captain's many priceless treasures disappearing out the hole and into the muddy river.

The *Nautilus* was a durable vessel, but she was also, in some ways, delicate. She wasn't built for broadside naval combat, not like the steel-reinforced zeppelin. The *Charnel House* could outlast a frontal assault far better than Captain Scott's old underwater ship. If I took her up again to the surface, away from the protection of the deep Hudson, we'd have maybe one chance to shoot before taking another full round of gunfire, and one more round would do us in. Our small guns just didn't have the firepower to take down a hulk like the *Charnel House*, and the *Nautilus*'s torpedoes didn't have the angle to hit an airborne target.

At that point the best I was hoping for was to distract the Gentleman long enough to give Jezebel a head start. She was still back at the Percy, and perhaps she'd even had enough time to find Merlin. Regardless, the bird was someone else's responsibility now. . . .

You will save the life of this girl you will meet, you will catch her before she falls into darkness and you will die as a result. First you, then the world.

This is precisely why I don't put much stock in prophecies— I'd saved Jezebel, and if the High Father was right, my own life was now forfeit. But here I was, alive and fighting still. Perhaps the High Father had been wrong, or perhaps my death was just waiting for me. Perhaps this next volley.

So be it. I'd made my choice and the world would live or die because of it. When it had come down to it, there was no way I would let Jezebel die.

For what it's worth, I'd grab her every time, even if it meant the world dying. Even if it meant a hundred worlds dying.

I cranked the wheel to port and dove deeper into the murky river. I had one last idea and I needed depth if it had any hope of working—a crazy, dangerous plan—but one that might just bring down the *Charnel House*. The water in the cabin had already risen to my knees. This wasn't the plan of a seasoned Explorer; this was the plan of a cornered street thief—desperate and dirty.

I found myself whistling as I angled the ship's nose upward. Just as it should be.

The engineer moved faster than Jez would have thought possible, but he wasn't fast enough to avoid the net. With a pressurized thunk the net wrapped the engineer up tight, and the force of the shot sent him reeling backward and through a window, falling to the gunner's deck below. Jez cringed at the thought of his body hitting the boards—she hadn't meant to kill him. But when she looked down, she saw that he was still moving and she wondered if he'd actually ever been truly alive. What had Tommy called them? *Near*-dead?

She didn't have time to worry about it. Already several Grave Walkers had spied the engineer's fall and were climbing the rigging after her. She removed the mayfly from her pocket. Bernie had said that the little device was capable of destroying a portal—Jez could imagine what it might do to an engine. She gave the ball a twist and there was the sound of something clicking into place. Immediately the ball began to vibrate in her hand. She was so startled she nearly dropped it before tossing it into one of the engine's many vents. Then she began her climb back along the rigging as fast as she could manage.

From deep within the engine she heard the sound of buzzing, like an angry bug in a jar. It was getting louder.

Just then Jezebel heard a great cry go up from the Grave Walkers, and as she looked down she saw Tommy's submarine shooting up out of the river. It was nearly vertical, launching into the air on jets of water like a rocket. No, more like a missile—a missile aimed for the heart of the *Charnel House*. He was going to crash the sub into the zeppelin.

The rigging around her shook with the impact, and Jezebel barely managed to hang on. The whole ship quivered and quaked; countless Grave Walkers spilled over the railings into the churning water below. The *Charnel House* groaned and settled for an instant before the world around her cracked and burst into flame.

I held on to the wheel with one arm wrapped around the spokes as I searched frantically for the control panel. The water was rushing away from my feet, the near-vertical angle of the dying *Nautilus* causing the excess to wash to the back, drowning the aft engines and effectively killing them.

The viewport, and indeed the entire nose of the *Nautilus*, was mangled, crushed in places and torn in others. Not a foot from my face a large section of the *Charnel House*'s hull had splintered through the *Nautilus* like a giant spike—any closer and it would have taken my head off at the neck. The sounds of cables snapping, of metal grinding, filled the air with so much noise that I could barely think. But luckily I didn't have to think. I just had to *do* and hope that the ship had enough life left in her to accomplish her last task.

Despite the pain of a hundred little cuts made by shredding, flying debris, my fingers found the button I'd been searching for.

I couldn't really hear my own voice over the destruction, but I shouted the order anyway.

One last hurrah before I died.

"FIRE TORPEDOES!"

CHAPTER TWENTY-FOUR

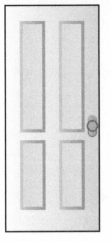

JEZEBEL
NEW YORK, TODAY

The ringing subsided, but her ears still felt like they were filled with cotton. At first she thought she was just dizzy from the blast, but she soon realized that what she was seeing was the motion of the *Charnel House* tossing about on the waves—the zeppelin had fallen from the sky into the Hudson below. Large sections were on fire, but the giant airbag and gunner's deck had broken away from the ship proper and landed in another part of the river, floating on the rough waves; the rest of the ship looked like some great, sinking water beast spouting flame and smoke. Jez could hear the mayfly buzzing in the distance, tearing apart chunks of machinery in its fury even as it sank beneath the surface. The portal still twisted, darkly, above them.

But it wasn't Jez's mayfly that had brought the *Charnel House* down. This destruction had been caused by something else. Some kind of explosion when Tommy's submarine had impacted with the zeppelin.

Jez was tangled in the rigging, suspended just a few feet above the dark water. The storm waves crested below her, and her shoes dangled in the surf. A long bloody rope burn cut across one cheek where a snapped line had whipped her on the way down, but otherwise she was miraculously uninjured. Charred and broken bodies of Grave Walkers floated everywhere, some still struggling to swim despite having lost a limb or two. The near-dead were, ironically, frustratingly hard to kill.

But one body in particular caught her attention. It floated near a broken ship's wheel, its hand lashed to one of the spokes. Panic rising in her chest, Jezebel managed to pull herself free from the rigging and dropped into the river. When she reached the wheel she grabbed it for support and cradled Tommy's head in her arm, pulling his head free of the water. She kicked with her feet, netgun slung over her shoulder, Tommy in her arms, and paddled back to the gunner's deck, which was still afloat. It took all her strength to haul Tommy up out of the churning water and onto deck, but she did so. For once she was thankful he was so small.

She rolled him over onto his back, but his face was white and his lips already blue. A long splinter of metal protruded from his chest. Three inches of steel had entered his heart. Tommy Learner was dead.

"Such a shame to go like that," said a voice in her ear. "I'd hoped to have the pleasure myself."

The Dead Gentleman was standing before her. He was nothing more than a grinning skull in an immaculate black business suit, but his voice sounded like it was right next to her ear. He had Merlin clutched in a bony fist.

Her face was wet with river water and sudden tears. She wanted to shout something at him, tell him to shut up, but she couldn't get the words out of her tight throat. Tommy Learner was dead.

The Gentleman bowed his skull and put one ghostly hand over his chest. "To our honored opponent. Our fallen foe, I salute you!"

Behind him, a few survivors had assembled, a motley group of wounded Grave Walkers. And in the middle was Macheath the vampire. He had removed his filthy cap, but his face was nothing but a gloating sneer. In the other hand the vampire held Tommy's Cycloidotrope, the one they'd confiscated back in the Gentleman's cell a hundred years ago. He was spinning it in his palm like a toy.

"A moment for Tommy Learner," said the Gentleman. "You gave your life to bring down my ship, but it was all for naught—my victory is at hand!"

The Gentleman reached out toward Tommy's body. Jezebel felt a chill descend around her. "May you serve me better in death than you fought me in life."

"NO!" Jezebel screamed, finding her voice. "You won't take him! You won't make him one of you!"

She slid off the netgun and took aim. The Gentleman chuckled. "Well, aren't you something? All dressed up for the part. You even have one of their ridiculous weapons. You sure that thing still works, my dear? It must be an antique, by now.

"Macheath," he said. "She's yours. The last Explorer is yours to feed on. You've waited long enough."

Jez fired. Two shots—one at the Gentleman and one at Macheath and the Grave Walkers. The nets expanded as they flew, and Macheath cursed as one twisted around him and he fell, caught in a mass of kicking Grave Walkers. The Cycloidotrope clattered across the deck.

The second hit the Gentleman squarely in the chest, but he tore it away like it was so much paper. "Useless," he said, glancing back at his tangled henchmen. He took two long strides and backhanded Jezebel. She rolled and cracked her head, hard, against the rail.

"You'll both serve me soon enough," said the Gentleman. "But I'll waste no more time on children. My hour is at hand!"

The Gentleman reached up and with a bony finger stroked Merlin's head. "Such a rare thing, this artifact! I have found you at last, *Brother Theophilus!*"

With that he popped the little bird's head back with a click, opening it up like a pill bottle. Inside was a ball of soft golden light.

"How do you live forever?" asked the Gentleman. "Brother Theo thought he'd found the answer. He gave up his physical self—his fragile, feeble flesh and blood—for something more durable. An immortal soul in a body of brass and gears, so he could be an Explorer till the end of time."

With two fingers he scooped out the light, cupping it gently in his palm. He let Merlin fall to the ground, a hunk now of dead metal.

He held up the little ball of light. "How does the song go? *If I only had a brain . . .*"

The Gentleman peered up at the heavens. "This world abhors what I am." The sky was already lightening in the east; the storm was waning and dawn threatened to break through. "The soulless cannot exist here for long. Already I can feel myself begin to dissipate. As the sun rises, my power wanes."

He looked back at Jezebel, his skull's grin seeming to get wider. "A soul in a bottle—that's what Brother Theophilus made himself into. And I will gladly swallow him whole!

"Bon appétit!" he said, and then he plopped the ball of light into his mouth.

At once he began to shine. First it was just a dull glimmer in the hollows of his cheeks and the dark sockets of his eyes. But the light continued to brighten and expand until Jezebel had to turn away.

When she looked back, after the light subsided, the Gentleman was gone. In his place was a handsome young man. He had pale cheeks and thick, coal-black hair. His mouth was unusually red, but his eyes were dark and cruel.

He hesitated at first, as if touched by fear, but then he took a long, deep breath. It came back out with a loud, full-throated laugh. He shouted as he raised his arms to the sky.

"THE DEAD GENTLEMAN . . . LIVES!" he cried.

Just then the sun broke free from behind the clouds and Jez heard Macheath cursing as he struggled against his bonds. But the Gentleman ignored his servant and turned his face toward the light, shouting in defiance.

"The Gentleman lives, but the rest of this world will die," he cried. "In time, I alone, in all of creation, shall possess the gift of life. I will burn like a fire in the heart of a great black darkness. *I alone!*"

Jezebel covered her ears as a whip-crack of thunder rocked the heavens, and she looked up to see the prow of a second black zeppelin coming through the swirling portal. And another. And another. The curling vortex was expanding, making way for a thousand-thousand ships and their crews of grinning, leering Grave Walkers.

Jezebel crawled over to Tommy and laid her head down next to his. They'd failed. The Gentleman had stolen Merlin's life, his soul. That was the secret the Gentleman had been after all this time—he'd been plotting to steal the bird's soul so that he might live. Now the sun could not harm him. Now his army would kill everything else. Everything.

Something caught Jez's attention; something flickered out of the corner of her eye. She lifted her head and saw the Cycloidotrope lying a few feet from her. It sparkled softly despite the gloom. Jezebel grabbed the little device and looked at the Gentleman. His arms raised, he was still shouting his triumph, and the ship around them began to rise out of the water. Fires died and shredded metal began to knit itself back together. Under the Gentleman's power, the *Charnel House* was rebuilding itself. Even the sunlight seemed weak and ineffectual in this new world—the Gentleman's world. Jezebel imagined what must be happening all over the city. She pictured the things that were crawling out of the dark spaces, and the millions of people who slumbered fitfully in their beds, unaware of the danger.

She looked down at the little cube. It lit up in her hands. She willed herself to see Tommy and there he was, still alive. In the cube Tommy was clinging to the wheel of his ruined ship as a wall of metal exploded into his chest. Next, he was fighting the wheel as the floor filled with water.

The Cycloidotrope was going backward.

"Yes!" she said. "Show me Tommy."

He appeared before her in a hologram of light. His back was to her, but she still felt her throat catch when she saw him moving about, shouting orders at no one in particular as he flipped a row of switches and brought his ship around to aim at the *Charnel House*'s belly. There was that swagger in him, even at the end.

A glance at the Tommy here and now—his cold lips, his dusty-gray skin. The first time he'd visited her, he'd used the Cycloidotrope to project his image to the future so that he could communicate with her. He'd told her that the future was malleable, changeable, but that the past was fixed. You cannot alter events in your own life, you cannot change what has already happened, and to do so risks great danger.

"Tommy," she said. He didn't hear her. "Tommy!" she shouted, but he wasn't seeing her. He was busy fighting to control his ship. He was going to drive it straight up into the *Charnel House*.

She had to stop him. He didn't need to sacrifice himself to bring down the Gentleman's ship—the mayfly would have taken care of that. He didn't have to die.

She gently laid Tommy's head down on the deck—she was glad that she didn't have to close his eyes.

"I'll see you in a minute," she whispered, and then she leapt, one more time, into the light.

CHAPTER TWENTY-FIVE

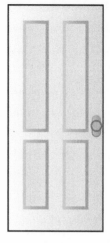

JEZEBEL

NOW.

"You okay?" whispered Tommy.

"Huh?" asked Jez, blinking.

"I asked if you're okay."

"Sure," answered Jez, rubbing her eyes. "For a minute there, I . . . you're alive!"

Jezebel grabbed Tommy and wrapped her arms around him in a giant bear hug.

He tried to shush her. "Keep your voice down! Of course I'm alive. We've already been through this. I did like you asked. I have to say, I'm pretty impressed at your sabotage. I didn't think you had it in you."

Jezebel let him go and looked around her. They were on the Gentleman's ship, hidden away behind a crate of gun shells. The sky above was still dark, but there was the pink of early dawn in the east. The zeppelin tossed about on the waves of the river, but it wasn't sinking. Grave Walkers were scurrying overhead, desperately trying to put out a fire that had originated in the engine but was quickly spreading to consume the airbag itself. The *Charnel House* had been forced to make an emergency landing on the river.

It was strange. Jezebel could remember everything that had happened to her—the explosion, finding Tommy's body, using the Cycloidotrope to jump into the past. But she also had memories of bringing down the ship with the mayfly grenade, of hiding from the Grave Walkers and of Tommy's surprise at seeing her appear inside his ship. She'd persuaded him not to attack. She explained that she'd sabotaged the *Charnel House*'s engine, though she had more trouble explaining how she got aboard the *Nautilus*. Luckily there wasn't much time for questions, as the Gentleman's ship came tumbling out of the sky and Jezebel and Tommy, alive and well, snuck aboard the wreckage.

It was like these two sets of memories were trying to occupy the same space in her brain. In one, Tommy died and the Gentleman won. In the other, she stopped Tommy's suicide run. They were competing for room, and when she tried to focus on just one it felt like someone was digging around in her skull with an ice pick.

She'd done it. She'd actually changed her own past. "It worked," she said, squinting against the pain.

"What worked?" asked Tommy. "You're starting to worry me, Jez."

"Never mind," she said, suddenly self-conscious at her own confusion. "I'm fine."

"Well, you've bought us some time, but we still need to find Merlin."

"The Gentleman's got him."

"You keep saying that," said Tommy. "But are you sure?"

"I'm sure," Jez answered. "Look, you said that the Gentleman could never conquer Earth because the undead can't exist here for long—they cannot walk in the sun, because the undead don't have souls."

"That's right."

"Well, I think he's found one. He's going to steal Merlin's."

"Merlin's a gadget," said Tommy. "He doesn't have a soul."

"Does the name Brother Theophilus mean anything to you?"

"Sure, Fat Theo," Tommy answered. "He's a founder of the Explorers' Society. He discovered Merlin, actually."

"Merlin is Brother . . . eh, Fat Theo. Somehow the guy put his soul into that bird so that he could live forever, and now the Gentleman is about to steal it for himself."

Tommy was thinking it through, Jez could tell. He was chewing the side of his cheek as he looked for holes in her theory. But Jezebel couldn't tell him that it wasn't just a theory. She didn't want to tell him that she'd broken the rule about changing your own timeline. She didn't want him to know that she'd done it to save him.

The ice pick was stabbing at her brain.

He was still struggling to make sense of the Gentleman's plan. "But even if you are right, even if he wants to get a soul—to be alive—what good would it do him?" he asked. "He'd be here on Earth, but what about his army?"

"You said yourself that his army is the *near-dead*. That's why he's been gathering them from all sorts of different worlds. Their bodies are decomposing and gross, but they must still have their souls—he's keeping them just on the brink of death so that they can be his servants in the daylight. There are hundreds, thousands of ships full of them waiting just on the other side of that big portal. And I think the more killing they do, the more things that die—the stronger he'll become."

"He's going to kill everything," Tommy said.

"No, he's not," said Jez. "This time we're going to stop him. Come on!"

"This time?" asked Tommy, but Jezebel ignored him.

They came out of their hiding place in time to see the Gentleman emerging from his quarters. Bloody Macheath loped along at his side, squinting nervously up at the weak sunlight that had managed to peek through the clouds. Again, he was holding the Cycloidotrope in his palm.

"We've lost the *Nautilus*, sir," he said. "She surfaced for a minute after we set down on the river, but then she went under again. We're assuming she's too damaged to make another attack."

"I wouldn't make such an assumption," answered the Gentleman. "But it's no matter. Captain Scott's toy boat is little threat now."

"Can't say I care much for that sun, either, Captain," said Macheath, shielding his eyes against the sky. "You won't mind if I scurry on back belowdecks?"

"Once I have the soul, my power will be such that you will not need to worry about the sun ever again," said the Gentleman. "But every minute I spend here without it uses up vast reserves of energy. If I remain as is, I shall surely perish." As he spoke Jezebel noticed that he did seem weaker, somehow. There was a haze about him, almost a transparency to his bones.

"BRING ME MY PRIZE!" he called, and a pair of Grave Walkers crossed the deck to him. One of them carried Merlin in his hands. One of the bird's wings was bent sharply in the wrong direction and flapped uselessly at its side.

"You have a plan?" asked Tommy.

"I have an idea," admitted Jez. "But I don't know if it'll work. We need to create a distraction."

Tommy nodded. "No worries." He pulled a cylinder from his belt pouch. It was a funny-looking thing with a strange crank on the side. He flicked his wrist and it extended to several feet.

"Spare Tesla Stick," he said. "Grabbed it off the *Nautilus*. Just hope it didn't get too wet." He turned the little crank and the end of the staff sparked blue.

"Wait, Tommy," said Jez, but it was too late.

"See you soon," he said, and smiled as he leapt across the deck, shouting as he ran at a full charge toward the Grave Walkers.

"Stupid boy," she muttered as she began circling around. She hadn't meant for him to charge them head-on, but perhaps she could take advantage of the chaos and get close enough to grab Merlin.

The Grave Walkers turned and met Tommy's charge. The Gentleman was shouting at them to ignore the boy and bring him the bird, but Tommy had already stunned the first one with his Tesla Stick and was threatening the other, who still held Merlin tight. Tommy's attention was fixed on the Grave Walker, however, and he didn't see Macheath sneaking up on him from behind, a long blade in his pale hand.

"Tommy, look out!" shouted Jez. *Oh well*, she thought. *So much for stealth.*

Tommy turned just in time to deflect Macheath's attack, but it gave the Grave Walker an opportunity to escape. The black uniformed cultist ran for his master, Merlin in hand.

"Bring it here!" the Gentleman cried. "Quickly!"

Jez remembered the netgun slung over her shoulder. She took aim at the running Grave Walker and fired. The shot flew wide and struck the deck where the cultist had just been standing. Bernie had warned her—four shots only. That meant she had one left. This time Jez aimed in front of the Grave Walker and fired.

He fell to the floor in a heap of tangled filaments. The Gentleman let out a howl of rage. As he did so, Jezebel noticed that the cloud cover was disappearing in the east and pink-orange sky was just barely visible on the horizon. The Gentleman's grip on this world was slipping. The sun was coming out. He was racing against the dawn.

Merlin rolled from the Grave Walker's fingers. He hopped away, flapping his useless, crippled wing. Jez ran for the bird, tossing the spent netgun away as she went. She dove, skidding along the deck and skinning her arms and legs. But her fingers found Merlin.

"Gotcha," she said, and she was greeted with a tweet in response.

"An impressive shot, and a brave move," said a cold voice. "But now what are you going to do?" The Gentleman stood over her, his skull face more ghostlike than ever. "The battle is finished. What can you possibly do to stop me from taking that from you and crushing your soft head between my fingers?"

Jez fought down the brutal wave of panic. Every nerve in her being was filled with the intense desire to beg for mercy before this dark creature. But she struggled through the pain in her head as she remembered what the other Gentleman had done, in a different time. She pictured where he'd placed his fingers near the bird's throat.

"I'm so sorry," she whispered, and Merlin gave her a soft, reassuring chirp. It didn't struggle when she placed two fingers under its chin and found the indentation there. She pressed down and heard a metallic click. The shine went out of the bird's eyes as its head flipped back on its hinged neck, revealing the soft ball of light underneath.

Jezebel heard the Gentleman's gasp.

She threw Merlin as hard as she could over the side of the ship and into the river. As it flew through the air, the ball of light separated from its metal body and drifted up while the rest sank beneath the water's surface. For an instant it hovered there, a glowing orb. But then the light shifted, coalescing into a smiling, fat face before fading away into nothing.

A lightning flash lit up the sky; a thunder crack rattled Jezebel's teeth, it was so close. She looked over her shoulder at the portal and saw that the funnel cloud had reversed itself—it was shrinking, collapsing in on itself and on the fleet of black ships. As she cupped her hands over her eyes to see, Jezebel realized that she was squinting in the bright glare of the morning sun, which had broken through at last.

The Gentleman bellowed at the day, screaming, as Jezebel began to crawl away, scooting on her hands and feet. But he saw her and easily blocked her path. His skull's face was barely visible in the glare of the sudden sunlight, but his eyes still burned with anger—two great black pits that threatened to swallow her whole. His long, skeletal fingers wrapped around her throat and he squeezed.

And nothing happened. His fingers, his arm, his everything had become as insubstantial as shadow. In the light of day, with his powers disappearing, the Gentleman was reduced to nothing more than a ghost. You wouldn't have known it from his expressionless face, but Jezebel felt it—the Dead Gentleman was afraid.

He dashed past Jezebel, but he had no more power than a cold gust of wind. He began shouting orders to the crew. A familiar rumble started in the bowels of the ship as the crew of the *Charnel House* began, desperately, to prepare to open a new portal. They were fleeing.

Jezebel screamed as a hand grabbed her shoulder.

"It's me," said Tommy. "Come on!"

Macheath was gone. A steaming skeleton was all that was left of the vampire, his bones already crumbling to dust under the bright sunlight. Tommy's Tesla Stick was broken in two and he had the beginnings of a second black eye, but otherwise he seemed unhurt.

The pair ran together through the chaos that had taken hold of the Gentleman's crew. The Grave Walkers seemed more interested in escaping than in stopping the two of them, and those that weren't trying to get the ship moving seemed to be dying before their very eyes. As their master faded, so, too, did they.

As they ran, Tommy pulled the little brass compass out of his pocket and flipped open the lid.

"I'm calling the *Nautilus*," he shouted. "There, to port!"

"Where?" asked Jez.

"The left! To the left!"

They reached the rail and, without stopping, Tommy pulled Jez over the side and into the river. But the splash Jez was expecting never came. They landed instead on a hard metal surface and tumbled into an open hatchway.

"You all right?" asked Tommy.

"My butt," groaned Jez.

"You can sit in a bucket of ice later! Close the hatch behind us and come on!"

They were inside Tommy's submarine. Jez pulled the spherical door closed and gave the wheel-shaped handle a turn, just like she'd seen them do in the movies. Then she followed Tommy down a long hall and into a large room—the ship's bridge. She'd been there before, but the memory stabbed at her skull.

"You get the door closed?" asked Tommy as he took his place behind the Captain's wheel.

"I think so," answered Jez. "I've never actually closed a submarine door before."

"A what? This is the *Nautilus*. An underwater ship! A one-of-a-kind."

"Yeah, but . . . ," started Jez. "Never mind. What are we doing?"

Tommy pulled a lever and a large viewport opened up front. They could see the *Charnel House*. On the deck, a group of Grave Walkers were wheeling the Gentleman's portal archway, the one she'd seen them use to leave the Hollow World, into position.

"They're going to open a new portal beneath the ship—they're making an emergency escape," said Tommy. "All hands prepare to fire torpedoes!"

"Who are you talking to?" asked Jez.

"My crew."

"Your crew?"

"Okay." Tommy shrugged. "You."

The *Nautilus* gave a little shudder, and Jezebel watched as two objects launched through the water at the Gentleman's ship. The first explosion tore a hole in the back, and the second cracked the ship in half. The rear half sank fast beneath the still-tossing waves.

Tommy lowered a periscope sight from the ceiling and pressed his face against the viewer.

"Here," he said, gesturing to Jezebel. "Look."

Through the magnified sights of the periscope she could see a shadow clinging to the broken prow of the sinking ship. It looked like a flutter of black cloth in the wind, but Jezebel knew it was the Gentleman. It writhed and curled under the bright sun, but it had nowhere to go. Just as the last of the ship sank from view, the shadow seemed to catch fire and explode into a weak puff of smoke.

"He's gone," said Jez.

In a few minutes the rest of the ship sank beneath the river, and all that remained to remind them of the *Charnel House* was the scattering of debris upon the waves.

CHAPTER TWENTY-SIX

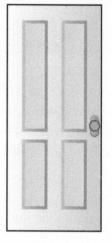

JEZEBEL
NEW YORK, TODAY

During the worst thunderstorm in a hundred years, Jezebel Lemon had been sitting comfortably in Bernie's apartment having a nice cup of tea while her father was out in the gale-force winds searching for her. He'd been grateful to find her safe and sound, of course, if slightly annoyed at his own drenched state. He, like the rest of New York, was saddened to hear of the explosion that sank a barge on the Hudson, but they were thankful that it was unmanned when it broke free from its moorings and drifted out into the stormy waters. It could have been a real disaster had anyone actually been on board.

This was how the Veil worked, explained Tommy. The Veil softened her father's panic and fuzzied his recollection, so that as the days went on he asked fewer and fewer questions about where she'd disappeared to that night. And he was as anxious as she was to keep the whole thing from her mom—he didn't want her to know that he'd lost their only daughter for a night. Soon the whole incident was a distant, unexciting memory. Her parents were still too tangled in the Veil, in their own tiny war, to see that their daughter had been a part of a real war. And she'd won. She might even have saved the whole planet.

There were some who'd come close to the truth, of course. There were those who'd heard strange sounds rattling beneath the stairs, or who might've glimpsed terrible things watching them from the shadows. There were even a very few who had looked out their windows at the Hudson River and seen, instead of a fierce lightning storm, a ferocious naval battle between some kind of submarine and a towering black zeppelin. But these were told by their parents to stop making up stories, or else they were told by their peers to seek professional psychiatric help.

The Storm of the Decade would go down in the history books, but the real story would be recorded in only one place—the *Encyclopedia Imagika*.

Every other weekend at her dad's, Jezebel helped Bernie write up the story of the Battle of the Hudson, as well as update the entries on Thomas Learner, Merlin aka Brother Theophilus, and the Dead Gentleman (she took a special joy in denoting the Gentleman as "destroyed," since "deceased" would have been redundant). Together they wrote the sad final fate of the Academy, but they did leave room for an entry to be titled *New Academy*—after all, as long as there was still a single Explorer, the Academy was not gone, not entirely.

The trickiest entry of all was the one titled *Lemon, Jezebel*. With Tommy's help, she'd dictated the details of her adventures to Bernie, believing that it would be more honest to then let him write it. But she couldn't help suggesting an extra adjective here or there, such as "fearless" or "ingenious." After a while Bernie shut the door on her and forbade her from interrupting until he was finished.

Tommy showed little interest in the *Encyclopedia*. By day his legs twitched incessantly and he shifted about like he had saddle bugs in his pants. But at odd hours, Jezebel spotted him scribbling away in a notebook of his own. She tried to catch a peek at the contents, but the boy's handwriting was nearly illegible and his spelling atrocious. But she did manage, with some difficulty, to decipher the words on the cover. In bold, messy boy-scrawl they read:

The Incredible Life and Times of Tommy Learner, Explorer.

When Tommy saw that Jezebel had spotted his secret project, he surprised her by looking at his shoes and speaking in a very un-Tommy-like way. A soft, almost self-conscious whisper.

"A dumb idea," he'd said. "That encyclopedia is so ridiculously huge, I just can't stand the idea of making it any bigger. So this is a rough draft of all the important stuff I've seen. People I've met. Put some of the Captain's learning to use. Thought maybe I could go back someday and polish it up, when I've got more words under my belt, and prettier ones to tell it all with. Or at least the good parts."

Jezebel didn't try any more peeks after that. She let him go about his secretive composition and pretended not to notice, though she dearly wished that if he ever did finish, she might make it in as one of the "good parts."

He stayed with Bernie for a few months—they told everyone that he was Bernie's grandnephew in for a visit. On the weekends when Jez stayed with her dad, she took Tommy out to show him the modern world. She took him to the movies and introduced him to the Internet, and though he enjoyed these things (well, he enjoyed the movies—the Internet just made him angry), he quickly got bored. Jez supposed that after you'd seen the things that Tommy Learner had seen, 3-D must seem a little dull.

Tommy insisted on visiting the Bowery, though he quickly got lost. And he spent long hours walking the Brooklyn Bridge and staring at the passing barges below. Those were quiet moments, and Jez suspected Tommy was seeing things she couldn't. He was looking for ghosts.

During the weeks when Jez was at her mom's place across town, Tommy worked on repairing the *Nautilus*, sneaking aboard at night and parking her on the river bottom during the day. He'd become quite the engineer under Captain Scott's tutelage, and what he couldn't fix outright he worked around. By the end of a few weeks the ship might not have been as pretty as she once was, but she was working just fine.

Which meant that he'd be leaving soon. Tommy didn't belong in this century. He probably didn't belong in his own century, either—he'd seen too much. He belonged out beyond this world, exploring.

With the Gentleman gone, Jezebel's closet was back to being just a closet, though Jez kept a nightlight burning in there constantly just for good measure. Tommy had theorized that since the mysterious mural portal had led to the *Charnel House*, which was now little more than wreckage on the river bottom, the portal itself would stay broken, and also stay closed, from now on. The mural had returned to being just a painted glade, and during one of Jezebel's weeks away her father had found the time to surprise her and finish it—unicorn and all. The truth was that despite Tommy's reassurances, Jezebel still found it hard to sleep in that room, and the gentle-looking unicorn actually seemed to help in a strange way. It was silly, it was childish, but for the first time it felt a little like home.

There had been no teary goodbyes or drawn-out farewells when Tommy left. There was never any discussion of whether Jezebel would go with him—after all, she had parents who loved her and a life here, such as it was. All Tommy had was being an Explorer. So one night Tommy informed them that the last of the tests on the *Nautilus* had checked out and that he'd be sailing for something called the Lemuria Outcropping, which to Jezebel sounded like some kind of nasty skin condition. He shook Jez's hand, patted Bernie on the shoulder and disappeared. He did leave Jez a version of his homing compass. She was to stand facing due north and press the button should she ever need help. And he told Bernie to keep the *Encyclopedia*, since he never had much time for reading, anyway.

On another rainy Saturday, several months later, Jezebel found herself pacing her room. Her father was working in his studio and she'd knocked on Bernie's door, but he was somewhere else in the building attending to a clogged drain or a stubborn radiator. Summer had come to a close, and they were well into fall. The first truly frosty days had arrived. In a building as old as the Percy, the hot-water heating system was temperamental at best and the winters were either freezing cold or boiling hot. She wouldn't mind a little renovation on the heating system.

She listened to the rain splatter against her window for a few minutes, noticing that some of the water was already turning to ice, and then made up her mind. She just couldn't bear to be cooped up in her room during a rainstorm. No way. Too many memories.

She grabbed a piece of notebook paper and a black magic marker from her desk drawer and scribbled "Be Back Soon" across the front. She would head out to a coffee shop for a mocha-something and wait out the storm there. She looked at the note for a minute and then added "Love, Jez" at the bottom.

She pulled on her rain slicker and had just started out the bedroom door when something moved in the mural. At first she thought it was a trick of the eye—that had happened before; several times, in fact, over the last few months—but when she looked a second time she was sure that the scene had changed. The sky was lighter; the unicorn seemed farther to the right than he'd previously been . . .

Jezebel was surprisingly calm when the mural began to shimmer and an ancient man with a cow's tail stepped through. She knew at once that this was the High Father, even though when she'd seen him last he'd been just a little boy. That was, of course, a hundred years ago.

"*Broken portal*, my butt, Tommy Learner," she muttered.

"Good afternoon, Jezebel," said the High Father. "It is good to see you are still alive."

"Uh, yeah. Good to see you are still alive, too, only . . . older," she said. "It worked, you know. Jumping through the Cycloido-trope with Tommy into the future. You were right."

The High Father smiled and nodded, but he looked troubled. The last time she'd seen him they were preparing for a zombie attack, but he hadn't seemed nearly as grim then. Jezebel told herself that it was just his age, but the High Father seemed weighted down. Troubled, even.

"Yes, the peculiarities of time travel are mysterious even to the very wise. There are great forces at work there that even I do not claim to fully comprehend; thus we have strict rules. We break them at our own peril, and yet sometimes, break them we must."

At the mention of time travel, Jez felt her cheeks redden. She'd broken the greatest rule of all when she'd gone back and saved Tommy. Even now if she tried to remember those events, the ice pick returned to stab at her brain.

She decided to change the subject. "You know, every time I saw the Gentleman he looked different, like a different kind of dead. And now, you look different, too. Only, you're alive, of course." Jez smiled and plopped down on the edge of her bed. She knew she was beginning to babble.

"Two sides of the same coin, you might say." The High Father nodded. "Though my cycle of rebirth moves along at a far slower pace than the ever-changing nature of the Dead Gentleman. It has always been so, and it seems that it *will* always be so."

Something in the High Father's words set off an alarm in Jez's head. What had he just said—*that it will always be so?*

"Wait a minute," she said. "The Gentleman was destroyed. I saw it happen."

"Yes, you are correct. He found himself trapped in a place he did not belong, and without the protection of Merlin's stolen soul. One Gentleman was totally and utterly destroyed. But another Gentleman emerged from the battle triumphant. You also saw that. A Gentleman who won."

"What are you talking about?"

The High Father wobbled over and sat down next to her on the bed. He patted her knee with a wrinkled, liver-spotted hand.

"I don't blame you for what you did to save Tommy," he said slowly. "But the universe is not as forgiving as I am. You went back in time and changed the events of your own life. You caused a schism in the timeline and, in effect, created two different, competing realities. In one of these realities you managed to save Tommy Learner and save your world in turn. But in the other, Tommy died and the Gentleman won."

"No," said Jez. Her heart was beating wildly in her chest, her thoughts spinning in her head. "That didn't happen! I went back and made sure that it didn't happen!"

"You cannot unmake that which has already occurred," said the High Father. "It doesn't work that way. You changed nothing. You merely splintered this Earth off into another path and another reality. An alternate universe. In one universe your Earth dies and the Gentleman is triumphant, even as he is defeated and destroyed in another. We've just witnessed the birth of the *multi*verse."

Jezebel didn't know what to say. For months now she'd been thinking of herself as a hero.

The High Father smiled at her. "It's possible that this new universe, this new Earth—the one in which the Gentleman rules supreme—will stay safely locked away, undiscovered, forever."

"But it's also possible that the Dead Gentleman will find us, that he'll find a way to come through and see there is a whole new Earth to invade, a whole new Earth to kill. And it's all my fault!"

The High Father looked into her eyes, and in an instant the pain in her head was gone. Staring into those deep, soulful eyes, her heartbeat returned to normal and she felt at peace.

"Without you," he said, "there would be only *one* reality— one where the Gentleman ruled over a dead Earth. By creating another world you *saved* an entire world. You did the only thing you could do. The consequences could not be helped."

Jezebel understood, but she still felt that she should've done something differently. If she'd acted quicker or been smarter, then all of this could have been avoided.

"You are a hero," he said. "Enjoy it. And what a hero you are! In all of existence, Jezebel Lemon, you may be unique."

"Huh?"

"That pain you feel when you try to remember the events surrounding the schism—that is because you can feel the pull of the two realities. You alone have knowledge of both of them. You are one of a kind."

"But you know about all of this," Jez said. "If I'm unique, if I'm the only one who knows it, then how can you be saying all this?"

He shrugged. "I'm the High Father. I know things. But trust me, Jezebel, you are special."

He stood up and stretched. "Ah, I'm getting old, my dear. Another twenty or thirty years and I may have to be born again. It's the gout, you see. It gets unbearable." He winked at her, but Jez still felt that he was putting on a show by lightening the mood. What he'd told her was very serious.

He leaned forward and tapped her on the forehead. "Protect what's in there. They're your greatest tool, your wits. But you now also carry around knowledge of the most dangerous sort, and that must not fall into the wrong hands. Tommy's a brave boy, but he's brash and often vengeful and he could lead you into trouble. Keep him in line, won't you? You do balance each other well."

"Tommy left without me," Jez said, feeling a little pang at the mention of Tommy's name. "He's gone. I doubt I'll see him ever again."

"That so?" said the High Father, returning to the painted wall. "Remember what I said before, I know things! Take this mural, for instance. You might assume that this is just a regular old painting.

Or you might assume that it was a totally random portal that led to the one place you needed to get to—the Gentleman's ship. Or you might instead assume that this is a special portal, given to you by a very special, a very *old* friend, and it will lead you to wherever your heart wants to go. If that were the case, I would hope that you would consider it a precious gift, and use it wisely." The High Father winked at her.

"Be seeing you, Jezebel Lemon," he said.

With that he stepped through the mural and she watched as it shimmered and glowed, dissolving and swirling into a sun-lit glade—a real sunlit glade. The High Father walked along the grass toward a cool green forest beneath a pink twilight sky. Then the colors blurred and she was once again staring at the still life of a unicorn.

The High Father was gone, and Jezebel was left with an uneasy, empty feeling in her gut. The wind had picked up outside and the rain was a steady drumbeat against the window. She imagined Tommy sailing an alien ocean somewhere, probably heedless of some obvious danger in front of his very eyes. She smiled at the thought of Bernie wrestling with a lug nut on a radiator upstairs, cursing under his breath as he did battle with the metal monstrosity, but happy, nevertheless, in his element. She saw her father struggling with the same painting he'd been working on for years. He'd probably want to order in tonight. Maybe pizza. He'd ask her questions about Mom, pretending not to really care, and Jez would play dumb and pretend not to know the answers.

She looked down at the note she still clutched in her hands— "Be Back Soon. Love, Jez"—and set it carefully on her pillow.

EPILOGUE

TOMMY

HOPELESSLY LOST, TODAY

The problem, as I saw it, was that I was a captain without a crew, and therefore, a captain without a navigator. Bernard had taken on that role back in the old days, and though it was true that Scott had managed to find his way around just fine for many years without the bespectacled Bernard, Scott had always been more of a jack-of-all-trades type of captain. Me, on the other hand, I'm a specialist captain. I specialize in engineering, I specialize in adventuring, I even specialize in *captaining*. I do not specialize in maps.

I found myself, at the conclusion of my great adventure with Jezebel Lemon in which we saved the Earth, the universe and everything, sitting alone surrounded by hundreds of unfolded maps and navigational charts that might as well have been written in ancient Atlantean. According to my best guess, I'd entered the Lemuria Outcropping at the exact coordinates needed to transport me to the Borderlands of Faerie, and by my figuring I should've been sailing along the midnight-black waves of the Duskwaters right now. But the problem was that the steaming, swampy green muck outside the viewport looked nothing like the Duskwaters. This looked more like a giant ocean of pond scum, and I hadn't found anything labeled "pond scum" among the *Nautilus*'s charts.

I braced myself as something collided with the ship, again. Whenever I took a moment to slow down and study the charts to find a way out of this giant sewer world, this thing—whatever it was—would catch up and begin banging away at the hull. In the filthy muck water I couldn't even get a good look at it, so firing a warning shot wasn't an option.

The ship rattled again and the maps went flying. It was getting annoying. A couple more hits like that and the *Nautilus* would start to take some real damage.

Of course, Jezebel hadn't wanted to come, and, truth be told, I was glad of it. Exploring was a dangerous profession and I could ill afford to look after the two of us. Historically, I'd had enough trouble keeping my own self alive. Besides, she had her father. She had a life in that towering, gleaming New York of hers. She even had Bernie.

The old man would look after her. I was relieved beyond words to discover that my old partner, Bernie's father, hadn't betrayed me after all. My only regret now was that Bernard Senior had died without the two of us making amends. Bernard Billingsworth had been an Explorer, regardless of rank or position. On that Scott had been wrong—Bernard had had the stuff after all.

Jezebel had the stuff, too, but she had other things to worry about. Explorers couldn't worry about family. The Veil protected the Explorers from outside prying eyes, but her father would certainly catch on if Jez disappeared again, and even if she tried to show him the truth he wouldn't believe it. He wouldn't be able to—he'd been under the Veil for too long; his own mind wouldn't allow him to see the real world now.

I, on the other hand, was lucky that no one was waiting for me—no one out there to worry about me. Very, very lucky.

The ship rocked as whatever it was took another strike, and the *Nautilus* threatened to bank into a menacing-looking blob of floating gunk just off the starboard side. I barely managed to grip the wheel and steer the ship into a narrow near miss.

And there was another thing about Jezebel Lemon—secrets. How had she gotten into the *Nautilus?* I'd pressed her on this point several times, and she'd always carefully avoided the question. Her first claim that she'd followed me all the way from the Percy and managed to stow away didn't hold water. I know when I'm being followed—years on the street had given me a sixth sense about that sort of thing. But nevertheless, she'd appeared on the ship's bridge and talked me out of my admittedly desperate plan to ram the *Charnel House*. But she wouldn't tell me how she'd gotten there. Not the truth, anyway.

Too many questions. Too many secrets. True, I knew how to keep a secret of my own—like the future I saw in the Cycloidotrope, the vision of the dead Earth the High Father showed me. But I defied the vision and everything turned out all right in the end. Jezebel and I *both* lived, and the world was safe from the Gentleman forever, so why bring it up? The vision could go jump off a cliff for all I cared. The High Father, too.

Then why did I still feel so uneasy? As if something was wrong but I couldn't remember what it was. Like I'd tied a string round my finger and forgotten why. Like I'd told this story before with a different ending.

Even today, I still find myself looking over my shoulder at shadows.

The ship rolled again. I would have to do something about this creature out there. Whatever it was.

"Battle stations!" I shouted.

"Aye, aye, Captain," answered a voice.

Jezebel was standing behind me. She was saluting, which seemed awfully out of place for her. More so, even, than her sudden appearance.

"Huh," I said. "Don't suppose you're going to tell me how you got here this time?"

"Sure I will," she answered. "The mural in my room. It's really a portal that can take me anywhere. I just have to picture the place and it appears. It was a gift from the High Father."

Now this was worth considering. A portal that went anywhere opened up endless possibilities for profit—if I ever decided to go back to my old ways, that is. But the fact that it was located in Jezebel's bedroom was a bit inconvenient. A thought occurred to me.

"So you just hopped through the portal to here?"

"Yep."

"And how are you getting back?"

Jezebel's smile faded at once. I bit back a chuckle as she frantically scanned the bridge, looking for the signs of a portal home.

"Here's your first official Explorer lesson—never take what the High Father says at face value. Beware immortal monks bearing gifts."

"But I thought . . . I mean, when he said I could go anywhere

I just assumed it went two ways. . . . Look, I came here to visit, not to stay!"

I grabbed a handful of charts from the floor. "Here. You know how to read these?"

"No," she answered, turning a chart this way and that.

"Well, you'd better learn. Because you've got to find us a portal back to Earth so that I can get you home."

There was another loud crash as the ship sustained a direct hit. Alarm whistles went off, and the two of us had to grab ahold of each other just to keep from falling.

"Get us home, Navigator," I said. "Hope we survive the trip!"